The Bungalow

**Center Point
Large Print**

**This Large Print Book carries the
Seal of Approval of N.A.V.H.**

The Bungalow

Sarah Jio

CENTER POINT LARGE PRINT
THORNDIKE, MAINE

This Center Point Large Print edition
is published in the year 2012 by arrangement with
Plume, a member of Penguin Group (USA) Inc.

Copyright © 2011 by Sarah Jio.
All rights reserved.

The text of this Large Print edition is unabridged.
In other aspects, this book may vary
from the original edition.
Printed in the United States of America
on permanent paper.
Set in 16-point Times New Roman type.

ISBN: 978-1-61173-369-3

Library of Congress Cataloging-in-Publication Data

Jio, Sarah.
The bungalow / Sarah Jio.
pages ; cm
ISBN 978-1-61173-369-3 (library binding : alk. paper)
1. Older women—Fiction. 2. Reminiscing in old age—Fiction.
  3. United States. Army Nurse Corps—Fiction.
  4. World War, 1939–1945—Fiction.
  5. Americans—French Polynesia—Fiction.
  6. Bora-Bora (French Polynesia)—Fiction.
  7. Life change events—Fiction. 8. Washington (State)—Fiction.
  9. Large type books. I. Title.
PS3610.I6B86 2012b
813′.6—dc23

                                                    2011050274

For Jason,
with memories of our own island bungalow.
I love you.

Tuck a slip of paper into a flimsy envelope, seal it with a swipe of the tongue, then send it on its way. That letter might be handled by dozens of people and journey a thousand miles before reaching the intended mailbox, where it nestles anonymously between pages twenty-nine and thirty of some unwanted catalog, lying in wait for its unsuspecting recipient, who tosses the catalog, with its treasure tucked inside, into the recycle bin with a flick of the wrist. There, next to poorly rinsed milk cartons, an empty wine bottle, and yesterday's newspaper, a life-changing piece of mail quietly awaits.

That letter was for me.

Prologue

H ello?"

Startled, I opened my eyes at the sound of a familiar voice—pleasant, but sorely out of place. Jennifer, yes, my granddaughter. *But where am I? Or rather, why was she here?* I blinked a few times, disoriented. I had been dreaming of sandy beaches and coconut palms—the place my unconscious mind always tries to visit, but this time I was lucky enough to find it in the archives of my memories.

He was there, of course—in uniform, shyly smiling at me as the waves fell into the shore. I could hear them—their violent crash, followed by the fizz of a million bubbles kissing the sand. Closing my eyes tighter, I found him again, standing there amid the fog of sleep that was lifting, too quickly. *Don't go,* my heart pleaded. *Stay. Please stay.* And he obediently appeared again with that beckoning grin, those arms outstretched to me. I felt the familiar flutter in my heart, the longing.

And then, in an instant, he was gone.

I sighed and looked at my watch, scolding myself. *Half past three.* I must have dozed off while reading. Again. Spontaneous sleepiness was the curse of the elderly. I sat up in my lounge chair, a bit embarrassed, and retrieved the novel I'd been reading before the exhaustion hit. It had fallen from my hands to the ground, spine side up, its pages fanned out in disgrace.

Jennifer walked out onto the terrace. A truck barreled by on the street, further disturbing the peace. "Oh, there you are," she said, smiling at me with her eyes, smoky brown, like her grandfather's. She wore jeans and a black sweater with a light green belt around her slim waist. Her blond hair, cut to her chin, reflected the sun's rays. Jennifer didn't know how beautiful she was.

"Hi, honey," I said, reaching my hand out to her. I looked around the terrace at the pale blue pansies in their simple terra-cotta pots. They were pretty enough, peeking their heads out of the dirt like shy, repentant children who'd been caught playing in the mud. The view of Lake Washington and the Seattle skyline in the distance was beautiful, yes, but cold and stiff, like a painting in a dentist's office. I frowned. How had I come to live here, in this tiny apartment with its stark white walls and a telephone in the bathroom with a red emergency call button beside the toilet?

"I found something," Jennifer said, her voice prying me from my thoughts, "in the recycle bin."

I smoothed my white, wispy hair. "What is it, dear?"

"A letter," she said. "It must have gotten mixed in with the junk mail."

I attempted to stifle a yawn, but it came anyway. "Just leave it on the table. I'll look at it later." I walked inside and sat down on the sofa, turning my gaze away from the kitchen to the reflection in the window. *An old lady.* I saw her every day, this woman, but her reflection never ceased to surprise me. *When did I become her?* My hands traced the wrinkles on my face.

Jennifer sat down next to me. "Has your day been any better than mine?" In her last year of graduate school at the University of Washington, she had chosen an unusual subject for a class-assigned article: an obscure work of art on campus. Donated in 1964 by an anonymous artist, the bronze sculpture of a young couple had a placard that read simply, *Pride and Promises.* Transfixed by the sculpture, Jennifer hoped to profile the artist and learn the story behind the work, yet an entire quarter's worth of research had turned up very little.

"Any luck with your research today, dear?"

"Nada," she said, frowning. "It's frustrating. I've worked so hard to find answers." She shook her head and shrugged. "I hate to admit it, but I think the trail's gone cold."

I knew something about being haunted by art. Jennifer didn't know it, but I'd spent the majority of my life searching in vain for a painting that I'd held in my hands a very long time ago. My heart ached to see it again, and yet after a lifetime of working with art dealers and collectors, the canvas eluded me.

"I know it's hard to let go, honey," I said delicately, knowing how important the project was to her. I tucked my hand in hers. "Some stories aren't meant to be told."

Jennifer nodded. "You may be right, Grandma," she said with a sigh. "But I'm not ready to let it go. Not yet. The inscription on the placard—it all has to mean something. And the box, the one that the man in the statue holds in his hands, it's locked, and the people in the archives don't have record of a key, which means"—she paused and smiled hopefully—"there may be something inside."

"Well, I admire your spirit, sweetheart," I said, clutching the gold chain around my neck, the one that held the locket I'd worn and kept safe for so many years. Only one other soul knew what was tucked inside beyond the protective guard of the clasp.

Jennifer walked back to the table. "Now, don't forget this letter," she said, holding up an envelope. "Look at this gorgeous stamp. It's from"—she paused, reading the postmark— *"Tahiti."*

My heart rate quickened as I looked up, squinting to see the letter in Jennifer's hands.

12

"Grandma, *who* do you know in Tahiti?"

"Let me see it," I said, inching closer.

I scanned the simple white envelope, damp from its brush with a milk carton and speckled with crimson dots from last night's cabernet. No, I did not recognize the handwriting, or the return address. *Who would be writing me from Tahiti? And why? Why now?*

"Aren't you going to open it?" Jennifer said, hovering over me in anticipation.

My hands trembled a little as I turned the envelope over again and again, running my fingers along the exotic stamp, which depicted a Tahitian girl in a yellow dress. I swallowed hard, trying to purge the memories that were seeping into my mind like rising floodwater, but mere mental sandbags could not keep them out.

Then, powerless to resist, I opened the envelope with one swift tear.

Dear Mrs. Godfrey,

Forgive me for my intrusion. It has taken me many years to find you. I understand that you were an army nurse stationed in Bora-Bora during the war. If I am correct, if you are indeed the woman I seek, I urgently need to speak with you. I was raised in the Tahitian islands, but have only now returned, with a mission to solve a mystery that has troubled me since girlhood. A horrific murder occurred on a quiet stretch of beach on Bora-Bora one evening in 1943. I am haunted by the tragedy, so much so that I am writing a book about the events that preceded a happening which, in many ways, changed the island forever.

I was able to locate the army employment records and I noticed that you were blocked out on leave that day, the day of the tragedy. Could you, by chance, remember something or someone on the beach that night? So many years have passed, but perhaps you recall something. Even a small detail may help in my search for justice. I pray that you will consider my request and get in touch. And, if you ever plan to visit the island again, there is something of yours I found here, something you might like to see again. I would love nothing more than to show it to you.

Yours Truly,
Genevieve Thorpe

I stared at the letter in my hands. Genevieve Thorpe. No, I did not know this woman. *A stranger.* And here she was, stirring up trouble. I shook my head. *Ignore it.* Too many years had passed. How could I go back to those days? How

14

could I relive it all? I closed my eyes tightly, willing the memories away. *Yes, I could just ignore it.* It wasn't a legal inquiry or a criminal investigation. I did not owe this woman, this *stranger,* anything. I could throw the envelope into the garbage can and be done with it. But then I remembered the last few lines of the letter. "If you ever plan to visit the island again, there is something of yours I found here, something you might like to see again." My heart, already in poor condition, raced at the thought of it. *Visit the island again? Me? At my age?*

"Grandma, are you all right?" Jennifer leaned in and wrapped her arm around my shoulder.

"I'm fine," I said, composing myself.

"Do you want to talk about it?"

I shook my head and tucked the letter safely inside the book of crossword puzzles on the coffee table.

Jennifer reached for her bag and began fumbling inside. She retrieved a large manila envelope, wrinkled and worn. "I want to show you something," she said. "I was going to wait until later, but"—she took a deep breath—"I think it's time."

She handed me the envelope.

"What is this?"

"Look inside," she said slowly.

I lifted the flap and pulled out a stack of black-

and-white photos, instantly recognizing the one on top. "That's me!" I cried, pointing to the young woman dressed in white nurse's garb, with a coconut tree in the distance. Oh how I had marveled at the palms the first day I set foot on the island, almost seventy years ago. I looked up at Jennifer. "Where did you find these?"

"Dad found them," she said, eyeing my face cautiously. "He was going through some old boxes and these were tucked inside. He asked me to return them to you."

My heart swelled with anticipation as I flipped to the next photograph, of Kitty, my childhood friend, sitting on an overturned canoe on the beach, her feet kicked out like a movie star's. Kitty *could* have been a movie star. I felt the familiar pain in my heart when I thought of my old friend, pain that time hadn't healed.

There were several more in the stack, many of them scenes of the beach, the mountains, lush with flora, but when I reached the last photograph, I froze. *Westry. My Westry.* There he was with the top button of his uniform undone, his head tilted slightly to the right with the bungalow's woven palm wall in the background. *Our bungalow.* I may have taken thousands of photographs in my life, and so many of them were forgotten, but not this one. I remembered everything about the snapshot, the way the air had smelled that evening—of seawater and

16

freesia, blooming in the moonlight. I could recall the feeling I had in my heart, too, when my eyes met his through the lens, and then there was what happened in the moments that followed.

"You loved him, didn't you, Grandma?" Jennifer's voice was so sweet, so disarming, that I felt my resolve weaken.

"I did," I said.

"Do you think of him now?"

I nodded. "Yes. I have always thought of him."

Jennifer's eyes widened. "Grandma, what happened in Tahiti? What happened with this man? And the letter—why did it affect you in the way it did?" She paused, and reached for my hand. "Please tell me."

I nodded. *What would be the harm in telling her?* I was an old woman. There wouldn't be many consequences now, and if there were, I could weather them. And how I longed to set these secrets free, to send them flying like bats from a dusty attic. I ran my finger along the gold chain of my locket, and nodded. "All right, dear," I said. "But I must warn you, don't expect a fairy tale."

Jennifer sat down in the chair beside me. "Good," she said, smiling. "I've never liked fairy tales."

"And there are dark parts," I said, doubting my decision.

She nodded. "But is there a happy ending?"

"I'm not sure."

Jennifer gave me a confused look.

I held the photo of Westry up to the light. "The story isn't over yet."

Chapter 1

August 1942

Kitty Morgan, you did not just say that!" I set my goblet of mint iced tea down with enough force to crack the glass. Mother would be happy to know that I hadn't spoiled her set of Venetian crystal.

"I most certainly did," she said, smirking victoriously. Kitty, with her heart-shaped face and that head full of wiry, untamable blond ringlets springing out of the hairpins she'd been so meticulous about fastening, hardly provoked anger. But on this subject I held my ground.

"Mr. Gelfman is a *married* man," I said in my most disapproving voice.

"James," she said, elongating his first name for dramatic effect, "is impossibly unhappy. Did you know that his wife disappears for weeks at a time? She doesn't even tell him where she's going. She cares more about the cats than she does him."

I sighed, leaning back into the wooden bench swing that hung from the enormous walnut tree in my parents' backyard garden. Kitty sat beside me then, just as she had when we were in grade school. I looked up at the tree overhead, its leaves tinged with a touch of yellow, hinting that autumn was imminent. *Why must things change?* It seemed like only yesterday that Kitty and I were two schoolgirls, walking home arm in arm, setting our books down on the kitchen table and making a dash to the swing, where we'd tell secrets until dinnertime. Now, at twenty-one, we were two grown women on the verge of, well, something—not that either of us could predict what.

"Kitty," I said, turning to face her. "Don't you understand?"

"Understand what?" She looked like a rose petal, sitting there in her dress brimming with pink ruffles, with those wild curls that were getting even more unruly in the late-afternoon humidity. I wanted to protect her from Mr. Gelfman, or any other man she intended upon falling in love with, for none would be good enough for my best friend—certainly not the married ones.

I cleared my throat. *Does she not know Mr. Gelfman's reputation?* Certainly she remembered the hordes of girls who had flaunted themselves at him in high school, where he had been

Lakeside's most dashing teacher. Every girl in English Lit had hoped to make eye contact with him as Elizabeth Barrett Browning's "How Do I Love Thee?" crossed his lips. That was all girlish fun, I contended. But had Kitty forgotten about the incident five years ago with Kathleen Mansfield? How could she forget? Kathleen—shy, big breasted, terribly dim-witted—had fallen under Mr. Gelfman's spell. She hovered near the teachers' lounge at lunch, and waited for him after school. Everybody wondered about them, especially when one of our girlfriends spotted Kathleen in the park with Mr. Gelfman after dusk. Then, suddenly, Kathleen stopped coming to school. Her older brother said she'd gone to live with her grandmother in Iowa. We all knew the reason why.

I crossed my arms. "Kitty, men like Mr. Gelfman have only one objective, and I think we both know what that is."

Kitty's cheeks flushed to a deeper shade of pink. "Anne Calloway! How dare you suggest that James would be anything but—"

"I'm not *suggesting* anything," I said. "It's just that I love you. You're my best friend, and I don't want to see you get hurt."

Kitty kicked her legs despondently as we swung for a few minutes in silence. I reached into the pocket of my dress and privately clutched the letter nestled inside. I'd picked it up at the post

20

office earlier that day and was eager to sneak away to my bedroom to read it. It was from Norah, a friend from nursing school who'd been writing me weekly accounts from the South Pacific, where she'd been serving in the Army Nurse Corps. She and Kitty, both hot-tempered, had a falling out in our final term together, so I chose not to bring up the letters with Kitty. Besides, I couldn't let on to her how much Norah's tales of the war and the tropics had captivated me. They read like the pages of a novel—so much so that a part of me dreamt of taking my newly minted nursing degree and joining her there, escaping life at home and the decisions that awaited. And yet, I knew it was just a fanciful idea, a daydream. After all, I could help with the war efforts at home, by volunteering at the civic center or collecting tin cans and assisting with conservation projects. I shook my head at the thought of traipsing off to a war zone in the tropics mere weeks before my wedding. I sighed, grateful I hadn't uttered a word of it to Kitty.

"You're just jealous," Kitty finally said, still smug.

"Nonsense," I retorted, pushing Norah's letter deeper into my pocket. The sun, high in the summer sky, caught the diamond ring on my left hand, producing a brilliant sparkle, as arresting as a lighthouse's beacon on a dark night, reminding me of the unavoidable fact that I was engaged. Bought and paid for. "I'm marrying Gerard in less than a month," I said. "And I couldn't be happier."

Kitty frowned. "Don't you want to do something else with your life before you"—she paused as if the next few words would be very difficult, very displeasing to say—"before you become Mrs. Gerard Godfrey?"

I shook my head in protest. "Marriage, my dear, is not suicide."

Kitty looked away from me, her gaze burrowing into a rosebush in the garden. "It might as well be," she murmured under her breath.

I sighed, leaning back into the swing.

"Sorry," she whispered, turning back to me. "I just want you to be happy."

I reached for her hand. "But I will be, Kitty. I wish you'd see that."

I heard footsteps on the lawn and looked up to find Maxine, our housekeeper, approaching, tray in hand. In heels, she walked steadily across the lawn, requiring only a single hand to bear a laden silver platter. Papa had called her graceful once, and she was. She practically floated.

"May I fetch you girls anything?" Maxine asked in her beautiful, heavily accented voice. Her appearance had changed very little since I was a girl. She was petite, with soft features, great big sparkling green eyes, and cheeks that smelled of vanilla. Her hair, now graying slightly, was pulled back into a tidy chignon, never a strand out of place. She wore a white apron, always clean and freshly starched to a remarkable stiffness, cinched tightly around her small waist. Lots of families in the neighborhood had servants, but we were the only household that employed a *French* housekeeper, a fact Mother was quick to point out at bridge parties.

"We're fine, Maxine, thank you," I said, weaving my arm through hers.

"There is something," Kitty said conspiratorially. "You can convince Anne not to marry Gerard. She doesn't love him."

"Is this true, Antoinette?" Maxine asked. I was five years old the day she came to work in our home, and after a quick once-over, she said declaratively, "You do not have the face of an Anne. I shall call you Antoinette." I had felt very fancy.

"Of course it's not true," I said quickly. "Kitty is just in one of her *moods*." I gave her a sideways glance of disapproval. "I'm the luckiest girl in Seattle. I'm marrying Gerard Godfrey."

And I *was* lucky. Gerard was tall and impossibly handsome, with his strong jaw and dark brown hair and eyes to match. He was quite wealthy, too, not that it mattered to me. Mother, on the other hand, frequently reminded me that at twenty-seven he enjoyed the distinction of being the youngest vice president at First Marine Bank, a title that meant he would come into a fortune when he took over for his father. You'd have to be a foolish woman to turn down a proposal from Gerard Godfrey, and when he asked for my hand, under this very walnut tree, I nodded without a moment's hesitation.

Mother had been giddy upon hearing the news. She and Mrs. Godfrey had planned the union since I was in infancy, of course. Calloways would marry Godfreys. It was as natural as coffee and cream.

Maxine picked up a pitcher of iced tea and refilled our goblets. "Antoinette," she said slowly, "have I ever told you the story of my sister, Jeanette?"

"No," I said. "I didn't even know you had a sister." I realized that there were many things I didn't know about Maxine.

"Yes," she said quietly, looking thoughtful. "She loved a boy, a peasant boy from Lyon. They were madly in love. But our father and mother pushed her toward another man, a man who made a decent wage in the factories. So she parted with her farm boy and married the factory worker."

"How heartbreaking," I said. "Did she ever see him again?"

"No," she replied. "And she was miserable."

I sat up and smoothed my dress, blue crepe with

a delicate belt on the bodice that was just a trifle too tight. Mother had brought it home from one of her European shopping trips. She had a habit of buying clothing too small for me. "Well, that's very sad, and I'm sorry for Jeanette. But this does not have any application to my life. You see, I *love* Gerard. There is no one else."

"Of course you love Gerard," said Maxine, reaching down to pick up a napkin that had fallen on the grass. "You've grown up with the boy. He is like a brother to you."

Brother. The word had an eerie pulse to it, especially when used to describe the man I was going to marry. I shivered.

"Dear," she continued, catching my eyes and smiling, "it is your life and your heart. And you say there is no one else, and that may be true. I'm simply saying that maybe you haven't given yourself enough time to find him."

"Him?"

"Your one true love," she said simply. The four words rolled off her tongue in a natural, matter-of-fact way, implying that such deep, profound feeling was available to anyone who sought it, like a ripe plum dangling from a branch, ready for the picking.

I felt a chill come over me, which I blamed on the breeze that had just picked up, and shook my head. "I don't believe in fairy tales, or in knights in shining armor. I believe that love is a choice.

You meet someone. You like them. You decide to love them. It's that simple."

Kitty rolled her eyes. "How horribly *unromantic,*" she groaned.

"Maxine," I said, "what about you? Were you ever in love?"

She ran a cloth along the side of the tea tray, wiping up the rings our goblets had left. "Yes," she said, without looking up.

Blinded by curiosity, I didn't stop to consider that maybe the memory of this man was painful for her. "Was he an American or a Frenchman? Why didn't you marry him?"

Maxine didn't answer right away, and I instantly regretted my line of questioning, but then she opened her mouth to speak. "I didn't marry him because he was already married to someone else."

We all looked up when we heard Papa's footsteps on the terrace. Puffing on a cigar, he crossed the grass toward the three of us. "Hi, kid," he said, smiling at me through his thick gray mustache. "I didn't think you were coming home until Tuesday."

I returned his smile. "Kitty talked me into taking an earlier train."

I had finished my college courses at Portland State University in the spring, but Kitty and I had stayed on for an additional two months of training to obtain our nursing licenses. What

26

we'd do with these credentials was of great concern to our parents. Heaven forbid we actually use them.

Gerard, on the other hand, found the whole business of being engaged to a trained nurse, in a word, amusing. Our mothers didn't work, nor did any of the women we knew. He joked that the cost of hiring a driver to chaperone me to my hospital shifts would amount to more than any paycheck I'd ever make, and yet if donning the white cap and tending to the sick was what I wanted to do, he promised to support me.

In truth, I didn't know what I wanted to do. I'd chosen nursing because it stood in stark contrast to everything I'd grown to detest about the lives of the women I knew—Mother, who devoted herself to luncheons and the current state of ladies' hemlines; and my school friends, who had spent months luxuriating in Paris or Venice upon high school graduation, with nary a worry, save finding a rich husband so they could perpetuate the lifestyles of their youth.

No, I didn't fit that mold. Its confines stifled me. What spoke to me was nursing, in all of its gritty rawness. It promised to fulfill a part of me that had lain empty for the majority of my life, a part that longed to help others in a way that had nothing to do with money.

Maxine cleared her throat. "I was just leaving," she said to Papa, picking up the tray with one fluid swoop. "Can I get you anything, Mr. Calloway?"

"No, Maxine," he said. "I'm just fine. Thank you." I liked the way he spoke to Maxine, always kind and gentle, never cross and hurried, which was the way of Mother.

She nodded and made her way across the emerald lawn, disappearing into the house.

Kitty looked up at Papa with concerned eyes. "Mr. Calloway?"

"Yes, Kitty?"

"I heard about another wave of men being drafted"—she gulped—"for the war. I read about it in the newspaper on the train. Do you know if any from Seattle have been notified?"

"It's still very early, Kitty Cat," he said, using the name he'd given Kitty when we were in grade school. "But the way things are progressing in Europe, I think we'll see a great deal of men going off to fight. I just ran into Stephen Radcliffe in town and heard that the Larson twins are shipping out Thursday."

I felt a tightness creep up in my chest. "Terry and Larry?"

Papa nodded solemnly.

The twins, a year younger than Kitty and me, were going off to war. *War.* It hardly seemed possible. Wasn't it only yesterday that they were tugging at my pigtails in grade school? Terry was shy and had cheeks speckled with freckles. Larry, a bit taller and less freckled, was a born comedian. Both redheads, they were rarely seen apart. I wondered if they'd be allowed to stand next to each other on the battlefield. I closed my eyes as if to try to suppress the thought, but it lingered. *Battlefield.*

Papa read my mind. "If you're worried about Gerard shipping out, don't," he said.

Gerard was as strong and gallant as any man I knew, surely, but as hard as I tried, I couldn't imagine him anywhere but in a suit at the bank. And yet, as much as I wanted him spared from fighting, a secret part of me longed to see him in uniform, to see him stand for something other than dollars and cents.

"His family's position in the community is too important," he continued. "George Godfrey will see that he isn't drafted."

I hated the conflict brewing inside my heart— the fact that I took comfort in Gerard's protected position and detested it at the same time. It wasn't right that men from poor families had to fight a nation's war while a privileged few dodged the draft for frivolous reasons. Sure, George Godfrey, a bank mogul now in failing health, was a former senator, and Gerard was the next in line to fulfill his duties at the bank. But even so, it was unsettling to imagine the Larson twins fighting in a European bunker in the dead of winter while Gerard rested comfortably in a heated office with a leather chair that swiveled.

Papa could read the anxiety in my eyes. "Don't let it worry you. I hate to see you worry."

Kitty stared at her hands in her lap. I wondered if she was thinking of Mr. Gelfman. *Will he join the war too?* He couldn't be more than thirty-eight, surely young enough for combat. I sighed, wishing I could will the war to an end. The ill tidings of conflict hovered, creeping in and spoiling even the most perfect summer afternoon.

"Mother's eating in the city tonight," Papa said, glancing toward the house with a look of uncertainty that had all but disappeared by the time his eyes met mine. "Will I have the privilege of dining with you ladies this evening?"

Kitty shook her head. "I have an engagement," she said vaguely.

"Sorry, Papa, I'm having dinner with Gerard."

He nodded, suddenly looking sentimental. "Look at you two, all grown up, with big plans of your own. It seems like only a moment ago that you girls were out here with your dolls."

Truth be told, I longed for those easy, uncomplicated days that revolved around paper dolls, dress-up, and tea parties on the terrace. I buttoned my sweater against the wind on my skin—winds of change.

"Let's go inside," I said, reaching for Kitty's hand.

"OK," she said sweetly. And just like that, we were Kitty and Anne again.

• • •

My eyes burned from the haze of cigarette smoke hovering like a low cloud over our table. The lights were dim in the Cabaña Club, the place everyone in Seattle went dancing on Saturday nights. I squinted, trying to make out the scene.

Kitty pushed a box wrapped in blue paper toward me. I eyed the gold ribbon. "What's this?"

"Something for you," she said, grinning.

I looked at her quizzically, and then at the box, and carefully untied the ribbon before peeling off the wrapping. I lifted the lid of a white jewelry box and pushed aside the cotton lining to reveal a sparkling object inside.

"Kitty?"

"It's a pin," she said. "A friendship pin. Remember those little rings we had as children?"

I nodded, unsure if the stinging in my eyes was from the smoke or the memories of simpler times.

"I thought we needed a grown-up version," she said, pulling a lock of hair away from her shoulder to reveal a matching pin on her dress. "See? I have one too."

I eyed the silver bauble, round and dotted with tiny blue stones that formed the shape of a rose. It glistened under the dim lights of the club. I flipped it over, where I found an engraving: *To Anne, with love, Kitty.*

"It's perfectly beautiful," I said, pinning the piece to my dress.

31

She grinned. "I hope it will be a symbol of our friendship, a reminder to us both that we'll never keep secrets from one another, that we'll not let time or circumstances change things between us."

I nodded in agreement. "I'll wear it always."

She grinned. "Me too."

We sipped our sodas and scanned the bustling club, where friends, schoolmates, and acquaintances reveled in what could be the very last Saturday night before whatever waited in the wings scooped them up. War. Marriage. The unknown. I swallowed hard.

"Look at Ethel with David Barton," Kitty whispered in my ear. She pointed to the two of them huddled together at the bar. "His hands are all over her," she said, staring a little too long.

"She ought to be ashamed of herself," I said, shaking my head. "She's engaged to Henry. Isn't he away at school?"

Kitty nodded. But instead of mirroring my disapproving gaze, her face told a different story. "Don't you wish someone could love you *that* much?" she said wistfully.

I scrunched my nose. "That, my dear, is not love."

"Sure it is," she said, planting her cheek in her hand. We watched the couple saunter hand in hand out to the dance floor. "David's crazy about her."

"Crazy, sure," I said. "But not *in love* with her."

Kitty shrugged. "Well, they have passion."

I retrieved the pressed powder from my purse and dabbed my nose. Gerard would be there soon. "Passion is for fools," I said, snapping the compact closed.

"Maybe," she replied. "But just the same, I'll take my chances with it."

"Kitty!"

"What?"

"Don't talk like that."

"Like what?"

"Like a *loose* woman."

Kitty giggled, just as Gerard arrived at our table with his friend Max, a colleague from the bank— short, with curly hair, a plain, honest face, and eyes for Kitty.

"Do share your joke, Kitty," Gerard said, grinning. I loved his smile, so charming, so confident. He towered over the table in his gray suit, adjusting a loose cufflink. Max stood at attention, panting like a German shepherd, eyes fixed on Kitty.

"You tell him, Anne," Kitty said, daring me with her smirk.

I cleared my throat, smiling deviously. "Yes, Kitty was just saying that, well, that she and Max made a better dance duo than the two of us, Gerard." I shot Kitty a victorious look. "Can you believe that?"

Gerard grinned, and Max's eyes lit up. "Now,

we can't have her carrying on like that, can we, dear?" He looked toward the dance floor and held out his hand. "Shall we?"

The band began playing, and Max fumbled to his feet, grinning from ear to ear. Kitty rolled her eyes at me as she took Max's outstretched hand.

Gerard clasped his arms around my waist, smoothly, elegantly. I loved his firm grasp, his confidence.

"Gerard?" I whispered in his ear.

"What is it, sweetheart?" He was an excellent dancer—precise in the same way he was about finances, never missing a penny in his budgeting.

"Do you feel . . . ?" I paused to consider what, exactly, I was asking him. "Do you feel *passionate* about me?"

"Passionate?" he said, stifling a laugh. "You funny thing, you. Of course I do." He squeezed me a little tighter.

"Really passionate?" I continued, dissatisfied with his answer.

He stopped and lovingly pulled my hands toward his chin. "You're not doubting my love for you, are you? Anne, you must know by now that I love you more than anything, more than anything on earth."

I nodded, and closed my eyes. Moments later, the song stopped and another began, this one slower. I nestled closer to Gerard, so close I could feel the beat of his heart, and I was sure he could feel mine. We swayed to the clarinet's haunting melody, and with each step, I assured myself that we had *it*. Of course we did. Gerard was head over heels for me, and I for him. What nonsense these feelings of uncertainty were. I blamed Kitty for planting them. *Kitty.* I glanced over at her dancing unhappily with Max, when, out of nowhere, Mr. Gelfman appeared on the dance floor. He walked straight toward her, said something to Max, and took her into his arms as Max, crestfallen, scurried away.

"What is Kitty doing with *James Gelfman?*" Gerard asked, frowning.

"I don't like it," I said, watching as Mr. Gelfman twirled her around the room like a doll. His hands were too low on her waist, his grasp too tight. I thought of Kathleen, poor Kathleen, and winced.

"Let's go," I said to Gerard.

"So soon?" he said. "But we haven't even had dinner yet."

"Maxine left some sandwiches in the icebox," I replied. "I don't feel like dancing anymore."

"Is it Kitty?" he asked.

I nodded. I knew there was no stopping Kitty now. She had made that much clear. But I'd be damned if I was going to watch my best friend give away her heart, her dignity, to a man who wasn't worthy of her—a *married* man who wasn't worthy of her. But there was more to the story, something my mind wouldn't acknowledge just then, though my heart already knew: I envied Kitty. I wanted to *feel* what she was feeling. And I feared I never would.

The doorman handed me my blue velvet coat, and I tucked my hand into the crook of Gerard's arm. Warm. Safe. Protected. I told myself I was very lucky.

On the drive home, Gerard wanted to talk about real estate. Would we buy an apartment in the city or something in Windermere, the opulent neighborhood of our youth, near our parents? The apartment would be closer to the bank. And how gay it would be to live on Fifth Avenue, he crooned. But the Buskirks would be selling their home this fall, the big Tudor with the four dormers in front. We could buy it and renovate; build a new wing for the help and a nursery for the baby. For the *baby*.

Gerard droned on and suddenly the air in the car felt warm. Too warm. The road blurred in front of me and the street lights multiplied. What was wrong with me? *Why can't I breathe?* Dizzy, I clenched the door handle to steady myself.

"Are you all right, darling?"

"I think I just need a little air," I said, rolling the window down.

He patted my arm. "Sorry, honey, am I overwhelming you?"

"A little," I replied. "It's just that there are so many decisions to make. Can we take them one at a time?"

"Of course," he said. "No more talk of homes for now."

He turned the car in to Windermere, passing the stately, lit columns flanking the entrance. Within was a well-tended sanctuary, where gardeners spent hours manicuring lawns and grooming flowerbeds, not a petal askew, and governesses tended to children in a similar fashion. We passed Gerard's parents' home, the gray gable mansion on Gilmore Avenue, and the Larsons' white colonial, with the clipped boxwood hedges and stone urns shipped from Italy. *What is wrong with me?* Here was a man who loved me, who wanted to give me a beautiful, comfortable life, a life I was accustomed to. I scolded myself.

Gerard parked the car in my parents' driveway, and we walked into the house and straight to the darkened kitchen. "Maxine's probably gone to bed," I said, looking at the clock. Half past nine. Maxine always retired to her downstairs quarters at nine.

"Would you like a sandwich?" I offered.

"No, I'm fine," Gerard said, consulting his watch, a Rolex—my gift to him on his twenty-fifth birthday.

We both looked up when we heard footsteps.

"Papa?" I said, peering around the corner, where I detected a female form coming down the stairs in the darkness.

"Mother?" I turned on the hallway light and realized I'd been mistaken.

"Your mother isn't home yet," Maxine said. "I was just stocking your bathroom with towels. Francesca wasn't here today, and I wanted you to have some for the morning."

"Oh, Maxine," I said. "Look at you worrying about *my towels* at this late hour. I will not hear of it! Please, get some rest. You work far too hard."

When she turned her head to look at the clock, I thought I detected a glint of moisture in her eyes. *Has she been crying or is it just the day's exhaustion?*

"I think I shall say good night," she said, nodding. "Unless you need anything."

"No," I said. "No, we're fine. Sweet dreams, Maxine." I wrapped my arms around her neck the way I had done as a girl, taking in a breath of her vanilla cheeks.

After she'd left, Gerard kissed me, gently, quickly. *Why can't he kiss me longer?* "It's getting late," he said. "I suppose I should be on my way too."

"Do you have to go?" I said, pulling him toward me, eyeing the couch in the living room with other intentions. *Why must Gerard be so practical?*

38

"We need our rest," he said, shaking his head. "Tomorrow's going to be a big day."

"A big day?"

"The party," he said, looking at me suspiciously. "Have you forgotten?"

Until that moment, I had. Gerard's parents were hosting an engagement party for us at their home, on that enormous lawn, trimmed so perfectly that it resembled the ninth hole at Papa's country club. There would be a band, croquet, ice sculptures, and platters of tiny sandwiches served by white-gloved waiters.

"Just put on a pretty dress and be there by two," he said with a grin.

"I can do that," I replied, leaning into the doorway.

"Good night, darling," he said, walking out to the driveway.

I stood there watching as his car motored away, until the sound of the engine was swallowed up by the thick quiet of the August night.

Chapter 2

M axine!"

I opened my eyes, blinking a few times, trying in my deep state of grogginess to place the voice—loud, shrill, a bit angry, but mostly annoyed, and definitely frustrated.

Mother. She was home.

"I told you Anne would wear the blue dress today—why isn't it pressed?" The voice was nearer now, right outside my bedroom door.

I pushed the quilt aside and sat up, reaching for my robe before setting my feet down reluctantly on the cool hardwood floors. *Poor Maxine.* She didn't deserve to be shouted at. Again.

I opened the door. "Mother," I said cautiously. I knew better than to contradict her fashion decisions. I walked slowly into the hallway. "I thought I'd wear the red one today. The one you bought in Paris."

She smiled, a few paces away on the landing, yanking the drapes open with a vexed glance at Maxine. "Oh, good morning, dear," she said, walking toward me. "I didn't know you were up." She reached out her arms and cradled my face in her hands. "You look tired, love. Were you out late last night? With Gerard?" She always said his name with a tone of excitement, the way one might gush about a chocolate cream pie. It had occurred to me at least once that Mother might like to marry Gerard Godfrey herself.

I shook my head. "No, it was an early night."

She pointed to the puffiness under my eyes. "Then why the dark circles?"

"I couldn't sleep," I said.

Maxine approached timidly, with a dress on a hanger. "Antoinette," she said. "Is this the one?"

I nodded.

"I wish you wouldn't call her that, Maxine," Mother snapped. "She's not a girl anymore. She's a woman, and about to be married. Please use her given name."

Maxine nodded.

"Mother," I squeaked, offering my hand to Maxine, "I *like* to be called Antoinette."

Mother shrugged. A new pair of diamond earrings swung from her lobes. "Well, I suppose it doesn't matter now. Next month you'll be Mrs. Gerard Godfrey, the most important name of all."

I felt a prickly sensation in my underarms. My eyes met Maxine's, and we shared a knowing look.

"Must you wear the red dress, darling?" Mother continued, tilting her head to the right. She was a beautiful woman, far prettier than I would ever be. I'd known it since I was young. "I'm not sure it's your color."

Maxine looked Mother straight in the eyes, something she didn't do often. "I think it's perfect on her, Mrs. Calloway," she said, leaving no room for further argument.

Mother shrugged. "Well then, wear whatever you wish, but we need to leave for the Godfreys' in two hours. You had better start getting ready." She was halfway down the hall when she turned back to Maxine and me. "And put your hair up, dear. Your profile looks so much more becoming that way."

I nodded in compliance. Mother subscribed to all the fashion magazines and attended the runway shows in New York and Paris each year. She cared a great deal about appearances, in a way that other mothers didn't—always designer dresses, perfect hairdos, the latest accessories. And for what? Papa hardly noticed. And the more clothes she amassed, the unhappier she seemed.

When Mother was out of earshot, I rolled my eyes at Maxine. "She's in a *mood,* isn't she?"

Maxine handed me the dress. Her eyes told me she was still smarting from Mother's dismissive tone. We walked back to my room, and I shut the door.

I draped the dress against my body. "Are you sure this one will look all right on me?"

"What's bothering you, Antoinette?" she asked. I could feel her eyes piercing my skin, demanding an answer I wasn't yet prepared to give.

I gazed down at my bare feet on the hardwood floor. "I don't know," I said, hesitating. "I worry that it's all happening so fast."

Maxine nodded. "You mean the engagement?"

"Yes," I said. "I love him; I really do. He's such a good man."

"He is a good man," she said simply, leaving room for me to continue.

I sat down on the bed and leaned my weary head against the headboard. "I know a person can't be perfect and all," I said, "but I sometimes wonder if I'd love him more, feel more deeply for him, if he'd do the right thing."

Maxine hung the dress up against the door. "And join the war?"

I nodded. "I just wish some things were different about him, about us."

"Like what, dear?"

"I want to feel proud of him the way the other women feel about their men joining the fight," I continued, pausing for a moment to think of other couples I knew. "I want to feel passionate about him." I giggled nervously. "Kitty thinks we don't have enough passion."

"Well," Maxine said expectantly, "do you?"

"I don't know," I replied, before shaking off the thought. "Listen to me going on like this. What a terrible fiancée I am even to speak this way." I shook my head. "Gerard is a dream come true. I'm lucky to have him. It's time I start playing the part."

Maxine's eyes met mine. I could see a fire brewing inside. "You must *never* talk that way, Antoinette," she said, making each word as clear and firm as she could muster with her heavily accented voice. "You can never play a part in life, especially not in love."

She wrapped her arm around my shoulders the way she'd done when I was a child, nuzzling her cheek against mine. "You be yourself," she said. "And never ignore what your heart is telling you,

43

even when it hurts, even when it seems like following it will be very difficult or untidy."

I sighed and buried my face against her shoulder. "Maxine, why are you telling me this? Why now?"

She forced a smile, her expression oozing regret. "Because I didn't follow my heart. And I wish I did."

Gerard's mother, Grace Godfrey, was a formidable woman in appearance. Her dark eyes and sharp features, which looked so handsome on Gerard, manifested in the female form as alarming, jarring. But when she smiled, the edges softened. As a child, I often wished Mother could be more like Mrs. Godfrey—practical, down-to-earth, despite her wealth and her position. In a time when women in her class offloaded much of the child rearing to hired help, Mrs. Godfrey did not. During their childhood, if one of the Godfrey boys skinned their knees, she'd shoo the nanny away and swoop in to bandage it herself, kissing the injured child gently.

"I don't know why Grace Godfrey doesn't let her nanny do her job," I overheard Mother complain to Papa when I was in grade school.

And true to form, as my parents and I walked across the lawn at the Godfreys' that afternoon, Grace could be seen assisting the waitstaff in carrying an ice sculpture—a large duck with three ducklings trailing precariously behind—from the terrace to a table on the lawn.

"Let me help you with that," Papa called out from behind me.

"Grace, be careful," Mother chimed in. "You'll put out your back."

Mrs. Godfrey relinquished her hold on the duck, which looked perilously on the verge of collapse, just as Papa dove in to assist.

"Thank you," she said, before turning to Mother. "Hello, Luellen, Anne. Isn't it a lovely day for a party?"

"Yes," I replied, peering up at the blue sky, a single fluffy white cloud its only resident. Tables covered the expansive lawn, and in every vase atop the lilac-colored table linens were five stems of purple hydrangeas. "It's . . ." I paused, suddenly overcome with emotion for the display of love for me, for Gerard, for our impending union. "It's all so beautiful."

"I'm glad you like it," Mrs. Godfrey said, entwining her substantial arm in mine. "Gerard's on the terrace waiting for you, dear."

I could see him in the distance, stretched out on a chaise longue, puffing on a cigar with his father. Smart, handsome, strong, he could have stepped from the pages of one of Mother's magazines. When he saw me, he stood up quickly and snuffed the celebratory smoke. "Anne," he called, waving, "I'll be right down."

I adjusted the sash on my dress, and Maxine's words rang in my ears: "You can never play a part in life, especially not in love." *But everyone plays a part, don't they? Mother. Papa. Kitty, in some ways. Even Maxine. Why should I be expected to behave any differently?*

Moments later I felt Gerard's arms around my waist. "You," he said, whispering in my ear, "are the most beautiful woman I have ever laid eyes on."

I blushed. "Do you really think so?"

"I know so," he replied. "Where did you get that dress? You are a vision."

"I wore it for you," I said. "I wanted you to—"

"Wait, is that Ethan Waggoner?" He squinted at the entrance to the garden as a man and his very pregnant wife walked through the gate. "Sorry to interrupt, sweetheart, but it's an old friend from college. Let me introduce you."

The afternoon was so filled with introductions and how-do-you-dos that I hardly saw Gerard, except for an occasional wave from across the terrace or a kiss on the cheek in passing. Engagement parties were not for the engaged.

As the dinner bell rang, I looked around for Kitty, realizing that I hadn't seen her all afternoon. *That's strange; she's known about the event for weeks.* Throughout dinner, her spot at the head table next to Gerard and me remained curiously empty. And when the band started to play the first song of the night, "You Go to My Head," I began to worry.

"Gerard," I whispered in his ear as we swayed on the dance floor, feeling what seemed to be a thousand pairs of eyes staring at us through the warm night air. I tried to ignore them. "Kitty hasn't shown up. I'm worried about her."

"She's probably just running behind schedule," he said, without a trace of concern. "You know Kitty."

True, Kitty was often late. But not *five hours* late—to the engagement party of her best friend. No, something was wrong. I felt it.

I rested my head on Gerard's lapel as he led me around the dance floor in perfect form. I closed my eyes and let him lead me, as I always did, never taking the reins for a moment, as I listened to the words of the song.

You go to my head and linger like a haunting refrain. . . . Did *Gerard* go to my head?

"Gerard," I whispered, "have you thought much about the war? About joining?"

He pulled back to look at me. "Sweetheart, if you're worried about me being drafted, please don't. Father's already taken care of that."

I frowned. "Oh," I said, pausing to choose my words carefully. "But, don't you ever worry that . . ."

"Worry about what?"

My thoughts were interrupted by motion,

detected in the corner of my eye, at the entrance to the garden. Someone was waving, trying to get my attention. The lights from the dance floor blurred the periphery, but I squinted hard to bring the person into focus. *Kitty.* There she was, standing behind the garden gate. *Is it locked? Why isn't she coming in?* She dabbed a handkerchief to her eye. *No, something is wrong.*

The song ended and several other couples joined us on the dance floor. I leaned in close to Gerard and whispered, "Do you mind sitting this one out?"

He gave me a confused smile, but nodded, before I raced through the gate, where I found Kitty seated on the sidewalk, slumped over, head buried against her knees.

"Kitty, what happened?" I noticed her face first, the tear-smeared makeup down her cheeks, eyes red from crying.

"You must think I'm a terrible, terrible friend," she sobbed, burying her face again.

I smoothed her hair, tucking whatever stray locks I could back into her hairpins, but it was no use. Her curls were disheveled in a way I'd never seen before. "Of course I don't, dear," I said. "What's wrong? Tell me."

"I'm so sorry, Anne, for standing you up like I have," she sniffed. "You must consider me a wretched friend. And I am. I am a miserable, unworthy friend." More sobbing ensued, and I pulled out a fresh handkerchief from the fold of my dress and handed it to her.

"You are not an unworthy friend," I said. "You are my dearest friend."

Kitty blew her nose, and looked up at me with frightfully grief-stricken eyes. Her gaze telegraphed sadness, that was certain, but also a glint of desperation. Here was a woman on the verge of a drastic move. I looked away.

"I arrived hours ago," she said. "But I just couldn't come in."

"Why on earth not?"

She blew her nose again. "Because I can't bear to see you off," she said.

"But I'm not going anywhere, Kitty."

"That's just it," she said. "You are. You're getting married. You're changing. And I know I should be happy for you, but all I can think of is how I'm losing you."

"Oh, Kitty," I said. "You'll never *lose* me!"

She nodded. "But I will. And it's the way it has to be. I just haven't gotten used to it yet." She pointed to the party on the other side of the hedge. "It's why I couldn't join in tonight. I'm so sorry, Anne."

I reached for her hand. "No," I said firmly. "You mustn't apologize." I used the hem of my dress to blot an errant tear from her cheek.

"Anne," she said, a little distantly. "There's something I need to tell you."

I let go of her hand. "What?"

"You're not going to like it."

"Tell me anyway," I said, bracing myself for whatever was coming.

"I've made a big decision—about my future," she said. She cleared her throat. "You're moving on, and so must I."

"Kitty, whatever do you mean?"

She took a deep, calming breath. "You remember the pact we made when we signed up for nursing school together?"

I nodded. "Yes. We swore we wouldn't end up like our mothers."

"Exactly," she said, staring straight ahead. "And that we wanted a different life, a more meaningful life."

I frowned. "Kitty, if you're implying that by me marrying Gerard I'm—"

"No," she said quickly. "I don't mean that at all. I'm just saying that it occurred to me that there is something *I* can do with my life, with my skills—something of great meaning. I've been thinking about it for a while now, ever since we first heard rumors of the war, but tonight, Anne, it's clear what I need to do."

I clenched my hands tightly in my lap.

"I'm going away," she said. "Far away—to the South Pacific. I'm joining the Army Nurse Corps to assist with the war efforts. I was downtown today at the volunteer registration center. Anne, they need trained nurses. They're desperate for them. This could finally be a chance for me to do something of value."

My heart surged with emotion. I thought of the stories recounted in Norah's letters about the islands—the muggy nights with the stars so close you could touch them, the beauty and the mystery, the fear of destruction, of war, lurking around every corner. The men. And though I'd only dared to dream about what it would be like, I had no idea that Kitty had been quietly making plans to go.

I kicked a pebble, sending it flying into the street. "Are you sure?"

"Yes," she said softly.

I sighed.

"Listen," Kitty continued. "You're getting married. Everyone's getting married, or going to school, or going somewhere. I won't sit here idly and watch while everything changes. I want to be a part of the change."

Yes, change was happening to both of us, whether we wanted to participate or not. The closer we came to it, the more painful it felt. And now that we were staring it in the eye, it produced an ache in my heart that I could not ignore.

"Mother hates the idea, of course," Kitty continued, "of me running off to an untamed island, to mingle with *savages,* to live among army men, but I don't care. I don't care what anyone thinks, except"—her tone became more cautious—"well, you."

I couldn't bear to think of Kitty out there either, but not because of the "savages" or the men, though the latter did concern me a fair amount. No, I couldn't stand it that Kitty was leaving, flinging herself to another part of the world—without me.

"I've been corresponding with Norah," I finally confessed.

Kitty looked displeased, but then her eyes brightened. "Isn't she in the South Pacific now?"

"Yes," I said. "She's been after me to sign up."

Kitty grinned. "Well, she's wasting her time on the wrong girl."

"Maybe not," I said quietly.

I thought about the wedding, just weeks away. All the little details ran through my mind like the frames of a film. My dress, French silk. The blue garter. A five-tier cake, with fondant. Doilies. Bridesmaid bouquets. White peonies and lavender roses. I shuddered. *How can I get married without Kitty standing by my side?*

I sat up straighter and nodded to myself. "I'm going with you," I said matter-of-factly.

Kitty beamed. "Anne! No, you can't mean that. What about the wedding? We'd have to leave in under a week, and the commitment is at least nine months, maybe longer."

I shrugged. "They need nurses, don't they?" My heart pounded—with excitement, with anticipation, and also with fear.

Kitty nodded through her sniffles. "They do," she said. "The recruiter says the action in the Pacific is heating up, and they're in dire need of nurses."

I smiled. "What kind of friend would I be if I let you set off on the adventure of your life without me?"

Kitty threw her arms around me, and we sat there on the sidewalk together for the next song, and then another. The music from the party sounded as if it might be a world away, and in some ways it was. The clipped laurel hedge represented the border between the certain and the uncertain.

"Gerard will never forgive me," Kitty said, "for stealing his fiancée away on the eve of his wedding."

I shook my head. "That's nonsense. You're not taking me prisoner. I'm going because I want to."

I looked over my shoulder at the party behind us. My decision would come with consequences; I knew that. Mother would be beside herself. Papa would warn against it. And Gerard . . . *Gerard.* I sighed. He would find this hard to take—his fiancée going off to a battle zone while he stayed comfortably at home. I knew he'd also be hurt, which is what worried me most of all.

But I couldn't think about that, not now. If he loved me, truly loved me, he would wait—and if he wouldn't, well, then I'd cross that bridge when I came to it.

As each moment passed, I felt my resolve strengthen. I needed to go to the South Pacific with Kitty. Why, exactly? The answer was still hazy. And yet one thing was certain: In this new adventure, I would not be simply playing a part.

Chapter 3

Kitty jabbed her elbow into my side, and I groaned, opening my heavy eyelids. "Look out your window," she said, squealing with delight. "We're almost here!"

It had been a forty-five-minute flight from an island to the north, where we'd arrived by ship. I'd been seasick for a full four days and longed to be on land again. I looked around the cabin of the small plane, so gray and mechanical. A place for men. Yet, other than the pilots in the cockpit and a single soldier, a tall, gangly fellow with strawberry-blond hair and a freshly pressed uniform on his way back from an extended medical leave, the plane was filled to capacity with nurses.

"Look!" Kitty exclaimed, holding her hand to

her heart. "Have you ever seen anything more beautiful?"

I leaned over Kitty to have a look out the tiny window. I gasped as my eyes met the scene below—the impossibly light blue water against white sand and the lush, emerald-green hillside. I hadn't expected to catch my breath at the sight. Frankly, I hadn't expected much. Sure, Norah, now on a ship headed stateside, had talked of the islands' allure, but newspaper articles from home told a different story, one of an unrelenting tropical heat, squalor, and misery, where men fought in mosquito-infested swamps described in letters as "a living hell." And yet the view from the window didn't seem to fit that description. No, this island was something else, something entirely different.

My thoughts turned to Gerard and the look on his face when I boarded the plane—sad, unsure, a little frightened. He had been wonderful when I told him, the day after the party, that I was going. But there had been something concerning in his eyes too.

Of course, he tried to talk me out of going, but eventually he squeezed my hand and forced a smile. "I'll be here for you when you return. Nothing will change that," he said.

After a long talk before I left, we decided to postpone our wedding a year. Mother was devastated when she heard the news, running to her bedroom to weep. Papa was a little more difficult to read. I waited until the evening after the party at the Godfreys', right before supper, when he was sipping a scotch in his study. Little beads of sweat had appeared on his forehead. "Are you sure you want to do this, kid?"

"I'm sure," I said. "I can't explain it other than it just feels *right*."

He nodded, then lit a cigar, puffing the smoke toward the open window. His eyes glimmered. "I wish I had your courage."

"Papa—"

"Well, that's that," he said abruptly, snuffing out the cigar in an ashtray and any emotion lingering in the air. "We don't want to miss dinner. Maxine is making *croque monsieur*." And yet, Papa managed to take only one bite that night.

I straightened my dress. How had mine gotten so rumpled when Kitty's looked freshly pressed? I frowned. *Have I made a mistake coming here?* I folded my hands in my lap and eyed the landscape below—my new home, for a good portion of a year, at least.

Constance Hildebrand, the charge nurse who would be our superior on the island, stood up in the front of the plane and looked sternly at the group of young nurses. She was a portly woman with gray hair tucked severely under a nurse's cap clipped so tightly it looked painful. If she had a gentle side, she kept it under lock and key. "We are almost to the island," she said. It was loud in the airplane, and even though she spoke in a shout, I still had to read her lips to understand her completely. "Don't be fooled by its beauty; it isn't a place of luxury," she continued. "You will work harder and perspire more than you can imagine. The heat is harsh. The humidity is suffocating. And if the mosquitoes don't get you, the natives will. The ones close to the shoreline are friendly, but don't venture farther than that. Cannibal colonies still exist not far from the base."

I glanced at the other women near the aisle, wide-eyed and frightened, as Nurse Hildebrand cleared her throat. "I know you are tired, but there is work to be done," she said. "You will find your quarters, wash, and meet me in the infirmary at fourteen hundred hours. And, a word of warning: There will be a great many men watching your arrival, men who haven't seen women in a very long time, aside from the *wahine*." She shook her head for emphasis. "Do not oblige the men with eye contact. They must be made to behave like gentlemen."

One of the girls in the row in front of us whipped out her compact, dusting her nose with a bit of powder before applying a fresh coat of red lipstick.

Kitty leaned in toward me with a grin. "There

are two thousand men on the island," she whispered. "And forty-five of us."

I frowned at Kitty. How could she let her mind turn to men when all I could think of were Nurse Hildebrand's chilling warnings? "Do you really think there are *cannibals?*"

"Nah," Kitty said confidently. "She's just trying to scare us."

I nodded to reassure myself. "Besides," I added, "Norah didn't say anything about mosquitoes in her letters."

Kitty nodded in agreement. "Meredith Lewis— you know, Jillian's sister—was on another island near here. She arrived with the first wave of troops and said the cannibal stories are all fiction."

But instead of comforting me, Kitty's words hit my heart like shrapnel. Meredith Lewis had been in Gerard's class in high school. She'd stood next to him in his yearbook photograph, and the memory made me long for home. My heart swelled with uncertainty, but the thoughts quieted as the plane began to shudder and jolt.

Kitty and I held hands as we touched down with a thud, speeding down a runway that appeared dangerously close to the ocean. For a moment, it seemed a very real possibility that we would catapult right into that great body of water like a speeding torpedo. I quietly crossed my heart and said a prayer.

"Here goes," I whispered under my breath a few moments later, as I filed in with the other women to exit the plane.

I felt Kitty's hand on my shoulder behind me. "Thank you for coming with me," she whispered. "You'll be glad you did, I promise."

One by one, we walked down the stairs onto the airstrip. The breeze hit my face—warm and humid, and when I took a breath, I could almost feel steam rising in my lungs. A nurse to our right, who had powdered her nose right before stepping off the plane, now looked dewy and shiny-faced, and I noticed a bead of perspiration roll down her cheek. I resisted the urge to retrieve the compact in my handbag, reminding myself that it didn't matter how I looked; I was engaged.

I looked across the airstrip and saw that Nurse Hildebrand was correct—about the men, at least. A sea of dark green uniforms swarmed like hornets. The bold ones whistled; others just leaned up against trucks behind lit cigarettes, staring.

"You'd think they had never seen women before," Kitty whispered, batting her eyes at a soldier in the front of the crowd, who puffed up his chest and smiled at us confidently. "He's cute," she said, a little louder than she should have.

Nurse Hildebrand turned to face us. "Ladies, allow me to present Colonel Donahue," she said, turning toward a man in uniform decorated with at least a dozen medals and pins. As he crossed the tarmac, his men moved into formation. A hush came over the crowd, and the nurses watched in fascination as he approached. The colonel was about forty, maybe older, with golden skin, dark hair with specks of gray, and undeniably striking eyes. He looked powerful in uniform, and a little frightening, I thought.

"Nurse Hildebrand, ladies," he said, with a tip of his hat. "I would like to formally welcome you to Bora-Bora. We are grateful for the service you are bestowing on the country, and I can assure you that your work will not go without a heartfelt thanks from the men stationed on this island, myself included." He turned to the men and shouted, "At ease," and the men erupted in applause.

"What a perfect gentleman," Kitty said in a whisper, without taking her eyes off of the colonel.

I shrugged. The sun felt even hotter now, its rays pelting us with an intensity I hadn't noticed when we first stepped off the airplane. It radiated off the pavement, causing heat to swirl around us, unrelenting. Kitty's body swayed slowly next to mine. At first I thought she was moving to the Ella Fitzgerald recording playing from a jeep nearby, but when I turned to face her, I could see that her cheeks had gone white, and her arms limp. "Kitty," I said, reaching for her hand, "are you all right?"

Her eyes fluttered just as her legs buckled underneath her body. I was able to catch her as she fell, but her bag, overstuffed with dresses too formal for the island, was the real saving grace, cushioning her head against the unforgiving tarmac. She lay in a crumpled heap on the hot cement airfield with her head in my lap.

"Kitty!" I screamed, instinctively pulling the hem of her blue dress lower on her legs.

"Smelling salts!" Nurse Hildebrand ordered, pushing through the circle of hovering women. She produced a green glass vial and held it under Kitty's nose. "The sun has gotten to her," she said without emotion. "She'll become accustomed to it in time."

Colonel Donahue appeared at Nurse Hildebrand's side. "Get her a stretcher!" he shouted to a man near the airplane. "And quick."

"Colonel Donahue," Nurse Hildebrand said, "we're dealing with a simple case of heatstroke. She'll be fine, this one."

He eyed Kitty with a possessive look. "Just the same, I'd like to make sure she's comfortable."

"Suit yourself," Nurse Hildebrand replied.

Two men appeared moments later with a stretcher and lifted Kitty, now conscious but groggy, onto it.

"Anne," Kitty said, turning to me, "what happened?"

Colonel Donahue swooped in by her side before

I could respond. "It's always the prettiest ones who faint in the tropics," he said with a grin.

I didn't like his tone, but Kitty beamed. "How terribly embarrassing. Was I out long?"

The colonel smiled in return. The crowd around us was so thick I could no longer see through it. "Just long enough to miss the news that we're having a dance tonight in honor of your arrival," he said, phrasing the statement as if the dance might be solely for her.

Kitty smiled, much too flirtatiously to address a ranking colonel. "A dance?" she muttered weakly.

"Yes," he said, "a dance." He turned to face the crowd. "You heard that right, men, tonight at twenty hundred."

"Thank you," Kitty said, unable to stop smiling.

"My pleasure," he replied gallantly. "I'll just ask for one favor."

"Of course," Kitty said, still beaming.

"That you save a dance for me."

"I'd love to," she replied dreamily as the men began wheeling her through the crowd.

Kitty always knew how to make an entrance.

The rest of the crowd began moving. I looked down at my suitcase and Kitty's enormous bag and groaned. The men had scattered, and now I was left to carry both.

"Can you believe that?" a woman said from behind me. I turned around to find one of the new nurses. Her soft auburn waves resembled Rita

Hayworth's in *Life* magazine, but that was where the similarity ended.

"I'm sorry?" I said, unsure of her meaning.

"Your friend pulled quite a stunt there to get the colonel's attention," she said, smirking. A bit of lace protruded above the top button of her dress. I wondered if the reveal was purposeful.

A second later, another nurse, this one with shiny dark hair and a meek smile, appeared at her friend's side with a look of agreement.

"Oh no, no," I said. "You're not implying that Kitty fainted intentionally, are you?"

"It's exactly what I'm saying," the auburn-haired nurse replied, clearly the alpha of the pair. "Scenes like that don't happen *spontaneously*. She staged it."

"She most certainly did not," I said in protest. "If you ask me, I think you're jealous."

The dark-haired nurse gasped, as the other woman shrugged confidently. "You'll thank us someday," she said.

"For what?" I asked suspiciously.

"For warning you of what your little friend is capable of. I wouldn't trust that one as far as I could throw her around any man of mine."

I shook my head and continued walking, as fast as I could with two heavy bags, one more so than the other.

"How rude of us," the auburn-haired nurse spoke up. But the apology I had anticipated wasn't coming. "I almost forgot to introduce myself. I'm Stella, and this is Liz," she said, pointing to her brunette friend.

I kept walking, disregarding the introduction.

"And you are?"

"Anne," I barked, marching onward without turning around.

Our quarters in the nurses' barracks were simple, meager at best, just two crudely constructed beds, a dressing table, and one closet for the two of us to share. The flimsy cotton drapes, discolored to a pale yellow from the hot sun, seemed inadequate to block the light or the men's line of vision. I arrived to find Kitty standing on one of the beds, hammering a nail into the wall. "What do you think of this spot for a picture?" she asked, tilting her head a little. "I was thinking of hanging a photo of Mama and Papa."

I set her bag down with a thud and wiped my brow. "I think it's fine," I said blankly. "You're feeling better, I see."

"Yes, thanks, dear," she said. "I feel badly for leaving you in the crowd like that. But Colonel Donahue insisted."

I was beginning to dread the sound of *the colonel*'s name, but I was careful not to let it show. "I'm just glad you're OK."

Kitty flitted like a spring bird around our little second-story room, chattering on about how we'd fix the place up. A spare sheet would make a perfect valance, she crooned, and we'd certainly be able to locate a coffee table, somewhere, for tea. *Certainly.* And the walls, weren't they such a lovely, soothing color? *Yes, infirmary beige— very soothing.*

In my view, however, the room was dank and strange. The two navy-blue-and-white-striped mattresses were bare and speckled with visible stains. Stacks of threadbare linens sat folded in neat little piles atop each. I longed for Maxine then, even though the thought made me feel childish. She'd have jumped in and made the beds, settling each of us with a calming cup of tea.

I was on my own now.

"Anne, can you believe there's going to be a dance tonight? A dance! And Colonel Donahue wants to dance with *me!*"

There was that name again. *Why does it affect me so? Do I distrust his intentions, or are my feelings misplaced?* I remembered what Stella and Liz had said on the tarmac. They were jealous. I hated to think that I was too.

Kitty had a way with men that I would never have. I thought of Gerard and twisted my engagement ring around my finger, which was swollen from the heat.

"Yes, won't that be fun?" I chimed in, working hard to sound cheerful.

"I'm going to wear my yellow dress," Kitty

65

said, running to her suitcase. She looked great in yellow, especially in the dress she held up for my approval. I'd seen her wear it a half dozen times—on the last occasion with Mr. Gelfman's arms wrapped tightly around the bodice. Funny, she'd been so heartbroken about the man when we left Seattle, but the island seemed to have erased her memory. I vowed to keep mine intact.

Kitty looked into the mirror, pressing the dress to her body, smoothing out the wrinkles, which the island humidity would soon erase. "I don't know," she said. "Maybe I should wear the blue one, the one we bought at Frederick and Nelson's last spring. It's a bit more conservative, I guess."

I shook my head. "No," I said, thinking of Liz and Stella. I was determined to prove—to myself, anyway—that I was not jealous, that I was being the best friend I could to Kitty. It's why I followed her here, I reminded myself. "Wear the yellow one. You look stunning in it."

Kitty would be the most beautiful woman at the dance. She'd have the time of her life. And I'd be happy for her.

The infirmary, a white building with a red cross painted above the entryway, smelled of soap and ipecac, with a touch of rubbing alcohol thrown in for good measure. Kitty and I, the last two to arrive that afternoon, nestled into the circle of women watching Nurse Hildebrand as she demonstrated, on a nurse's arm, the art of wound care in the tropics. Bandages were to be wrapped, she said, counterclockwise, not too tight, but snug enough to stop the bleeding. "The wound needs to breathe," she said. "Too much or too little air, and you get infection." She paused, looking out through the windows at the distant hills. "Especially in this godforsaken place."

We spent the rest of the session rolling bandages into tight little bundles, then tucking them away in crates pulled off the plane. I laid out the big bolts of taupe linen on the table, trying not to dwell on the wounds they would one day cling to. Kitty took one end, and I another. After an hour, my fingers ached.

We worked in silence, mostly in fear of Nurse Hildebrand, for we all had plenty to say. But when she left to attend a matter in the mess hall, the women began to find their voices.

"She's a tough one, that Nurse Hildebrand," said a woman to our left. A few years older than Kitty and me, she had hair the color of straw, freckles dotting her nose, and large, friendly eyes. Her smile revealed crooked teeth, which she tried, unsuccessfully, to keep hidden behind pursed lips.

"She is," I said in agreement. "I don't understand—if she hates this place so much, why did she volunteer?"

"She has a past here," she said.

"What do you mean, 'a past'?"

"All I know is what another nurse told me on the mainland." She lowered her voice to a whisper. "She was here before, a very long time ago. And something bad happened."

"What happened?"

"I don't know exactly, but it's some kind of scandal."

"You can't mean that she's a criminal!" Kitty exclaimed.

The woman shrugged. "Who knows? But I wouldn't want to be caught on Nurse's bad side," she said. "I'm Mary," she continued, nodding to Kitty and me.

"I'm Anne."

"And I'm Kitty."

Mary tucked another rolled bandage into the crate on the table. "What brings you here?"

Kitty opened her mouth, but I spoke first. "Service to our country," I said simply.

Mary smirked. "Isn't that what we all say? No, why are you *really* here? We're all running from or searching for something. What's your story?" She looked down at my engagement ring, perhaps because I was tugging at it.

But this time, Kitty responded before I could. "Anne was engaged," she began, but I cut her off.

"*Is* engaged," I corrected her.

"Yes, Anne *is* engaged, but she delayed the wedding to come with me." Kitty nuzzled her shoulder against mine, a gesture of gratitude. "I was in a horrible romantic mess before we left. I felt I needed to escape."

"Me, too," Mary said, holding up her bare left hand. "My fiancé broke off our engagement. He came by one day and told me he didn't love me. Now, what were his exact words, again?" She looked up at the ceiling as if to scan her memories. "Yes," she continued. "He said, 'Darling, I love you but I am not *in love* with you.' If that wasn't enough, he then announced that he was going to marry my best friend. Apparently they'd been seeing each other for months. I'll be honest, girls, it almost sent me to the loony bin, that ordeal. When I was coherent enough to think about my next move, I knew I had to leave town. I wanted to go to the farthest corner of the world to dull the pain. Our wedding was going to be in the fall, at the Cartwright Hotel in San Francisco." She looked down at her hands and sighed. "It was going to be *grand*."

"I'm so sorry," I said.

"Thank you," she replied. "I don't mind talking about it now, not really." She began working on another bandage roll. "We were going to move to Paris," she continued. "He was—well, is— joining the Foreign Service." She shook her head wistfully. "I should never have fallen in love with Edward. Mother was right. He was much too good-looking for me." She shrugged, replacing the hurt in her eyes with practicality. "And now I'm here. And you?" She looked at me. "Do you love the man you're going to marry?"

"Of course I do," I said a little more defensively than I had planned.

"Then why are you here and not at home with him?"

Why am *I here and not home with him? Is the answer really that simple?* I pondered the question for a moment. *Is it adventure that I, like Kitty, seek? Am I listening to Maxine's words and giving myself a chance to wait for something— God help me, for* someone—*to come along before I seal my fate?* I shook my head, destroying the thought. *No, I am here for Kitty. Yes, that's it, plain and simple.*

"Because my friend needed me," I said, squeezing Kitty's hand.

"That's sweet," Mary said. "You're lucky, you know—to have each other. I don't have a friend like that."

Kitty, ever the generous spirit, smiled warmly at Mary. "You can have us."

Mary's charming grin revealed her imperfect teeth. "I'd like that," she said, tucking another bandage into the crate. We'd rolled at least a hundred, give or take. It was a small feat, yes, but I was proud of our accomplishment. A mountain of bandages on our first day on Bora-Bora. We were *doing something*. We were really living.

• • •

The nurses had two designated tables in the mess hall, a plain building with long cafeteria tables packed in rows. We were not to eat with the men, said Nurse Hildebrand. Even so, we were aware of their every move, as they were of ours. Their eyes bore into us as we ate—Spam and beans.

"This food is *awful*," Mary said, stabbing a green bean with her fork and holding it up to the light. "Look, this thing is petrified."

"We'll come home perfectly thin," Kitty said, smiling, ever the optimist.

Stella and Liz sat across from us, but after their comments about Kitty earlier in the day, I dismissed their presence. "Well, well," Stella said with dramatic flair, pointing to a corner table where three men sat. "Get a load of that!"

Mary and Kitty, unaware of my grudge, turned to see what the fuss was about. "He's the spitting image of Clark Gable," Kitty said in agreement. "I wonder who he is?"

"His name's Elliot," Stella said. "The corporal who carried my bag today introduced us. Isn't he dreamy?"

Mary nodded. "Very," she said, swallowing a bite of Spam with a strained gulp.

"It's too bad, though," Stella continued. "Word is that he's deeply in love with a woman back home. A married woman."

Our eyes widened in unison.

"He could have his pick of women here," she went on, shaking her head, "and yet rumor has it that he spends his leave holed up in his bunk writing in his journal, brooding about her."

"How romantic," Kitty said dreamily.

I nodded. "A man who loves a woman that much is very rare."

"Or very stupid," Stella rattled back. She went on about her plan to capture Elliot's attention, while I picked at my plate.

I took another look at the table, where this man, Elliot, sat. He did resemble Clark Gable. Handsome, with dark eyes and thick ebony hair that came to a curl at the front. Yet my eyes were drawn instead to another, seated to his left. Tall, but not nearly as built, with lighter, wispier hair and sun-kissed skin with a dusting of freckles. His left hand shoveled food into his mouth while his right cradled a book, one he was clearly engrossed in. As he turned the page, he looked up. His eyes immediately met mine, and the creases of his mouth formed an instant smile. I quickly snapped my head back around. *What has gotten into me?* I instantly regretted the breach of decorum.

I felt my cheeks burn as I forced a bite of Spam, trying my best to avert the gag reflex rising in my throat. Stella had seen the exchange, and she shot me a mocking glance, but I turned away, willing myself to regain composure.

Tropical nights were better than tropical days, I decided, even if there were mosquitoes. The break from the sun made the air more agreeable. And then there was the cool mist wafting off the sea, and the stars, those luminous stars, so close you could almost reach out and pluck one from the indigo sky.

Kitty and I walked arm in arm along the gravel path to the center of camp to join in the evening festivities, she in her yellow dress and I in my red one. Kitty had urged me to wear something more daring, and at the last moment, I'd conceded.

It wasn't much of a walk, maybe the equivalent of five city blocks, but it felt like a great distance in heels. We passed the infirmary and noticed an interior light shining. *Is Nurse Hildebrand inside?* We scurried past swiftly. As we neared the men's barracks, Kitty and I pretended not to hear the whistles from the men smoking outside.

A safe distance past, Kitty tugged at my arm. "Look," she said, pointing to a large green shrub erupting in the most breathtaking blossoms.

"They're beautiful," I said. "What are they?

She picked a red bloom from the bush. "Hibiscus," she said, tucking the flower behind her right ear, before offering one to me. "In French Polynesia, when your heart is taken, you wear the flower in your left ear," she said. "When it's not, you wear it in your right."

"How do you know that?"

Kitty grinned. "I just do."

I stared at the enormous bloom in my hands; its crinkly petals were a brilliant shade of crimson. "Then I must wear it in my left," I said, dutifully tucking the flower behind my ear.

"How lovely," Kitty said, pointing to a makeshift dance floor in the distance. It had been cobbled together from plywood. "Fairy lights."

Strands of tiny white lights hung above, crisscrossing the rafters constructed of palm fronds. Men huddled together on the sidelines, whispering among themselves, as a group of nurses made their way across the lawn. Five musicians took to the stage, tuning their instruments while an announcer wielded a microphone.

"I would like to welcome the corps of nurses to our little island," the announcer said. "Let's show them a good time, lads."

There was a round of cheering and applause before the band started, and for a moment, no one moved. "What are we supposed to do?" Kitty whispered. Her breath tickled my shoulder.

"Don't do anything," I said, wishing I had stayed behind in the room with a book.

Stella and Liz ventured forward a few steps, and two of the men followed suit, one bolder than the other. "May I have this dance?" a soldier with a southern accent and a swagger in his step said to Stella. The other sidled up to Liz. Both women obliged.

"Look at them," I said to Kitty. "So fast."

Kitty was too distracted to hear me. I knew whom she was looking for. Suddenly, though, a man approached us—well, approached Kitty. I recognized him from the morning on the airstrip. "I saw your flower," he said, bowing in an exaggerated way. Men did strange things around Kitty. "I'm Lance," he said, extending his hand to her, and she relinquished hers, allowing him to lay a mock kiss upon it.

I rolled my eyes. He was tall and athletic, with hair a forgettable shade of brown, sharp features, and a coy smile that made me distrust him instantly.

"I'm Kitty," she said, clearly flattered.

Lance grinned. "Would you like to dance?"

Kitty nodded, and he whisked her off to the dance floor, leaving me alone on the sidelines. I tapped my foot to the music. It was a fine band— for the middle of nowhere. I felt prickles on my arm when I heard a clarinet play the introductory lines to "A String of Pearls." I'd last heard the Glenn Miller tune on the Godfreys' lawn. At our engagement party. I sighed, suddenly feeling lonely. Out of place. Awkward. I tugged at my dress. I unfastened a wayward pin in my hair and clasped it back into place. *Where is Mary?* I

75

looked around, but saw only strange men staring at me. *Thank God for the flower.*

But oblivious to the ring on my finger or the code of the flower, a man approached me. His shirt looked wrinkled, and I could smell alcohol on his breath even before he opened his mouth. "Care to dance?"

"Thank you," I said politely, "but no. I think I'll sit this one out."

"You're much too pretty to be a wallflower," he protested. "Besides, I'm tired of *wahine*. I want to dance with a real American woman." He pried my hand from my side and led me out to the dance floor.

"Well, you see," I said, startled by his bravado, "I think I better not."

"Nonsense," he said, grinning. I could smell the sour odor of beer—too much beer—on his breath.

He pressed his cheek against mine and I could feel the scratchy stubble on his jawline. "You're pretty," he said, as the band struck up a melody. *Please, not a slow song.* His hands were hot and moist on my dress, and his embrace suffocating, yet I willed myself to endure; I could not cause a scene. I would have to make it to the end of the song.

But, to my horror, the song ended and another man approached, presumably a friend of my dancing partner's, and as the tempo hastened, I found myself caught between them. One twirled me by the arm, spinning me into the other. I bobbled back and forth like a ball on a tether. I looked around desperately for Kitty, and spotted her tucked into the arms of Lance. She looked happy, amused. *Don't cause a scene.* I felt a hand brush my breasts. *Whose?* I froze, even though my legs were still moving. My eyes darted from left to right, and another hand cinched my waist, this one firmer. The room began to spin, or maybe I began to spin. Men were all around me. Hot, sweaty. The humid air was thick. I felt my voice rising up in my throat, but nothing came out. And then, there was scuffling and a loud thud. Someone fell to the ground. The music stopped, and a crowd formed around my original dancing partner. Blood trickled from his nose. He was out cold.

I pushed my way through the crowd off the dance floor, self-consciously keeping my head down. I felt guilty, even though I'd done nothing wrong. I didn't want to be followed. I darted for the path back to the barracks, quickening my pace to a light jog when I passed the men's barracks. I felt tears welling up in my eyes as the wind whistled through the palms overhead. It was a lonely sound, so foreign, so strange. I missed the walnut tree. I missed Seattle.

Spooked by a sound in the bushes, I instinctively turned to the infirmary instead of continuing on. The poorly lit path and the island night seemed impossibly dangerous without Kitty by my side. *Kitty.* I worried about leaving her there. She'd be fine, though; Lance looked decent enough. Or so I convinced myself.

A light shone inside, and I expected to find Nurse Hildebrand at her desk. Seated there instead was a man, the very man I'd seen in the mess hall at dinner.

He smiled, and I offered a startled smile in return.

"Hello," he said from across the room. "Don't let me frighten you. I'm just looking for a bandage. I thought I could find one in here, but you all must have the place soldier-proofed."

I squinted, and could see that his hand was bleeding. I ran over to the box of bandages I'd rolled that afternoon. "Here," I said, pulling one out, "let me help you."

I told myself not to be embarrassed. I was a nurse. He was a patient. There was no reason to feel odd about the interaction, no reason to feel awkward about being alone with this man after dark.

"What happened?" I asked, dabbing his wound with gauze I'd soaked in rubbing alcohol.

He winced, but continued smiling. "You didn't see?"

"See what?"

"I couldn't bear to watch Randy Connors have his way with you on the dance floor," he said.

"Randy Connors? Have his way with me? I beg your pardon—"

"What? His hands were all over you."

He'd stated an obvious fact, but still I looked down at my feet, ashamed.

The soldier lifted my chin with his hand. "It's why I punched him."

I grinned. "Oh," I said, trying my best to compose myself. *Does he notice the tears in my eyes?* "It was you. Well, then I owe you my gratitude."

"You'll have to forgive the men," he said. "They haven't seen women like you all in months, some longer. We've been on this rock a long time."

I remembered the word the soldier had uttered, *wahine*. It had sounded dirty and harsh on his breath.

"Do you happen to know what *wahine* means?"

His eyes twinkled. "Why yes," he said. "That's Tahitian for *woman*."

I nodded. "Well, I don't care if these men have been away from women for a century. It's no excuse for barbarism."

"It's not," he said. "Which is why I avoid most of them. There are a few decent men here. You must learn to be direct with them. At home you can play coy; you can expect decorum and genteelness. Not here. The tropics bring out the savage in all of us. The island dulls your inhibitions. It changes you. You'll see."

"Well," I said dismissively, wrapping his knuckles with a linen bandage in just the way Nurse Hildebrand had instructed. "I, for one, don't believe that something can change you unless you *want* to be changed. Haven't you ever heard of free will?"

"Sure," he said, looking very amused. "I'm just saying that this place has a way of revealing the truth about people, uncovering the layers we carry and exposing our real selves."

I fastened the bandage with an aluminum bracket, and exhaled. "Well, I'm not sure about that," I said. "But you're all fixed up."

"I'm Westry," he said, extending his bandaged hand. "Westry Green."

"Anne Calloway," I replied, shaking his hand gently.

"See you around." He headed to the door without lingering.

"See you around," I said, catching a glimpse of red in his left hand. As the door clicked closed behind him, I reached up to my ear. The hibiscus was gone.

Chapter 4

W hat time did you come in last night?" I
asked Kitty the next morning from my bed
across the room. I'd been awake reading for at
least two hours, waiting for her to stir.

She took one look at the clock, then pressed her
head back into her pillow. "Late," she said, her
voice muffled by down stuffing.

"It's nearly nine," I said, remembering our good
fortune to have arrived on the island on a Friday.
Saturday was our only day of leave. "I won't let
you sleep away our only day off. Come on, let's
get dressed!"

She yawned and sat up. "I can't believe it's nine
already."

"Yes, sleepyhead," I said, walking to the closet.
I wanted to explore the beach today and I'd need
to wear something light.

Kitty stood up quickly. "I have to hurry," she
said. "Lance is taking me into town for the day."

My heart sank, and Kitty could tell.

"You can come too," she offered. "He invited
you."

"And be the third wheel?" I shook my head.
"No thanks. You go on your own."

Kitty shook her head, unbuttoning her nightgown and letting it fall to the floor, exposing her breasts, two perfect spheres. "You're coming with us," she said. "A few others are going too. Lance is taking a jeep. Elliot's coming, and Stella."

"What?" I said. "How did she wrangle him into going?"

"She didn't," Kitty said. "Lance did."

I pulled the curtains closed to hide Kitty's naked body from prying male eyes. "Is anyone else coming?" I thought of Westry.

"I think that's it," Kitty said, looking into the closet. "Wait, is there someone you were thinking of?" There was a hint of teasing in her voice.

I shook my head. "I was only thinking of Mary."

Kitty didn't look up from the closet.

"I didn't see her last night, did you?"

"No," she said, pulling out a powder blue dress with short sleeves. "What do you think of this one?"

"It's fine," I said, less concerned about Kitty's wardrobe than the safety of our new friend. "Don't you think we ought to check with Nurse Hildebrand to see if Mary's all right?"

Kitty shrugged, holding up a pair of tan heels for inspection. "Yes or no?"

"No," I said. "Wear the blue ones. Your feet will thank me later."

She clasped her bra and stepped into a white silk slip, before putting on the dress.

"Tell me about Lance," I said a little cautiously, zipping her up. "Do you like him?"

"Yes," Kitty said, though I thought I detected a note of hesitation in her voice. "He's great."

"Did you ever dance with the colonel last night?" I asked, selecting a glaringly simple tan dress from the closet.

Kitty nodded. "I did," she said, smiling. "And it was divine. Lance wasn't too happy, but he could hardly challenge his superior."

I took a look at myself in the oval mirror on the wall. My cheeks were flushed from the morning heat and my hair looked limp. In a battle with the humidity, the humidity had won. I shrugged and pulled it back into a clip. I'd be wearing a sun hat anyway.

"Ready?" Kitty said, grabbing her handbag.

I stared back at her. Her cheeks were rosy, not ruddy like mine. Her hair, curlier and wilder than ever, looked alluring the way she wore it, pinned to the side.

The tropics became her.

"Ready," I said, following her out the door.

Lance drove much too fast. Kitty was unaffected, however, looking gay in the front seat while Stella, Elliot, and I were squeezed into the back like pickles in one of Maxine's canning jars. My legs began to sweat on the hot canvas seat, and I clutched my hat as Lance gunned the engine. The pothole-littered gravel road that encircled the island wasn't for the faint of heart. The dust was thick; I wished I'd brought a scarf.

"First to town center," Lance said, sounding like an overzealous tour guide. "And next, to the beach."

Kitty let out a little cheer, and Stella eyed Elliot, whose gaze remained fixed on the road ahead. "Do you get into town much?" she asked him sweetly.

He didn't respond.

"I SAID," Stella repeated, louder this time, competing with the engine noise, "DO YOU GET INTO TOWN MUCH?"

Elliot looked at us, at first startled, then confused, as if he wasn't sure which of us had spoken and why in such a shout.

"No, not often," he said briefly, before turning his gaze back to the road.

Stella huffed and folded her arms across her chest. The air smelled of dirt right after a rain, mingled with a sweet, floral scent I didn't recognize.

"You see that?" Lance said, pointing to a gated property to our left. He slowed the jeep, and I was glad to let go of my hat for a moment. My arm was beginning to cramp. "It's a vanilla plantation. Almost all the vanilla in the world comes from this island."

I wasn't sure if this bit of trivia was true, or if

84

Lance had just thrown it in to impress Kitty, but the idea of seeing a real, working vanilla plantation was incredibly exciting. I thought of Maxine. Was she happy living in the Windermere home day after day, waiting on my parents with little more than a "Thanks, Maxine" or "That will be all, Maxine"?

"An American owns the place," Lance continued. "He married an island girl."

Stella's eyes widened. "I thought they were all cannibals."

Elliot took his eyes off the road and gave me a knowing look before settling back into his quiet mind.

Lance continued on. Makeshift homes, constructed of scrap lumber, dotted the roadside, tucked in under the lush palms. Occasionally we'd spot a rooster or chicken pecking about, or a child running nude in front of one of the dwellings, but never an adult, and I was curious to see one of these natives that Nurse Hildebrand spoke of.

The jeep wound around the north side of the island and past a small turquoise cove with a ship anchored a way out. It might have been pulled from a page of *Robinson Crusoe*. Moments later, Lance pulled over to the side of the road. "Here we are," he said.

I stepped out onto the dusty ground and turned my gaze to the busy scene ahead, where one might never guess there was a war going on mere miles from the shore. There were rows of tables cluttered with exotic fruits and vegetables, handmade necklaces, packs of cigarettes, and bottles of Coca-Cola. The scantily dressed shopkeepers, with their olive skin and enigmatic eyes, sat behind their tables looking vaguely bored, or sleepy, or both, as soldiers buzzed about spending their hard-earned cash on whatever trinket caught their eye.

"Look," said Stella, gasping. She pointed to a native woman walking toward us. Bare-breasted, she wore her hair twisted into a single braid that rested between her breasts. A swath of green fabric hung around her waist, tied loosely, dangerously so. I noticed the flower in her left ear as she walked right up to us as if she knew us. I tried to look away, but her breasts, with nipples so dark, lured my eyes with magnetic power. Her presence had the same effect on Stella, Kitty, Elliot, and especially Lance.

"Mr. Lance," the woman said, setting down the bag she had been carrying. Her thickly accented voice was sweet and soft. She was maybe eighteen, possibly younger. Her breasts dangled and swayed as she bent down to the bag and produced a pack of Lucky Strikes. "Your cigarettes," she said, offering him the pack.

How does Lance know this woman, or rather, woman-child?

"Thank you," Lance said. Kitty eyed him as he

tucked the pack into his shirt pocket. "*Atea* here is the only shopkeeper who can track down my Lucky Strikes. She saves a pack for me every Thursday."

Atea looked proud standing there, bare chested, not the least bit modest. Her eyes sparkled. She gazed at no one but Lance.

"Are you coming today?" she said, unaware of the awkward stiffness in the air.

"Not today, Atea," he said, dismissing her with a self-conscious nod. "You be a good girl and rustle me up some more, if you can. I'll be back in a few days." He tucked a coin in her hand and then reached for Kitty's arm. "Now, let's go see the rest of the market."

"That was strange," Stella said, leaning in to me a few moments later.

It *was* strange, but I wasn't going to discuss it with her, not when Kitty might overhear. "What's so strange about Lance buying cigarettes from a female?" I said instead.

Stella smirked and continued on, stopping at a table of brightly colored beads.

"You OK?" I said to Kitty, once Lance was a safe distance away.

"Of course," she said. "Why?"

Good. She wasn't upset by the interaction. Then I'll just leave it alone. "Oh, nothing," I said. "Just wanted to make sure the heat wasn't getting to you."

87

She took a deep breath of the humid island air and smiled. "I'm having the time of my life," she said gleefully.

Stella laid a blanket out on the beach, careful to secure a spot next to Elliot. "I'm starved, are you?" she said, attempting to catch his attention, but he merely shrugged and muttered, "I ate a big breakfast," before leaning back against a large piece of driftwood wedged into the sand, snuffing out all further conversation by pulling his hat over his eyes.

We'd driven back around to the other side of the island, close to base. Though we selected a spot beneath the shade of a palm for our picnic, the white sand still radiated heat. I shifted my legs uncomfortably as Kitty set out a loaf of bread, a cheerful bunch of miniature bananas, four bottles of Coca-Cola, and a wedge of cheese—our improvised lunch cobbled together at the market.

We ate in silence at first, watching the waves crash onto the shore. Then Kitty pointed to the sea and said what we all felt: "It's hard to believe there's a war happening out there. This corner of the world is too beautiful for destruction."

I nodded, helping myself to another banana. They tasted different than the bananas at home, a little tarter, with a hint of lemon. "But there is," I said practically.

"And a serious one, at that," Lance added. "Just

yesterday, the Japs shot down three of our planes."

Stella looked worried. "Do you think we'll see fighting right here on the island?"

"I think we might," Lance said gravely. "Colonel Donahue doesn't see it that way, though. He's a fool. I tell you, we'll be all asleep in our bunks when the Japs fly over, bombarding us when we least expect it."

Kitty looked up with concerned eyes, then shook her head. "Colonel Donahue will protect this island."

Lance shrugged. "If you say so." He smirked, before muttering, "I could run this operation better blindfolded."

The statement was too boastful for a man of twenty-five, but Kitty must have been unaffected by his arrogance, because she laid her head lightly in his lap. I could tell by his smile that he liked it.

Elliot began to snore. Stella brooded.

"I think I'll take a walk," I said, standing. Kitty's eyes were closed in pretend slumber as I adjusted the brim of my hat and kicked off my shoes. "I'll be back," I said, though I don't think anyone looked up.

I walked down the beach, stopping occasionally to examine a rock or a shell, or to marvel at the growth patterns of the palms, reaching out to the sea in horizontal fashion. Years of wind and tropical storms had sculpted their trunks, but I liked to think they grew that way because the sea was calling. It made me remember what Westry had said about the island changing people. *Will I be able to resist its force?*

I strengthened my footing in the sand and charged onward. After the morning at the market, it felt good to be alone with my thoughts and the quiet lull of the waves on the shore. The deserted beach seemed to stretch toward infinity. I walked closer to the water, relishing the feeling of the cool, sea-kissed sand on my feet. Each step left an inch-thick indentation.

A seabird squawked from its perch on a rock a few feet away, which is where I first noticed another set of footprints, fainter, older, but still relatively fresh. *Whose?*

It would be silly to follow them, I told myself. *What if they're a native's? A cannibal's?* I shook my head. *I'm alone. I should turn back.* And yet, they lured me farther down the beach, beyond the bend. *Just a few steps farther.*

The footprints stopped at a crumpled beige blanket, anchored to the sand by nothing but a book. I recognized the fabric instantly because I had the same standard military-issue on my bed in the barracks. *But who was here?*

I turned quickly when I heard a rustling sound in the thick brush behind the palms at the edge of the beach.

"Hello there," said a man appearing out of nowhere a few hundred yards away. He carried a large palm frond that shrouded his face, but when he moved it aside, I could see that it was Westry.

"Hello," I said, a bit surprised, but grateful to have avoided an encounter of a grimmer nature.

"Are you following me?" he said teasingly.

I felt foolish, then irritated. "Of course not!" I said, my voice thick with pride. *I can't have him thinking I'm chasing after him.* "I was merely taking a walk—which reminds me, I need to be going. My friends are expecting me."

Westry smiled. "Oh, don't go," he said, pushing the base of the palm branch into the sand and then sitting under it. "Look, the perfect shade. Won't you sit down? Just for a minute?"

His smile was impossible to resist. I hesitated, then felt the corners of my mouth turn upward, without my permission. "All right," I said, grinning in spite of myself. "Just for a minute."

"Nice day," he said, leaning back on his elbows.

"Quite," I said, pulling the hem of my dress lower on my legs.

"What brings you to my beach?"

"*Your* beach?"

"Yes," he said matter-of-factly. "I discovered it."

I let out a little laugh. "You're really something."

"It's all virgin coastline, you know," Westry continued. "Of course, the natives have been here forever, and it will always be theirs. But the rest of the world isn't onto it. For now, this little slice of heaven is mine." He looked at me. "Well, ours. I'll let you have half."

"Well, that's awfully generous of you," I said, playing along.

"Do you know what I'm going to do, after the war's over?"

"What?"

"I'm going to buy this stretch of beach," he said earnestly. "As much as I can afford. I'm going to build a house and raise a family, right here. My wife and I, we'll watch the sun rise every morning from our porch and listen to the surf crash onto the shore at night."

"It all sounds terribly romantic," I said. "But I think you're bluffing. You'd actually want to live *here* after"—I pointed out to the Pacific, where Japanese warships may have been taking up residence at that very moment—"after all this? After the war?"

Westry nodded. "Sure," he said. "It's paradise."

It *was* paradise, I reminded myself. "But don't you have a life waiting for you at home?"

"No," he said, without hesitating. "But *you* do."

It wasn't a question, but a statement. He'd seen the ring on my finger.

"I do," I said honestly.

"Do you love him?"

"What kind of question is that?"

"A simple one," he said, grinning. "So, what's the verdict?"

"Of course I love him," I said, looking away. *Why does he have to stare at me that way?*

"Is he a good man?"

I nodded. "I wouldn't marry any man who wasn't."

The waves crept in closer to the blanket, prompting Westry to stand up, and I followed. "We better shift our camp a bit, or else Old Man Sea is going to swallow us up."

I smiled. "I really should be getting back. My friends are waiting for me."

Westry nodded. "I'll walk you."

The shoreline looked different in reverse, perhaps because I was seeing it through Westry's eyes now. I imagined his life on the island years from now, with a house and a wife, and two or three barefoot children, and smiled to myself.

"How's your hand?" I asked.

He held it up, and I took it in mine, feeling a flutter deep inside that I told myself to ignore.

"I think I'm going to pull through," he said mockingly.

"It's filthy," I scolded. "You really must let me change the bandage when we get back. You'll risk infection."

"Yes, nurse," he said playfully.

Moments later Westry gestured toward something in the brush line, where palms grew thick. We walked closer and stopped, just as the beach ended and vegetation began. Birds sang and animals howled under the cover of shady green plants with gargantuan leaves, just as I'd always imagined a jungle.

"Do you see that?"

I shook my head. "What?"

"Look closer," he said.

"No," I whispered, "I don't see anything."

Westry reached for my hand, and I took it, only because I feared danger lurking, and I followed him a few paces beyond the beach, which is when I finally saw what he did: a thatched-roof hut, just beyond the thicket. Though constructed in as makeshift a manner as the homes along the roadside, this one had a charm all its own. The exterior was built of bamboo canes, into which someone had painstakingly cut holes to approximate ocean-facing windows. A small door dangled from a single hinge, creaking in the afternoon breeze.

"I don't know if we should be here," I whispered.

"Why not?" he said, grinning mischievously. "Now that we've found it, we have to see what's inside."

Before I could protest, Westry set foot on the little step to the front door. The sound of his shoe striking the wood startled me, and I jumped back a few feet.

He lifted the collapsing door off its lone hinge and set it down on the sand, peering inside before turning to me with a wink. "All clear."

He helped me up the step, and we surveyed the place in silence. The interior walls, made of woven palm branches weathered to a light shade of caramel, had been beautifully strung together in a V-shaped pattern. They provided a perfect backdrop to a dark mahogany chair paired with a small desk containing a single drawer. Westry reached for its handle and pulled out a book, some French coins and bills, and a piece of paper, yellowed and curled from the humidity. He held it up so I could have a look. "Can you read French?"

I shook my head. "I wish I'd paid more attention in school."

"Me too," he said, slipping the paper back in the drawer.

The bed, big enough for just one person, looked tidy, even with a layer of dust on top, as if someone had woken up one morning and tucked the linens in place in anticipation of a return that never occurred.

My eyes darted around the space, landing anywhere but on Westry's face. Here I was, an engaged woman, alone in a bedroom with a soldier I knew nothing of.

My reverie broke when a spider the size of my palm crawled out from under the desk and raced out the open doorway, causing me to leap on top of the bed in terror. "Did you see that thing?" I shrieked, certain that another would jump out at any moment.

"They're harmless," Westry said, grinning. "Plus, they eat the mosquitoes, so we ought to lay out a buffet table for the critters."

I cautiously stepped down from the bed. "Who do you think lived here?"

Westry looked out at the sea. "My best guess?" He turned back to the bungalow, studying it carefully. "A shipwrecked sailor."

I nodded. It sounded plausible enough. "But what happened to the ship?"

"Maybe it sunk."

"So how did he recover the paper and"—I opened the desk drawer and pulled out the book with its dark brown leather cover—"and this book?"

Westry touched his index finger to his chin, as if to ponder the fate of our shipwrecked sailor. "Maybe he had a knapsack packed with a few rations." He pointed to the lamp on the desk. "A lantern, this book, a tin of biscuits. And he managed to find a piece of wood to drift on until he reached the island."

"The book would have gotten wet," I said.

"So it may have," Westry conceded. "But he might have let it dry in the sun." He fanned the book's pages, and sure enough, they were covered in water stains. "See?"

96

I nodded. "But where was he heading? He was clearly French."

"And poor," Westry added, pointing to the small stash of coins in the drawer.

"Could he have been a pirate?"

Westry shook his head. "Domestic trappings would hardly hold the interest of a pirate."

I eyed the curtains on the windows, ragged from the weather, yet still a brilliant burgundy, as if the fabric had been soaked in wine.

"OK, so he's a poor, shipwrecked, French sailor who likes to read," I said.

"And likes to drink," Westry added, holding up a dusty green glass vessel, sealed with a cork. "Red wine."

"And appreciates art," I said, pulling away a scrap of burlap that covered a painting hanging over the bed. The canvas depicted an arresting scene: a bungalow, just like the very one we found ourselves in, nestled between impossibly blue water and a hibiscus bush flowering vibrant yellow. Two figures stood in the distance.

"My God," Westry gasped. "It's beautiful."

I nodded. "Do you know much about art?"

"A little," he said. "Let me have a closer look." He stood up on the bed to gaze at the painting. "It looks"—he scratched his head—"*familiar* somehow."

Mother had prided herself on teaching me about the French impressionists, and yet, I feared my artistic knowledge was still woefully inadequate. Even so, I reveled in the potential of the discovery.

"Do you think the artist lived *here?*"

"Maybe," Westry said, his eyes still fixed on the painting. "What year was that book printed?"

I thumbed the opening pages of the book for a date. "Here, found it. Copyright 1877."

"It might have been one of the master impressionists," he said.

"You can't be serious," I said, in awe.

"Well, it's as possible as anything," he replied, grinning. "I'm almost certain I've seen this one in books before, or maybe something similar. And this island, all of these islands in the Pacific, they were popular among the French artists. It could have been any one of the greats." His eyes were wild with excitement. "You know what this means, don't you?"

"What?"

"We have to protect this place."

I nodded. "But how?"

"It will be our project," he said, "while we're here. We'll restore it."

"It does need a good scrub."

"And a new door," Westry added.

"And the curtains are rags," I said. "I can make new ones."

"So you're in?" He was looking at me with slightly mischievous eyes.

Why not? It will pass the hours Kitty spends with Lance. "I'm in," I said. "But how will we ever find the time, and how will we get here?"

"We'll walk," he said simply. "The base is less than a half mile up shore. You can slip out and be back before anyone knows you've even left. There's a trail that leads up to the road, so I'll bring the tools and the wood out in a jeep, of course. It will take some planning, but we'll figure it out."

Westry turned to the door and a weak floorboard creaked and bowed from the pressure of his foot. He knelt down and pulled it up, exposing the rickety subfloor and a small alcove just below the surface. "Here," he said. "This will be our 'mailbox.' I'll leave you letters when I'm here without you, and you can do the same."

My heart leapt with excitement—for the bungalow, for the artist, for the prospect of letters tucked under floorboards, but especially for this man who held the key to it all.

Westry wrapped the painting in its burlap covering and carefully slid it under the bed for safekeeping.

"There's just one thing," he said.

"What?"

"We can't tell a soul about this place, not anyone."

It pained me to think of keeping a find this marvelous from Kitty, and yet, I couldn't imagine her here in the bungalow, a place that already felt special to me, sacred, even after only a few minutes. I touched my hand to Kitty's pin, and felt a pang of guilt. *Is it wrong to want to harbor this little hut to myself, especially after we've vowed not to keep secrets from each other?*

"What do you say?" Westry continued.

I let my hand fall to my side and nodded. "Cross my heart," I said, convincing myself that Kitty didn't need to know—not yet, anyway. "I won't tell a soul."

"Good. Shall I walk you back?"

"Yes," I said. "They're probably wondering if I drowned."

"Or got eaten by a shark," he added, grinning.

The beauty of the island wasn't limited to its turquoise waters or green hills. That was mere surface beauty. The real awe of the place was evident in its stories. There was one waiting beyond every curve of the shore.

Chapter 5

Westry seems nice," Kitty said as soon as we'd shut the door to our room later that day.

"He's all right," I said vaguely, taking off my hat and placing it on the top shelf of the closet.

"Where's he from?"

I shrugged. "Not sure. We only spoke for a moment. He was kind enough to walk me back."

I could sense Kitty's grin, even without looking up to confirm it. "Seems like you and Lance are getting along fine," I said, changing the subject.

"Yes," Kitty replied, leaning back against the headboard of her bed. "I do like him. Very much. It's just"—she paused and shook her head—"it's just, well, I don't care for the way he speaks of Colonel Donahue. Don't you think he should show him more respect than he does?"

I shrugged. I hadn't yet determined the lesser evil for Kitty: the cocky soldier or his overbearing superior.

"Well," Kitty continued, "I suppose it's a small detail. Lance has so many stand-out qualities."

Like his bravado. His philandering with the island women. His smug attitude. "Yes," I said instead. "So many."

"Anne," Kitty said, a little shyly. "I haven't had a chance to tell you, but on the night of the dance, Colonel Donahue—"

We both looked up, startled, when we heard a loud, rapid knocking at the door.

"Yes," I said, turning the knob.

Liz stood outside, panting and out of breath. "It's Mary," she said. "In the infirmary. Come quick."

We followed Liz down the stairs and out the barracks door, picking up a brisk pace once we reached the pathway outside. The infirmary wasn't far, but we arrived at its entrance wheezing from the sprint.

Inside, Nurse Hildebrand hovered over Mary's bed alongside Dr. Livingston, a middle-aged physician with thinning hair and spectacles. Mary looked unnaturally pale. Her eyes were closed, but the shallow rise of her chest told us she was still breathing.

"Dear Lord," I whispered. "What happened?"

The doctor produced a syringe and injected a clear liquid into Mary's arm; she didn't flinch when the needle pricked her skin.

"One of the women found her in her room," Nurse Hildebrand said, "collapsed by the bed. She'd been there at least sixteen hours. Malaria. Must have contracted it on her first day on the island."

"Malaria," I repeated. The word sounded so foreign, and yet the disease was right here, threatening to take the life of a terrific girl, one we'd just begun to know, a girl who had her whole future ahead of her, who had come to the South Pacific to start over, not to die.

"The fever broke," Dr. Livingston said, "but I'm afraid it weakened her heart. The only thing we can do now is wait."

My hands trembled. "But she's going to make it," I said. "She's going to pull through. She has to pull through."

Dr. Livingston looked away.

I thought of Mary, poor Mary. Tall, perhaps a little too tall. Teeth a bit crooked. Heart broken. Her fiancé had left her and she had felt alone; she'd told us so. *No, I will not let her die alone.*

"Kitty," I said, "will you run back to the barracks and fetch my reading glasses and anything you can find to read? Bring the damn *War Digest*, if that's all there is—whatever you can find."

Kitty nodded.

"We're going to hold vigil," I said. "May I pull up a bed and stay next to her tonight?" I asked Nurse Hildebrand.

She nodded in approval.

Kitty returned with two magazines, three books—two from Liz and another from Stella—a copy of the *War Digest*, and a nursing textbook, just in case.

"Good," I said, examining a book with a tattered spine. "We'll take shifts reading to her. We won't stop until she regains consciousness, or . . ."

Kitty reached for my hand. "Anne, you can't save her if she's—"

"I won't let her die alone," I said, wiping away a tear. "Nobody deserves that."

Kitty nodded.

I set down the book and picked up a copy of *Vogue* with Rita Hayworth on the cover. I turned to the first page, and began reading an advertisement: "Why not get a lovely figure for spring? If you want to dress inexpensively, and be able to wear standard fittings with charm and distinction, start now to get rid of that accumulated winter fat. With the help of nightly Bile Beans you can 'slim while you sleep' safely and gradually . . ."

I read for four hours, every word on every page in front of me, until my eyes began to blur. Kitty read next, turning on a little lamp on the table next to the gurney when the sun set, then passing the torch back to me a few hours later after her voice became hoarse.

We'd covered three magazines and three quarters of a novel by the time the sun's morning rays first shone through the infirmary windows, which is when Mary's eyes began to flutter.

She opened them slowly, then shut them again, and we watched with great anticipation as the next minute passed, and then the next, before she moved her arm, and then her legs, and then her eyes again, this time opening them and looking straight at me.

"Where am I?" she said weakly.

"In the infirmary," I replied, tucking a strand of her blond, straw-like hair behind her ear. "You've been stricken with malaria, dear," I continued, choking back tears. "But you're going to be fine now."

Mary looked around the room, then at Kitty and back to me. "I had the strangest dream," she said. "I kept trying to walk toward a bright light, and there was this voice always there. It kept luring me back."

"Did you turn around?"

"I didn't want to," she said. "I wanted to keep walking, but every time I took a step, the voice beckoned."

"Good," I said, holding a glass of water to her lips before tucking her cold arms back under the blanket. "Dear, we have all the time in the world to talk about it, but you need your rest now."

Our care of Mary didn't compel Nurse Hildebrand to congratulate us on our nursing skills, but she did excuse us from duty that day, and Kitty and I welcomed the opportunity to rest.

I slept until noon, when the sound of the lunch bell ringing from the mess hall woke me. My stomach growled, yet my exhaustion persisted and I was tempted to stay in bed.

"Kitty?" I said, without lifting my head. "Are you awake?"

I turned my heavy head expecting to see her fast asleep, and instead found her coverlet pulled tightly up over her bed and the two pillows fluffed and neatly stacked against the headboard.

Where is she? I sat up and stretched, then noticed a note on the dressing table.

Anne,
    I didn't want to wake you. I left at 10 to go canoeing with Lance. I'll be back this afternoon.

Love,
Kitty

Boating with Lance. Of course, it was a perfectly normal thing for her to do, and yet I felt uneasy. *We were granted the day off only hours ago, so when did she have time to make plans with Lance?* I thought of the bungalow, and realized our little dormitory room was already thick with secrets.

The lunch bell rang a second time—the last call. If I dressed and ran quickly I could make it in time. But I saw a shiny red apple on the nightstand and thought of a much better idea.

I slung over my shoulder a knapsack packed with the apple, a bit of bread Kitty had brought back from the mess hall, and a canteen filled with water, then I snuck past the entrance to the infirmary, stopping briefly to glance through an open window to where Stella and Liz and a few of the other nurses were working. They looked bored, at best. A few fussed over a lightbulb that needed changing, and a small group hovered over the only patient in the building, a man who looked like he had nothing more than a skinned knee. His smile indicated his enjoyment.

This wasn't the wartime life I'd expected. And yet, change was coming. I'd heard a rumor that Colonel Donahue had an operation planned, something big. I wondered how it might affect our work, our world.

I made my way to the path that led to the beach. Westry had said the bungalow was just a half mile north of the base. I hoped he was right.

I walked fast, and looked over my shoulder more than a few times. *What would people think of me sneaking away from the base like this, alone?* It didn't feel like something Anne Calloway would do.

Just around the bend, I began to make out the thatched roof of the bungalow, nestled in the thicket, just as we'd left it. As I grew nearer, I could hear the sound of a saw zigzagging.

My heart pounded in my chest. *Westry is here.*

"Hello," I said, knocking ceremoniously on the place where the door had once hung precariously. "Anyone home?"

Westry looked up, wiping his brow before brushing sawdust off his hands. "Oh, hi," he said. "Are you real or a mirage? I've been out here all morning without water, and I can't tell if I'm hallucinating or if there's really a beautiful woman standing in the doorway. Please tell me it's the latter."

I grinned. "You're not hallucinating," I said, pulling the canteen out of my bag. "Here, drink."

Westry took a long gulp, then exhaled, handing the canteen back to me. "I've almost got the door in working order," he said. "It didn't fit on the doorframe. The weather must have warped it. I had to take an inch off the side. See? I rustled up some old hinges from the supply yard." He held up the hardware proudly, as if it were treasure. "Our bungalow needs a proper, working door."

I smiled. I liked to think of it as *our* bungalow.

I pulled a box of Borax and some rags from my bag. "I thought I'd give the place a shine," I said.

"Glad you could join the work party," Westry said, turning back to his saw.

By three, the floors were fit to eat from, and Westry had the door fastened in place.

"I almost forgot," he said, plucking a scuffed brass doorknob from his knapsack. "It will just take me a second to fit it."

I watched him attach the knob, carefully fastening the screws in their holes.

"Our key," he said, holding up a shiny piece of steel. "Now, if we can just find the right hiding place for it."

I pointed to the open-air windows. "But anyone who wants in can just climb on through."

Westry nodded. "Sure. We'll get the windows installed soon enough. Besides, every home needs a proper, working lock. But where to hide the key, that's the question."

I followed him outside the hut, and we looked around near the front step. "How about here?" I suggested, pointing to a spot in the sand. "We could bury it."

Westry shook his head. "It's the first place someone would look. It's like the welcome mat— every crook knows to go there first." He paused as an idea struck. "Wait," he continued, running back inside and returning with a book he'd pulled from his bag. "We'll use this."

"A book?"

"Yeah," he replied, pulling out the ribbon attached to the spine. Its purpose might have been to mark the page for a reader, but Westry had other plans. He tied the ribbon securely around the lip of the key, tucking it into the book. "There," he said, sliding the book below the step. "Our secret spot."

The waves were crashing loudly now. "The tide's coming in," he said. "Want to watch it with me?"

I hesitated. "I probably should be thinking about walking back." I hadn't left a note for Kitty, and I worried that she could be concerned.

"C'mon," Westry said. "You can stay a few more minutes."

"All right," I said, caving. "Just a few."

"There," he said, pointing to a piece of

driftwood a few paces ahead on the beach. "Our perch."

He grabbed the wine bottle he'd found in the bungalow the day before and a tin cup from his knapsack and sat down next to me in the sand, our heads resting comfortably on the driftwood that had been smoothed into submission by the pulverizing surf. "A toast," he said, pouring the ancient wine into the cup. "To the lady of the bungalow."

He extended the cup to me, and I took a cautious sip, my face involuntarily contorting. "To sour hundred-year-old wine."

A bird sang in the distance as we sat together, mesmerized by the waves.

"I don't know anything about you," I said, turning to him a little abruptly.

"And I don't know anything about you," he retorted.

"You start."

Westry nodded and sat up. "I was born in Ohio," he began. "Didn't stay there long. Mother died of scarlet fever, and I moved west with my father, to San Francisco. He was an engineer, worked on the railroads. I tagged along with him, attending a different school every month."

"Far from a proper education," I said.

Westry shrugged. "I got a better one than most. I saw the country. I learned the way of the railways."

"And now what? After all of this, you said you wanted to come back here, to the island, but surely you have other aspirations, other things to attend to first?"

Westry's eyes were big and full of life, full of possibility.

"I'm not sure, exactly," he said. "I may go back to school, become an engineer, like Pop. Or maybe go to France, and learn to paint like the great impressionists. Or maybe I'll just stay here," he said, motioning with his head toward the bungalow.

"Oh, you can't do that," I said. "What a lonely life that would be!"

"Why would you call it lonely?" he countered. "I'd have everything I could possibly want. A roof over my head. A bed. The most beautiful scenery in the world. Some might call that paradise."

I thought about what he'd said about settling down and raising a family right there on the stretch of beach before us. "But what about companionship?" I said a little shyly. "What about . . . love?"

Westry grinned. "Easy for you to say. You already have that."

I looked at my feet, burrowing the tip of my shoe into the sand, which was so hot I could feel it radiating beneath the leather.

"Well," he continued, "I suppose I'll find her. Out there somewhere."

"What if you don't?" I asked.

"I will," he said, smiling at me confidently.

I turned away quickly.

"Now," he said, "let's hear about *you*."

I tugged at a loose thread on my bag until the silence felt strange. "Well, there isn't much to tell."

"I'm sure there is," Westry said with a leading smile. "Everyone has a story."

I shook my head. "I was born in Seattle. I lived there all my life. I got my nursing license, and now I'm here."

"And there you have it," he said dramatically. "An entire lifetime in three sentences."

I felt my cheeks get hot. "Sorry," I said. "I guess my life isn't quite as exciting as yours."

"I think you're bluffing," he said, sizing me up with his eyes. "The man you're engaged to," he continued, pointing to the ring on my hand, "why didn't you marry him before you left?"

How dare he ask me such a question? "Because I . . ." My voice trailed off without an answer. I thought of all the practical reasons: I didn't want to rush things; because Mother wanted a big affair at the Olympic Hotel; because . . . ; and yet, none were satisfactory. If I'd wanted, I could have marched down to City Hall, just like Gerard had suggested, and made it official. I could have become Mrs. Gerard Godfrey without a yearlong odyssey to the South Pacific as a hurdle that stood between us. *Why didn't I?*

"See?" Westry continued. "You do have a story."

"I assure you," I retorted, "you've created drama where there is none."

Westry winked. "We'll see."

Kitty wasn't in the room when I returned, so when the mess hall bell rang, announcing dinner, I walked out of the barracks alone, making a quick stop in the infirmary to check on Mary, whom I was happy to find sitting up and sipping orange juice through a straw.

"Hi, Anne," she muttered from her bed. Her voice, still quite weak, had perked up. There was strength in it that hadn't been there this morning.

"Hi," I said. "I'm headed to dinner. I was just wondering if I could bring you anything. You must be tiring of the liquid diet."

"I am," she replied. "A roll and a few packages of butter would be divine."

"I'll take care of it," I said, smiling.

I walked back out to the path that led to the mess hall, passing the hibiscus bush where Kitty and I had plucked flowers that first night. I kept walking until I could see the recreation dock. A dozen canoes bound by rope tethers bobbed on the water, waiting for off-duty soldiers to take them out to sea. Few did, even though Bora-Bora was a relative safe haven from enemy attack—so far.

I looked closer and spotted two figures

climbing out of a canoe. The tousled curls could have belonged to no other but Kitty, but the man helping her onto the dock wasn't Lance. I gasped when I saw instead the face of *Colonel Donahue*. She smiled sweetly at him as he stowed the paddles inside the canoe. They walked together, arm in arm, back up to the lawn, where he bid her adieu, and Kitty hurried along the trail back to the women's barracks.

Should I run after her? I decided not to; after all, she hadn't told me the truth about her date, and it was most likely because she thought I'd disapprove, *and I did*. But I couldn't have her thinking I was spying on her. No, she'd tell me in her own time. Instead, I turned back to the mess hall and spoke to the cook about getting a tray made up for Mary.

"How's Lance?" Stella coyly asked Kitty at breakfast. *Did she see her with the Colonel too?*

"Fine," Kitty said, picking at her scrambled eggs and grits, both the consistency of rubber. "We're seeing each other tonight."

Stella shook her head jealously, a gesture that might have put me on the defensive the day we met, but I had come to learn quickly that it was merely Stella's way. "My, do you have luck with men," she said, before sighing in defeat. "I've given up on Elliot. His head is much too tangled up with that woman from back home. He's either by himself taking photographs on the beach or holed up in the barracks writing poetry about her. She must be something else, that woman. Anyway, I met an airman last night. His name is Will, and he isn't half bad."

Liz approached our table with a tray and set it down. "Is Mary still on the mend?"

"Yes, thank God," I said. "She's much stronger today."

Liz gazed intently at an envelope she held in her hand. "This came for her today," she said cautiously. "And I can't help but notice the name on the return address. Didn't she say her ex-fiancé's name was *Edward?*"

I nodded. "Let me see it."

I held the envelope up to the light, unable to make out anything significant, just that the sender was indeed Edward. Edward Naughton, with a return address in Paris.

"Anne!" Kitty scolded. "You shouldn't read her mail. It's private."

"I will if I think it's going to compromise her recovery," I said. "Listen, if this man could leave her, almost at the altar, and send her into such a tailspin that she banished herself to a far-flung island on the other side of the world, imagine what a letter from him could do to her."

The other women nodded in agreement, and Kitty softened.

"Look," I said, "I'm not going to read it; I'm

115

merely tucking it away until she's ready. Her heart is weak. She needs to regain her strength first. I won't let this letter conflict with her recovery."

"All right," Kitty said. "But you really shouldn't meddle when it comes to love."

Is she giving me some kind of warning about her own life?

I scrunched my nose in displeasure and tucked the envelope into the pocket of my dress for safekeeping. "I'm not *meddling*," I said directly to Kitty. "This is a matter of health."

Kitty pushed her plate aside. "Well, girls, I don't think I can stand another bite of these overcooked eggs. I'm heading to work. Nurse Hildebrand says we've got a live one coming in today."

I stewed about Kitty's comments as we walked to the infirmary that morning, but forgot about the interaction entirely when we got word that a medic had radioed from another island that a wounded pilot was en route. The pilot would be our first real patient, aside from Westry, who was mine alone.

The airman arrived at a quarter past ten. It was as serious a case as any one of us could have imagined—shrapnel wounds to the head. Kitty, first to wheel the soldier into the operating area, worked alongside the doctor with steady hands, removing bits of blood-covered metal and piling them on a plate beside the operating table. Liz excused herself to vomit, yet Kitty didn't flinch. She handled the procedure with such skill and ease that the doctor requested she stay on for another hour to assist with the patient's care. She quickly agreed.

After our shift ended, I walked back to the barracks, eager to escape the sterile infirmary and relax in the comfort of the bungalow. I packed a little bag and tucked in scissors, a needle and thread, and a bolt of pale yellow fabric I'd found in a trash barrel outside the infirmary. Perfect for curtains, I'd thought, snatching it up before the enlisted men could haul it away with the garbage collection.

Westry wasn't inside when I arrived, so I retrieved the key from the book, remembering how he'd thought of the hiding place, and unlocked the door, setting my bag down on the old mahogany chair.

I immediately got to work on the curtains, measuring the width of the windows and calculating the length and width of each panel. I laid out the fabric on the floor, shooing a baby lizard away as I did, and commenced cutting. I listened to the birds' songs as I hemmed the curtains. I didn't have an iron to press them, but the seams would be fine for a beach hut, and in time, the warm, misty air would soften their creases.

As I stitched, I thought of Westry, so spirited and spontaneous, so unlike Gerard and his consistent, measured ways. *Why can't Gerard be more free, more of a lover of life?* And yet, as I pushed my needle and thread through the fabric, I realized the concerns I had harbored about him in Seattle seemed only to fester in the tropics. In particular, his ability to sidestep the war gnawed at my conscience. *Why didn't he disagree with his father's wishes and do the honorable thing?*

I remembered the painting resting under the bed as I fitted the rod into the first set of curtains on the window. I wondered about the subjects of the canvas, but mostly I wondered about the artist. *Who lived here so long ago? A man like Westry, with adventure in his soul?* I pictured Westry spending the rest of his days here on the island. Maybe he'd marry a native girl, like the one we'd met with Lance and Kitty at the market. *What was her name? Yes, Atea. But would he be happy then? Would a woman like that make him happy?* I grinned. *Yes, happy in* one *way, certainly, but would they be on the same intellectual plane?* Passion fades, yet love lives on. It's what I wished Kitty would come to believe.

Darkness fell on the bungalow just then, and I looked out the open-air window at gray, rain-soaked clouds looming in the sky, ready to drench the land below, whether it obliged or not. I scanned the beach, hoping I might see Westry bounding toward the bungalow, which is when I remembered the mailbox, or rather, the creaky floorboard in the corner. I walked over and lifted it, peering inside, and a white envelope caught my eye.

I tore it open with anticipation.

Dear Mrs. Cleo Hodge,

I suppose you're wondering who Mrs. Cleo Hodge is. Why, my dear, she is you. We need code names in case we're found out. Let's not forget, we are living in war times. So, you will be Cleo. I will be Grayson. What do you think? I considered the surname Quackenbush, but we'd fall to our knees in laughter every time we'd address each other and get nothing done. So, we shall be the Hodges, unless you have a better suggestion.

Yours,

Mr. Hodge

P.S. Look in the desk drawer. A surprise is waiting.

I giggled to myself, opening the drawer to find an orange. Its shiny, dimpled skin looked brilliant against the darkness of the mahogany drawer frame. I held it to my nose and inhaled the floral citrus scent before turning the letter over and writing a message to Westry:

Dear Mr. Grayson Hodge,

Today, I have been hard at work on the drapes, which I hope you will find satisfactory. Do you think we need a rug? A nice oriental? And how about a bookshelf and a place to sit, other than the bed? Perhaps, if we are lucky, a sofa will wash up on the shore. Thank you for the orange; it was perfect.

Yours,
Mrs. Hodge

P.S. Your imagination is uncanny. Where on earth did you come up with the name "Quackenbush"? I can hardly contain my laughter.

I tucked the note in the space below the floorboard and locked the door behind me. The wind had picked up since I had arrived, and the clouds overhead, now even darker, threatened rain. I hurried along the beach, nibbling on sections of the orange as I went.

I startled when, not far from the bungalow in the brush above the beach, I heard a rustling sound, causing every muscle, every tendon in my body to freeze. *What was that? Is someone following me?*

I took a few steps toward the jungle line, and waited. *There it is again, that sound. Rustling, and faint voices.* I crept closer, taking cover behind the base of a very large palm, and squinted. Two figures stood in the shadows of the lush jungle brush, one male, one female. Then I saw the telltale sleeve of an army dress shirt, and a bare female leg. I shrank back behind the palm before tiptoeing again onto to the beach and quickening my pace to a sprint, looking over my shoulder at every turn.

Once inside the room, I was disappointed to see that Kitty wasn't there waiting.

Chapter 6

"Can you believe it's been two months since we arrived?" Mary marveled, her cheeks tinged a rosy pink. It was good to see the color, the life back in her face. She had insisted that Nurse Hildebrand let her work morning shifts instead of making her continue on bed rest. Despite intermittent trembling in her hands, Mary continued to gain strength, and she eagerly volunteered to assist me in a round of immunizations that morning.

"I know what you mean," I said. "It sometimes feels as if we arrived only yesterday." I paused to count the vials of vaccine we'd be giving the men after breakfast. "Yet, so much has happened already. I hardly feel like the same girl who stepped foot on that tarmac the first day."

Mary nodded. "Me too. It's hard to imagine life back there."

I sighed. "I've almost forgotten what Gerard's voice sounds like. Isn't that terrible?"

"Not really," Mary said. "You still love him."

"Yes, of course," I said with extra emphasis, feeling guilty for not yet taking the time to write him.

"I've almost forgotten Edward's voice," Mary added. "But that's definitely not terrible." She grinned, and I nodded in agreement.

I remembered the letter I'd been keeping from her. *Is she ready yet?* I listened to her hum as she unwrapped the packages of vaccine and set them on the trays. *That letter could spoil everything.*

"Where's Kitty?" Mary asked. "I thought I saw her here earlier this morning."

"Oh, she's here," I said. "We walked down together."

"No," Nurse Hildebrand grumbled. "She said she wasn't feeling well, so I sent her back to the barracks."

That's odd. She looked fine this morning. I tried not to let my mind wander, but Kitty had been behaving strangely, almost since the moment we'd arrived on the island—saying she was going somewhere and turning up in another place; promising to meet me at breakfast or lunch only to disappear. She rarely spoke of Colonel

Donahue, and I hadn't mentioned witnessing their boat trip. That ship seemed to have sunk, yet she spent far too much time with Lance. Yesterday they stayed out until nearly midnight. Jarred from slumber, I'd eyed the clock sleepily when she finally stumbled into bed.

"She must have caught the virus that's going around," Mary said. "A terrible stomach illness."

I didn't believe that Kitty had a stomach illness. No, something else was going on. Our shifts in the infirmary didn't leave room for meaningful conversation, now that more wounded men were arriving from nearby islands, where the fighting was thick. They trickled in slowly, but the cases were grim. Knife wounds. Gunshots to the abdomen. And just yesterday, a nearly severed leg that needed an immediate amputation. The somber work of caring for fallen soldiers consumed our days, and when our shifts ended, we'd scatter like mice to our favorite hiding places. But where was Kitty's?

I thought about the other nurses. Stella had begun spending a lot of time in the recreation hall, where she'd taken a new interest in shuffleboard, or rather, in Will, who played shuffleboard. Of course, Liz dutifully tagged along. Mary, with little energy after a shift in the infirmary, went back to the barracks to read or write letters to friends at home, while I snuck away to the bungalow. Sometimes Westry would be there, sometimes not, but I always hoped to find him.

"Mail's here!" one of the nurses cried from the front door of the infirmary.

I left Mary with the vaccines and ventured over to the wooden crate filled with letters and parcels. Mail deliveries had been sparse. But this was a mountain of mail. It spilled out on the floor when I pushed the crate closer to the table—so many letters, like covert submarines, infiltrating our private world.

Stella received five; Liz, three; and Kitty, just two, both from her mother. And then I saw one addressed to me and I felt a familiar tugging at my heart when I recognized the handwriting. *Gerard.*

I opened it discreetly, prepared to tuck it away the moment Stella or another nurse crept up.

My love,
 The leaves are turning colors here, and I miss you so. Why did you have to go again?
 Seattle is the same, just as you left it, only it's lonelier without you. I suppose the war has something to do with the loneliness factor. It's all anyone can talk about. I worry about you out there. There will be great action in the Pacific. I pray that your island will be shielded from it.

The military minds who I've spoken to here believe it will be untouched. I pray they are right.

The war has taken the best of us. It's a ghost town at the Cabaña Club. You wouldn't recognize the place. Every able-bodied man has either joined up or been drafted, and I wanted you to know that even after all Father has done to protect me from the fight, I can't help but wonder if I should join too. It would be the right thing to do. The next wave of troops ships out on the 15th of October, and I'm thinking about voiding my exemption and going with them. I'd be spending two weeks in basic training at a base in California before heading to Europe.

Please do not worry about me. I will write you often to tell you how I am, and will dream of the day when we are reunited.

I love you with all my heart and think of you more than you know.

Yours,
Gerard

I held the letter to my heart and blinked hard. As much as I reveled in his burst of patriotism, I hated to think of him in danger, and cringed when I thought about the lapse in time between his sending the letter and my receiving it. *Could he be on a battlefield right now? Could he could be . . . ?*

I felt an arm on my back after I'd slumped over in my chair, trying to hide my tears from the other women. "What's the matter, dear?" Mary asked softly.

"It's Gerard," I said. "I think he signed up."

Mary patted my back as my tears dotted the crumpled paper in my hands, smearing Gerard's beautiful handwriting into patches of muddled black ink.

"What do you think it would be like to be a military wife?" Kitty asked me that night before bed. She sat in a pink cotton nightgown on top of her bunk, brushing her blond curls—and clearly feeling just fine—as I tried, unsuccessfully, to read.

I set the book down. "You can't be saying you're already thinking of marrying Lance, are you?"

Kitty didn't answer; she just continued brushing her hair. "I suppose the lifestyle could have its benefits," she said. "All the traveling and the excitement."

"Kitty, but you've only just met him," I said.

The evenings were the only time we talked anymore—at least, those evenings when Kitty wasn't out with Lance.

Kitty set her brush down on her bedside table and climbed into her bed, pulling the coverlet up to her neck, before turning to me. "Anne," she said. Her voice was childlike, curious, naive, tremulous. "Did you always know that Gerard was the one?"

The question caught me off guard in a way it wouldn't have in Seattle. "Well, yes, of course I did," I said, remembering his letter from earlier today. My devotion to him swelled. "I just knew."

Kitty nodded. "I think I have the same feeling," she said, turning her head to the wall before I could question her. "Good night."

Westry had been away on a mission to another island for thirty days, and when he returned on November 27, I waited near the men's barracks, pretending to gather hibiscus, in hopes of meeting him on the pathway. It was Wednesday, the day before Thanksgiving, and the buzz in camp revolved around two things: turkey and cranberry sauce.

"Hey, you, nurse!" one of the men shouted from a third-story window. "Do you think we'll get a bird?"

"Do I look like the cook?" I said sarcastically.

The soldier, barely nineteen, if that, smirked and recoiled. It had taken me months to become comfortable with the ways of men and war. No longer shy, I grunted at those who grunted at me and greeted inappropriate remarks with retorts that leveled the playing field. Mother would have been beside herself.

Twenty minutes of flower picking resulted in no Westry sighting, so I retreated to the barracks with a heavy heart and a bag full of hibiscus.

"The mail came," Kitty said, tossing an envelope on the bed. "It's from your mother."

I shrugged and tucked the envelope into my dress pocket as Kitty peeked into the flower-filled bag I'd set by the door. "They're gorgeous," she said. "Let's get them in water."

She plucked the blossoms from the bag and arranged them, one by one, in the water glass on her dressing table.

"They'll never keep," I said. "They're a terrible cutting flower. They'll wilt by morning."

"I know," she said. "But don't they look so pretty *right now,* just as they are?"

I nodded. I wished I could see the beauty in the moment the way Kitty did. It was a gift.

She stood back and marveled at the makeshift vase, packed with bright red blooms that would be limp by the time we came back from dinner, before glancing at her bedside table. "I almost forgot," she said. "I also got a letter from home. From Father."

Kitty tore the edge of the envelope and pulled out the letter, reading at first with a grin. But then a frown appeared, and a look of shock. Tears began a slow trickle down her cheeks.

"What is it?" I asked, running to her side. "What does it say?"

She threw herself on the bed, burying her face in the pillow.

"Kitty," I persisted, "tell me."

She didn't budge, so I picked up the pages of the letter that had fallen to the ground and read it myself, in the words of her father.

You should know, love, that Mr. Gelfman left for war in September, to Europe, and I'm afraid he was killed. I know this news is going to be hard for you to hear. Your mother did not want me to write of it, but I felt you should know.

I tucked the letter into Kitty's dressing table. *The damned mail. Why does it come and haunt us the way it does? We were getting along fine until the letters started arriving.* "Kitty," I said, leaning my face into hers. "I'm so sorry."

"Just let me be," she said quietly.

"I'll bring dinner up for you," I said, hearing the sound of the mess hall bell.

"I'm not hungry," she whimpered.

"I'll bring it anyway."

I heaped a pile of mashed potatoes on my plate and, with the cook's permission, I got an extra plate for Kitty, followed by sliced carrots and boiled ham that looked curled and dry under the warming lights. Still, at least it wasn't canned. I was glad of that.

Stella and Mary waved at me from the nurses' table, and I nodded and walked toward them. "I'm just grabbing a tray for Kitty and myself, to take back to the room. Kitty got a letter from home today. A bad one."

Mary frowned. "I'm sorry to hear it," she said. "Can you sit for a minute, though? You can't juggle both of those trays on the path back. You'll trip. Why don't you eat first?"

I thought it over, then agreed, sitting down next to Mary.

"They say there was a fight in the barracks today," Stella said in a hushed voice. "This island's really wearing on the men."

"It's wearing on all of us," I replied, attempting to cut the tough slice of ham with a dull knife.

Stella nodded. "I saw Lance at the market yesterday. He had his arm around that girl, that native."

I was grateful Kitty wasn't present. She'd experienced enough heartbreak for one day. "You mean *Atea*," I said. "She has a name." It irritated me that Stella held the island's indigenous population in such low regard.

"I guess that was her name," she said with a shrug. "Lance sure has a thing for her."

Mary looked doubtful. "Oh, Stell," she said.

130

"Just because he gets his cigarettes from her doesn't mean he's carrying on with her."

Stella shrugged. "I'm just telling you what I saw."

Poor Kitty. I won't tell her. Not yet. She needs time.

"All right, girls," I said, retrieving Kitty's tray, "I'm off to deliver a meal."

"Good night," Mary said.

Stella nodded and sank her teeth into a biscuit.

I waved flies from the tray as I followed the trail, pausing for a moment in front of the men's barracks, hoping, in vain, to find Westry gazing down from a window. Was his bunk on the second floor or the fourth? I scanned the second floor and my eyes stopped at an open window toward the middle of the building. There was rustling and movement inside. *A fight.* "Yes, sir!" a voice rang out. "Please, sir!" It was *Westry*'s voice.

My God! He's hurt. He's being beaten. I set the tray down on a bench and walked to the entrance to the barracks. I had to help him. But how? Women weren't allowed inside. I stood on the steps in desperation, listening to the sound of flesh pounding flesh and furniture breaking. *Stop. It has to stop.*

A moment later, it did. A door slammed, then heavy footsteps pounded in the hallway and down the stairs to the entrance of the barracks. My stomach turned when Colonel Donahue appeared in the doorway, clutching a bloodied hand. I shrank back against the hibiscus and watched as he walked directly to the infirmary.

My heart raced. "Westry!" I called out, in a panic. "Westry!" I said louder, pitching my voice into the open window.

There was only silence, and I feared the worst.

I ran to the mess hall, where many of the men were still eating, and found Elliot at a table near the entrance. His eyes met mine, and I motioned for him to come over.

"What is it, Anne?" he said, releasing a cloth napkin from his collar.

"It's Westry," I whispered. "He was beaten. By Colonel Donahue. He's in his room. He may be unconscious." My words shot out of my mouth like rapid fire.

Elliot's eyes widened. "I'll go," he said, pushing through the double doors and sprinting out to the trail.

I waited outside the barracks for a long while, alternately pacing and peering up at the second floor, trying to catch a glimpse through the window. Then I heard the door open and Elliot stepped outside.

"He's been beaten pretty bad," he said. "A laceration across his forehead's going to need stitches."

"Why won't he come down, then?" I said.

"He won't," Elliot continued.

"I don't understand. Why did Colonel Donahue do that to him?"

"He won't talk about it," he said, looking down the trail where the colonel had exited. "But something bad must have happened. Something's not right."

I rubbed my hand along my forehead. "Can you stay with him, then? Make sure he's OK, try to get him to go to the infirmary to get stitched up?"

Elliot nodded. "I'll do my best," he said, turning back to the door.

"Thanks," I replied. "And Elliot?"

"Yes?"

"Tell him I miss him."

Elliot grinned. "He'll like that."

Kitty's dinner tray was cold by the time I returned to the room, but it didn't matter. She still refused food.

"Can I do anything for you, dear?" I said, stroking her soft curls.

"No," she said meekly. "I just need to be alone."

"Yes," I replied, a little hurt. "I understand."

The sun had set, but the moon overhead provided an alluring amount of light. I eyed my knapsack. *The bungalow.* It's where I needed to be; my heart felt it.

"Kitty," I said softly, tucking a book into my bag. "I'm stepping out for a while."

She didn't answer, but I didn't fault her.

"I'll be back soon," I said, closing the door behind me.

The wind blew stronger than it usually did, tousling my hair as I trudged along the sand toward the bungalow. When I arrived, I unlocked the door and lay down on the bed. The new quilt I'd brought last week, found on the top shelf of our bedroom closet, felt warm and comforting on my weary body. I didn't bother checking the mailbox. Westry hadn't been back long enough to visit, and now he was holed up in the barracks nursing his wounds. I shuddered at the thought of Colonel Donahue's brutality. *Why did he hurt him so?* Whatever the reason, I was sure Westry hadn't deserved it.

I propped up the pillow behind my head and pulled out the letter from Mother that I'd tucked inside my pocket earlier.

My dearest Anne,

I write with a heavy heart, for it is I who must relate the most terrible news to you. Believe me, I pondered, for a very long time, whether to write you with this news or wait until you return. But, I feel you must know.

I am leaving your father. The circumstances are much too grave to discuss in a letter, but I will only say that despite our separation, I will love you as much as I always have. I will explain everything when you come home.

May your marriage to Gerard be more love-filled than mine has been.

I love you dearly and I hope this news doesn't hurt too much.

With love,
Mother

I felt the sting of salty tears in my eyes. *She's leaving Papa. Poor Papa. How could she?* "May your marriage to Gerard be more love-filled than mine has been." *What kind of rubbish is that?*

I heard a sound outside on the beach, followed by the slow creak of the bungalow door opening. My heart calmed when I saw Westry's face.

"I hoped you'd be here," he said, grinning.

"Look at you!" I exclaimed, ignoring my inhibitions and running to his side, where I instinctively reached my hand out to caress his cheek. "Why did Colonel Donahue hurt you?"

"Listen," he said firmly, "I need to make myself clear. You did not see Colonel Donahue today."

"But I did—"

"No," he said. "You didn't."

"But Westry, why?"

He looked conflicted and pained. "Please, don't ever mention it again."

I frowned. "I don't understand."

"It has to be this way," he said. "You'll understand someday." His face caught the light and I could see the severity of his wounds.

"You must let me take you to the infirmary."

Westry flashed a devious smile. "Now, why would I do that, when I have my very own nurse right here?"

I grinned, reaching for my knapsack. "Well, I should have a first-aid kit in here somewhere." I riffled through the bag until I found the little white case stocked with nursing essentials, then removed the suture set. I opened a white packet, pulling out an alcohol-soaked square of gauze. "This might sting a little."

I took his hand, feeling the familiar flutter inside when our skin touched, and led him to the bed. *What does it matter if we both sit here?* "Now," I said when we were seated, "hold still."

Elliot had been right. The laceration on his forehead was deep, and I doubted my ability to stitch it up. "It looks bad," I said, dabbing the wound with the gauze. Westry flinched but didn't say anything.

"You know," I said nervously, "we have a topical numbing cream at the infirmary. Let's go there. It will be less painful for you."

I began to stand up, but Westry reached for my hand and pulled me back. "I don't want to go," he said. "I want to stay. Right here."

His eyes were intense, tender. I nodded and

picked up the suture set. "All right, but this may hurt a bit."

Westry stared at the wall ahead as I made one stitch and then two. A third was all I needed to close the gap. I tied it firmly then snipped the edge. "There," I said. "Now, that wasn't too bad, was it?"

Westry shook his head. "You're a natural, Cleo Hodge," he said teasingly, gazing into my eyes with a look of concern. I smiled, then quickly turned away.

"You've been crying," he said. "Why?"

I thought of the letter from Mother. "Just some disturbing mail from home."

"What did it say?"

I hesitated. "It was from my mother. She's"—I choked back the tears that were coming again—"she's leaving my father."

He reached out and pulled me toward him; his arms wrapped around my back, and the side of my head nestled into his chest. I felt protected, encircled. "I'm so sorry," he said. His words reverberated in the little bungalow, floating on the air for some time, for neither of us spoke again for a great while.

I looked up to face Westry. He was here. Present. Now. And in that moment, nothing else mattered.

His hands moved up my arms, along my shoulders toward my neck and to my cheeks, where they pulled my face toward his. I felt something new stir inside me. Westry pressed his lips against mine so delicately, so perfectly. He pulled me closer, weakening any lingering resistance.

He held me in his arms, cradling me. November 27. It was an insignificant date, just a blip on the calendar. But it was also a life-changing occasion. It was the day I started loving Westry.

Chapter 7

The sun beat down without reprieve, which seemed unfair, given that it was Christmas Eve. At home, Mother would be trimming an enormous fir tree in the entryway. I could almost smell the evergreen, even if it was a figment, both because there were only palms in sight and because Mother had moved out of the house. Her most recent letter indicated that she'd taken an apartment in New York.

I thought of how jolly Papa was this time of the year, offering big mugs of mulled cider to carolers, stuffing Maxine's pastries and cookies into his mouth at every turn. *Maxine.* I'd wondered more than a few times why she hadn't written. The mail had slowed altogether, though, and the women waited expectantly every afternoon, hoping to catch sight of a jeep barreling across the lawn with a special delivery.

I hadn't heard from Gerard, which concerned me most of all. His silence had been welcome in some ways, leaving a place for my feelings for Westry to grow undisturbed. And yet, I worried about him every day, imagining him on a cold foreign battlefield, fighting for America. Fighting for me.

Kitty had grown to accept the death of Mr. Gelfman, though she didn't talk about it. Instead, she seemed to invest every fiber of her being in Lance. She frequently slipped off to meet him and stayed out much too late. But who was I to judge?

And suddenly it was Christmas Eve. I had time to head to the beach before the candlelight service at the chapel later that night, so I snuck away before Nurse Hildebrand could recruit me to help unpack the new shipment of supplies.

I was disappointed to find the bungalow empty. Westry had been on three missions in the past month, and I'd seen very little of him. I checked the mailbox under the floorboard, and giggled when I found an envelope waiting for me.

My darling Cleo,
Merry Christmas, my dear. I'm sorry we haven't seen much of each other lately. My commanding officer seems to have taken on all the qualities of a slave driver.

I had hoped to meet you here this morning, the only time I could break away, but no luck. So I will leave your Christmas present here for you to find. Maybe someday we'll have a real Christmas together.

Yours,
Grayson

My eyes welled up with tears as I read the last line over again. "Maybe someday we'll have a real Christmas together." *Will we?* The idea was frightening and exciting at the same time. My fingers worked fast to untie the red ribbon from the little box waiting below the floorboard, wrapped beautifully with tinfoil he must have stolen from the mess hall. I lifted the lid and found a gold, oval locket on a delicate chain. The inside was empty, but on the back, the inscription read: *Grayson and Cleo.*

I smiled, clasping the chain around my neck proudly, before producing a pen and a notebook from my bag.

My darling Grayson,
Thank you for the necklace. I love it. Do you know that in my 21 years, I have never owned a locket? I have always wanted one, and I will be very proud to wear it. In fact, I don't think I shall ever

take it off. My mind is filled with ideas about what to put inside. You'll have to help me decide.

I miss you so much, but being here helps. For even when we are apart, I can find you here. Your presence lingers in these four walls, and it warms me.

Merry Christmas.

With love,
Cleo

The mail arrived that evening, just before the Christmas Eve service. I eyed the crate with suspicion and caution, especially after Mother's last letter, which had been so surprising, so jarring. Leaving Papa with no explanation. Surely there was more to the story.

"Just one for you today, dear," Mary said, handing me a light pink envelope.

Pink. I felt my heart lighten. *Definitely not from Gerard.* I hated myself for feeling a sense of relief. It wasn't that I *didn't* want to hear from him. No, it was more complicated than that. I looked at the handwriting, so elegant, so perfect, and the return address on the envelope. *Maxine.* I tucked the envelope in the pocket of my dress and turned to the door. But when I heard church bells chiming from the chapel in the distance, I turned back around to see Nurse Hildebrand consumed in paperwork at her desk. *What will she be doing on this strange island, all alone, on Christmas Eve?* She never spoke of family, and if what the girls said was true, her past hadn't been a happy one. *She must be lonely this time of the year.* It was true that she hardly smiled or opened her mouth unless it was to bark orders at us. But it was Christmas. No one could be alone on Christmas. *Has anyone invited her to the candlelight service?*

I approached Nurse Hildebrand quietly. "Excuse me, Nurse Hildebrand," I began cautiously. "I'm leaving for the night. It's Christmas Eve—"

"I'm aware of the date," she snapped.

I nodded submissively. "It's just that I wanted to, er . . ."

"Make your point, Nurse Calloway," she said. "Can't you see I'm busy?"

"Yes," I said, "I'm sorry. It's just that I wondered if you knew about the candlelight service tonight. I thought you might like to attend, that's all."

She turned away from her files and looked at me for a moment—a good, hard look of amusement and maybe confusion, too.

"Run along, Nurse Calloway," she said briskly. "Your shift is over."

I nodded and walked back to the door, trying to hide my disappointment. *What does it matter?*

Kitty had promised to go with me to the service that night, but she wasn't in the room when I got back. After fifteen minutes of waiting and no sign of a note of explanation, I gave up and went to the closet to find something to wear, which is when I noticed that her yellow dress was missing—the one that clung to her body a little too suggestively. *Where is she going in that dress?* I chose a simple blue frock for myself, then retrieved Maxine's letter.

My dear Antoinette,

How are you, my dear? My, how I have missed you. The home isn't the same with you away. It's lonelier. It lacks life.

So much has changed since you left, and I'm afraid I don't know where to begin. But, we have always been honest with one another, so I will start with the truth. Bear with me, because the next few sentences may be very hard to take.

You must know, my dear, that I have loved your father for a very long time. It has been a love that I have fought, with all of my might, with all of my soul. But, you can't fight love. I know that now.

I never intended for this love to tear your family apart. And for many years, I was successful at hiding my feelings away, bottling them up so efficiently that even I was fooled. And yet, when I learned that your father returns my love, it pried open that cork that I'd been so diligent about keeping intact. It changed everything.

I do not know if you will ever speak to me again, or look at me in the same way you once did, but I pray that you will find it in your heart to forgive me. Your father and I want nothing more than your blessing.

After the war, we're going to France to be married. I know this probably sounds so strange and sudden. Give it time, dear Antoinette. For in time, I pray that we can be a family again.

With love,
Maxine

The pages drifted out of my hands, effortlessly, and fell onto the quilt on my bed, where I stared at them, studying Maxine's cursive. *Why does she loop her y's in such a strange way?* And that stationery, with the embossed edges—it was Mother's. *Who does she think she is? The lady of the house?*

Maxine and Papa. It didn't add up. *Have they loved each other my entire life? Did my mother know? No wonder she has been so cruel to Maxine—Papa's mistress living under her own roof. Poor Mother! How did I not notice it? How have I been so naive?*

I picked up the pages, crumpling them into a tight ball and tossing it into the wastebasket. I didn't need to read it again. I didn't want to see it again. And when I walked out to the hallway outside the room, I startled myself with the force with which I closed the door.

If Kitty wasn't coming, I'd go to the service alone. I couldn't stay in on Christmas Eve thinking about Papa and Maxine roasting chestnuts together back at home. I shook my head, and made my way down to the foyer. But before I could push open the doors and step outside, my ears perked up. Someone in a room upstairs must have found a radio, and even rarer, a signal out across the great blue ocean that carried the sweet, beautiful, pure sound of "O Holy Night" sung by Bing Crosby. My knees weakened as I listened to the song drifting over the airwaves like a warm breeze, comforting me, reminding me of Christmases in Seattle. With cider. Carolers. An enormous fir tree in the entryway. Papa smoking by the fire. Mother fussing about wrapping gifts. Maxine's sweets, though I didn't have the taste for them now. And Gerard, of course. I couldn't forget Gerard.

"Makes you feel sentimental, doesn't it?"

I turned around upon hearing Stella's voice behind me. "Yes," I said. *If she only knew.*

Her face appeared softer in the dim light of the entryway. *Has the island changed her?* "It hardly feels right," she continued. "No snow. Not even a tree. For the first time, I'm homesick. Really homesick."

"Me too," I said, locking my arm in hers. We stood there listening until the song ended and the radio frequency became garbled—the moment lost forever, swallowed up by the lonely Pacific.

"Are you going to the service?" Stella asked.

"Yes," I said. "I was just coming back to get Kitty. We planned to walk over together."

"Oh, I almost forgot to tell you," she said.

"Tell me what?"

"Kitty asked me to pass along a message that she's terribly sorry, but Lance had some special Christmas date planned for her tonight and she won't be able to attend."

"A *date*? On *Christmas Eve*?"

Stella shrugged. "You'd know better than I would. Seems like those two are spending an awful lot of time together, doesn't it? Every time I pass Kitty in the hallway, she says she's off to see Lance. Lance this, Lance that. But if you ask me, he's hardly worthy of her affection. The man is dangerous."

"Dangerous?"

"Yes," she said. "Everyone knows how he carries on with the *native* girls. Besides, that man has a temper the size of the USS *Missouri*."

I remembered the way Atea had looked at him, and the instinct I'd had about him shortly after. But I hadn't seen his temper flare. Could he really be *dangerous?*

"Well," I said, "he may have a wayward eye, but it's Kitty's prerogative. I've tried to get through to her about men before, and believe me, it doesn't work."

"You're a good friend, Anne," Stella said, eyeing me with a look of admiration.

I thought of my secrets. "Not as good as I should be."

"Want to head over to the chapel with me?" she asked, glancing at the clock in the hallway, which read a quarter past seven. "Mary and Liz are already there setting up. We can go meet them."

I smiled. "I'd love to."

As we walked outside, the radio's signal regrouped and began transmitting a weak version of "Silent Night" sung in a foreign language I didn't recognize. It sounded strange and lost, which was exactly how I felt.

Once inside the little chapel adjacent to the mess hall I let out a gasp. "Where on earth did they get a tree?" I eyed the fir standing at attention near the piano. "A Douglas fir, in the tropics?"

Mary grinned. "It was our big secret," she said. "The Social Committee has been planning it for months. One of the pilots brought it over with the supplies last week. Nobody thought of decorations so we had to get creative. The men deserve a tree on Christmas."

The choir began warming up to our left, as I looked at the fir tree, adorned with tinsel—handmade from finely cut tin foil—and red apples on each bow. Some of the women must have loaned out their hair ribbons, as there were at least two dozen white satin bows from top to bottom.

"It's beautiful," I said, blinking back a tear.

Mary draped her arm around me. "Everything all right, Anne?"

The choir, which was nothing more than a group of volunteer soldiers cobbled together by a lieutenant who was a music teacher back home, began singing "O Come, All Ye Faithful," and the hair on my arms stood on end. I closed my eyes and could see Gerard's face smiling at me with his kind, trusting gaze. Maxine and Papa looked on too, beseeching me for forgiveness as Kitty waved in the distance. And Westry was there in the midst. He stood on the beach, watching them all. Waiting.

I felt my legs weaken and my body sway, as Mary pulled me toward a pew. "You need to sit down," she said, fanning my face with a hymnal. "You're not looking good." Then she snapped, "Stella! She needs water."

The room seemed blurry and the choir sounded

as if it were singing the same lines over and over again. *O come let us adore him, o come let us adore him; O come let us adore him . . .*

Somebody handed me a mug and I took a sip, letting the water seep down my throat. "Sorry," I said self-consciously. "I don't know what happened."

"You're working too hard," said Mary. "That's what happened. I'm going to speak to Nurse Hildebrand about this. Look at you. Pale, thin. Did you eat dinner tonight?"

I shook my head.

Mary searched inside her purse until she found a candy bar. "Here," she said. "Eat this."

"Thank you."

Men began filing in, removing their hats at the door, and Stella nestled in next to us, followed by Liz. Partway through the service, I turned around to see if Kitty had come late, but instead I noticed Nurse Hildebrand seated in the back. She had a handkerchief in her hand, but quickly stuffed it into her dress pocket when her eyes met mine.

Shortly after the candles were lit and the choir began "Hark! the Herald Angels Sing," I heard some commotion and turned toward the back of the chapel. A door slammed. People shuffled in their seats. A nurse in the pew behind us let out a loud gasp.

"What's going on?" I whispered to Stella,

unable to get a good view of the scene through the crowd.

"That's what's going on," she said smugly, pointing at the center aisle.

There, walking toward us, was Atea—bare-breasted, beautiful Atea, with tears rolling down her face. She looked just as striking as she had the day at the market, though now her face was clouded in distress.

"Where is he?" she screamed, looking from left to right, scanning the pews. "Why he not here?"

One of the men stood up and took her arm. "Don't you see that you're disturbing this Christmas Eve service, miss?"

She wrenched her arm away from him. "Don't touch me! Where is he? He lie. I find him. I tell everyone."

The soldier regained his grip, this time tighter, and attempted to pull her toward the door. Atea screamed.

"Stop!" I shouted, waving my arms. I felt the blood rush from my head, but I steadied myself on the side of the pew. "I know this woman. Let me speak to her."

No one seemed to object, so I walked over to Atea and smiled warmly. Her big brown eyes, red from crying, searched my face for understanding, for trustworthiness.

"Would you like to talk outside?" I asked as if we were the only two people in the building.

She nodded and followed me through the double doors outside. We walked in silence along the gravel pathway that led to the beach. The wind was brisk, but neither of us minded.

Atea led me to a log on the beach, and we both sat down.

"I am fear," she said.

"You mean, you're *afraid?*"

She nodded.

"What, dear? What are you afraid of?"

"Him," she said simply.

Lance. My cheeks burned with anger. Stella had been right.

I nodded. "What did he do to you, Atea?"

"He hurt me," she said, pointing to a bruise on her wrist and another on her upper arm, purple and black.

"I'm so sorry," I said. "But why did you come here, to the chapel, tonight?"

Her eyes swelled with tears. "I tell everyone what he did," she said, "then he no hurt me again."

"Atea," I said, "you must leave this base. If he wants to harm you, he'll find a way. You must leave and stay far away."

She looked confused. "Where can I go?"

"Do you have someone you can stay with? Your mother? A grandmother? An aunt?"

Atea shook her head. "No," she said. "I have no one, except Tita."

"Who is Tita?"

"The oldest woman on Bora-Bora. She take care of all of us."

I nodded. Suddenly my own problems seemed unimportant. "Well," I said, "you can't stay here."

She looked unsettled about something. "But what will I do when he comes?"

"What do you mean, 'when he comes'?"

"He will come."

I patted her arm. "See that white building in the distance, and the window on the corner of the second floor, just near the palm?"

"Yes," she said meekly.

"That's my room. You call up to me when you need something, when you're afraid. We always leave the window open. I'll hear you."

She searched my face with her big, trusting eyes. "What if you not there?"

"Then run down this beach," I said, pointing my finger toward the shore. "About a half mile up there's a bungalow, a little hut a few steps into the thicket. The door is locked, but you'll find the key under a book beneath the steps. No one knows about it here. You'll be safe there."

Atea's eyes grew big. "The artist's home?"

I shook my head, confused. "I'm not sure I know what you mean."

"Yes, the painter. No one goes there. Tita say it's haunting."

"Haunted?"

"Yes."

"And do you believe it's haunted?" I asked.

Atea shrugged. "Maybe, but I go there if I must."

"Good girl."

Atea smiled.

"You're going to be fine," I said. "Everything will be fine. I'll see to that."

"Really?" Her eyes searched mine. She looked so beautiful, yet so innocent and afraid. I vowed to protect her. I'd speak to Westry about Lance. I'd make sure he never hurt her again.

"Really," I assured her.

She exhaled deeply and stood up to leave.

"Atea, there's something else," I said. "If you see Lance, you mustn't tell him about your visiting the base, or your chat with me. It will only anger him."

She looked confused, but nodded.

"Good night," I said.

"*Taoto maitai*," she said before disappearing into the moonlight.

Chapter 8

The morning sun was bright, streaming through the window with such force that two aggressive beams of light pushed through the curtains and danced unabashedly on the closet door. Kitty and I watched the rays from our beds.

"Can you imagine having a bright morning like this in Seattle—in January?" I said, turning to Kitty.

"No," she answered in a flat voice. "I miss the cold. I'm tired of all this sun."

"I don't know that I could ever tire of it," I said, sitting up and reaching for my robe draped over the foot of the bed. "Kitty? Can I confide in you?"

"Yes," she replied.

"I'm worried."

"Worried about what?" Her eyes looked tired, but not just because it was early. Deep exhaustion punctuated her face. We hadn't spoken of Lance since Christmas Day, when I'd told Kitty about what Atea had said. I'd warned her about Lance and yet the news hardly fazed her. Things were over between the two of them, or so it seemed. As each day passed, she grew quieter and more introspective, and I grew more concerned. Had Lance hurt her in the same way he'd hurt Atea?

"I'm worried that this island has changed us," I said.

Instead of looking at me, Kitty looked *through* me, right on to the wall behind my back. "It *has* changed us," she said simply.

"Kitty, it's just that I—" I stopped when I heard a sudden knock at the door.

"Who is it?" I called out.

"It's me, Mary."

I cinched the tie on my robe and opened the door to find Mary rosy cheeked and beaming. "Morning, lovelies," she said, poking her head into the room to catch Kitty's eye, with little success.

Mary had regained her strength after her bout with malaria, and she now hummed in the infirmary while the rest of us grumbled. Stella said Mary had been seeing a man named Lou, though Mary hadn't let on yet. I hoped it was true. She deserved happiness.

I felt a pang in my heart just then. *The letter. Mary's letter, from her ex-fiancé.* I looked at the shoe box under my bedside table, remembering that I'd hidden it there, promising myself I'd give it to her when I felt she was ready. I lifted the lid and reached inside the box and Gerard's most recent letter fell out onto the floor. My cheeks flushed and I hurriedly stowed it away. *How could Mary face her past if I couldn't even face mine?*

"I wanted to invite you to a little soiree tonight," Mary continued. Her eyes sparkled the way eyes do when one is in love, or rather, in *new* love. "A group of us are getting together tonight for a cookout on the beach. Stella, Liz, a few of the other nurses, and some of the men too. We're all piling into a truck at seven thirty for Leatra Beach. I think Westry's coming too, Anne."

She gave me a knowing look that I did not return. I hadn't spoken to Westry in three weeks, and I feared there was a silence growing between us. Sure, his commanding officer had kept him busy. Very busy. But I hardly found him in the bungalow anymore, even when I knew he was off duty.

Leatra Beach. It was just a stone's throw from the bungalow. Our bungalow. I felt my chest tighten. *What am I worried about?* Of course, no one would find it. No one knew it was there, except Westry and me. In fact, it sometimes felt that the little hut was visible only to us. And we spoke of that very thing the last time we were together there, when we'd spotted a soldier passing by on the normally quiet beach. The sound of his whistling sent shivers down my spine. Would he see the bungalow? Would he see us? I realized then how very much I loved this private little world of ours, and how much I hoped to keep it that way.

"Someone's coming," I had whispered in a panic to Westry.

We watched from the window that looked out

upon the beach as the man stumbled along the white sand. Probably drunk. The soldiers drank too much, and the island heat only amplified their intoxication.

"The coast is clear," Westry said a few moments later. "He didn't see us."

But why didn't he see us? The bungalow wasn't too far off the beach, only loosely hidden by palm fronds. Anyone with an ounce of curiosity would see it on second glance. So why hadn't others found it? How had it gone unnoticed after all these years and with an army base populated by a couple thousand men just down the shore? These were the questions that made me wonder if the bungalow was merely a figment. Our figment, a mirage in the French Polynesian sun custom made for Westry and me.

"So," Mary said expectantly, "will you come?"

I glanced back at Kitty. She looked disinterested, distant. "I'll go," I said hesitantly, "but only if Kitty joins me."

Kitty looked startled. "Oh, no," she said, shaking her head. "No, I can't."

"Why not?"

Kitty provided no explanation, just silence.

I folded my arms and forced a grin. "See? You don't even have a good excuse," I said, before turning back to Mary. "We're going."

"Perfect," she said. "Meet us down in the parking lot at seven thirty."

• • •

Kitty joined me, reluctantly. I took a good, long look at her before we left the room. What had changed about her? True, the color had left her cheeks, and her hair, always wild, was even wilder now, untamable. She didn't even stop to catch her reflection in the little oval mirror in our bedroom. And if she had, I wasn't certain that she'd even be able to see the change. It wasn't only her hair, but her figure. Last week, I'd heard Stella whispering to Liz in the mess hall about Kitty taking a second helping of mashed potatoes. "She's going to go home fifteen pounds heavier," she had said. Kitty did look plumper now, but her beauty still shone through the mussy hair, pale cheeks, and rounder appearance. Kitty would be beautiful no matter what.

"You look pretty," I said as we walked out of the barracks that evening.

"No I don't," she said. I didn't like the defeat in her voice.

"Stop it," I chided her. "I wish you would snap out of this mood you're in." I turned to face her. "I miss my old friend."

Kitty stopped suddenly on the trail, and when I looked up, I could see why. Colonel Donahue was approaching. He tipped his cap at us, but didn't say a word. A sick feeling came over me as I remembered the incident with Westry. That incident had made me despise the colonel, but

158

seeing the way he dismissed Kitty, without so much as a "Hello, how are you, Kitty?"— especially after the interest he'd taken in her when we'd arrived months ago—well, it made me fume. He was rumored to be seeing one of the other nurses—quiet, with dark hair and a figure that rivaled a pinup girl's. *He ought to be ashamed of himself.*

When the colonel was a safe distance away, I turned to Kitty. "I've never liked that man."

Kitty looked sad, which made me wonder if I'd said the wrong thing. "I didn't mean to—"

She reached for my hand and squeezed it tightly. "It's all right, Anne. You don't need to apologize. It's just that . . ." She paused, as if to collect her thoughts, or maybe to consider if anyone was listening from an open window in the distance. The men's barracks were nearing. "It's nothing."

"I wish you'd tell me," I said. "Are you sad about the colonel's new girlfriend? Stella says she's a real dimwit. Or is it Lance? Kitty, did something happen? Did he hurt you?"

She shook her head. "Anne, please don't."

"All right," I said, "but will you tell me when you're ready?"

Kitty nodded, but I feared it was an empty promise.

Just ahead, I spotted some of the men and women piling into a truck. Stella was there, with

Will by her side, as was Liz, and Mary, with her new beau, Lou.

Kitty and I climbed in. "Hi," I said, taking a seat next to Mary.

She beamed. "I'm so glad you two could come. Liz sweet-talked a mess hall cook into joining, and look at the loot!"

Mary pointed to a chest of ice with chicken and potato salad and corn for roasting. Another cooler held an enormous quantity of beer. I looked around the vehicle shyly, trying not to make eye contact with the men. There were many faces I didn't recognize, eager faces. And Lance was there, seated next to a blond nurse. *What's her name? Lela, yes.* I shuddered when I thought of Atea, poor Atea. Lance had used her, and hurt her. Perhaps in the same way he'd used Kitty. I hoped Kitty didn't see the way he was talking to the woman, flirting with her.

I refused to watch them; instead, I searched the vehicle for Westry. *Did he come?*

Mary must have read my mind. "Looks like he didn't make it," she whispered. "I'm sorry."

I shrugged. "Don't be," I said, tugging at my engagement ring. "There's nothing between us. Nothing at all."

I held on to Kitty as the truck sped along the bumpy island road. Each pothole punctuated the shame I felt. *How did I, an engaged woman, let myself become emotionally involved with Westry?*

I barely know him. What has this island done to my judgment? Kitty stared ahead. When the truck came to a stop a few minutes later, pulling up onto the beach, everyone but Kitty stood up.

"Kitty," I said, "let's go."

She nodded dutifully, rising as if it were an exhausting endeavor. Lance helped Lela out of the truck, scooping her in his arms and then plopping her onto the sandy ground. She giggled and batted her eyelashes at him. Kitty quickly looked away. *Was I wrong to bring her here?* I hardly wanted to be here myself.

Mary led the procession onto the beach, telling the men where to set out the blankets, the fire for the cook, the beverage station, and the radio. There were oohs and aahs when a lance corporal named Shawn pulled out a gray radio and extended its antenna. Even Kitty smiled a little. None of us were immune to the power of music.

"Now," Mary said, as the men and women found their places on the blankets. "If I can just get a signal." She worked on the tuner for some time, stopping momentarily when she heard the faint sound of a man's voice—an Australian accent—relating war news with such speed and intensity, I felt my body respond in kind.

"Japanese bombers stormed the north shore today, leaving a wake of death and destruction." We all leaned in closer to hear more. "Casualties are estimated in the hundreds, many of them

161

women and children." She quickly turned the dial. After a few seconds, the static parted to reveal a crystal-clear signal coming out across the ocean. The melody was soft and sweet, haunting. "How strange," Mary said. "We're picking up a French station."

The words were foreign, the melody unfamiliar, and yet it entranced me, and everyone else who was huddled together on the beach. Stella leaned in closer to Will. Lou reached for Mary's hand and asked her to dance. A few other nurses paired up with men I didn't recognize, even Liz. And Kitty didn't object when a soldier sat down beside her. She even grinned, biting into an ear of corn with gusto. The melody aroused a longing in my heart that I tried to squelch, a longing for Westry. I turned my gaze toward the ocean and the stretch of beach that led to the bungalow. It was getting dark now. *I shouldn't.* Besides, he wouldn't be there anyway. But as the music played on, the bungalow's pull became stronger, until I could no longer resist it. I stood up and walked quietly toward the beach. *I could just slip away for a half hour. No one would know. No one would miss me.*

I walked quickly, glancing back several times, just to be sure that no one followed. I slipped into the thicket and made my way to the steps of the bungalow. *There it is. Our bungalow.* The sight soothed me. I knelt down and felt around under the steps for the book and the key, but I heard the door creak open in front of me. I looked up, and there, standing in the dim light, was Westry.

A faint shadow punctuated his jawline, and his wet hair and unbuttoned shirt suggested that he'd just returned from a swim. He smiled. "I was hoping you'd come tonight," he said. "Did you see that moon?"

I nodded, gazing up at the sky, where an orange-tinged full moon dangled on the horizon, so close it almost kissed the shore.

I took a step closer. "I've never seen anything like it."

"Come in," he said, reaching for my hand. "I have something for you."

He closed the door behind us, and I sat down on the bed. I felt the pulse, the electricity in the air. I knew he felt it too.

"Look," he said, holding up a radio. "I got a signal." He turned the dial and there was that sound again—that beautiful, haunting foreign melody.

"Listen," he said, shaking his head. "French."

I closed my eyes and swayed to the music.

"This song," he said, "do you know it?"

I listened intently for a few moments, then shook my head. "No, I don't think I do."

"It's 'La Vie en Rose.'"

I raised an eyebrow. "How do you know it?"

"I heard it shortly before I left for the war," he

163

said. "A friend of mine works for a record label. No one knows the song yet, at least not anyone back at home. They're testing it on the radio before they release a record. But it's going to be a huge hit. Mark my words. Just listen." He sat down next to me. Our arms brushed, and I could feel the warmth of his body.

"What does it mean?" I asked, feeling Westry's gaze on my face. I stared ahead at the radio.

He took a breath. "It means, *Hold me close and hold me fast; The magic spell you cast; This is la vie en rose; When you kiss me, heaven sighs; And though I close my eyes; I see la vie en rose; When you press me to your heart; I'm in a world apart; A world where roses bloom; And when you speak; Angels sing from above.*"

"It's beautiful," I said, still unable to look at him. My hands began to tremble. I tucked them under my legs.

Westry stood up. "Will you dance with me?"

I nodded, taking his hand.

He held me close as our bodies swayed to the music, keeping his arms low on my waist, a perfect fit. I nestled my cheek into his chest.

"Westry," I whispered.

"You mean Grayson?"

I smiled. "My dear Grayson."

"Yes, Cleo?"

"Well, that's just it. I am Cleo; you're Grayson. But are we only pretending? Is this *real?* Why is it that when we're here together," I said, "everything feels so right, so perfect? But when—"

"When we're out there," he said, interrupting me, pointing toward the window, "it's different?"

"Yes."

"Because it is," he said simply. "This is our paradise. Out there, well, it's complicated."

"And that's just it," I said. "I almost didn't come tonight because I feared that you were growing distant. That night with Colonel Donahue—why haven't you spoken of it?"

He put his finger to my lips. "Would you believe me if I told you I was protecting you?"

I looked at him, confused. "Protecting me? From what?"

"It's a crazy world out there, Anne. War. Lies. Betrayal. Sadness. It's all around us." He cradled my head in his hands. "Next time you worry that I am growing distant, come here. Come to the bungalow and you will feel my love."

Love. *Westry loves me.* It was all that mattered. I pressed my body closer to his and felt something akin to hunger welling up inside, an unfamiliar longing I'd never felt with Gerard. *Passion. Is this what Kitty meant?*

Westry took a step back for a moment. "Look at you," he said. "You are a vision. I'm going to take your photograph." He retrieved a camera from his knapsack, and instructed me to lean against the

165

far wall. "There," he said after the flash went off. "Perfect."

"Now you," I said, lifting the camera from his hands. "I want one of you. I want to remember this night, this moment."

He obliged, leaning against the wall as I had done. I stared at his eyes through the lens, hoping to memorize the moment forever, before I clicked the button.

I set the camera down on the desk, and Westry lifted me in his arms and laid me on the bed, so effortlessly I felt like a feather in his grasp. I ran my hands along his arms. They were strong and firm. His lips touched mine, and my heart rate quickened as I took in the familiar scent of his skin, breathing it in, letting it intoxicate me. I unbuttoned his shirt completely and ran my fingers along his chest. His muscles quivered a little at my touch and he smiled. Something in me trembled too as he reached for the zipper of my dress. He undressed me with such delicate, loving hands, caressing my skin, and kissed me with such intention, I wondered if he'd dreamt about this moment a thousand times before, as I had done.

Our bodies fit together like they were made for each other. *Meant* for each other. I closed my eyes, vowing to remember every second, every breath, every sensation, and when it was over, we lay snugly in each other's arms, his warm chest pressed against mine. Our hearts beat in sync as the waves crashed into the shore outside the bungalow.

"Westry," I whispered.

"What is it, my love?"

"What will happen after all of this is over?"

"You mean, after the war?"

"Yes," I said. "When we go home."

"I wish I knew," he said, kissing my forehead.

I felt the cool gold of my engagement ring against my skin, and I instinctively pulled away from Westry.

"You're thinking of him, aren't you?"

I sighed. "It's all so complicated."

"Not when love is so certain," he said.

For Westry, it was that straightforward. We loved each other. That was that. And yet, I had made a promise to Gerard. Gerard, who might be fighting for his life on a battlefield right now. Gerard, who was waiting for me to be his wife. *How could I do this to him?*

I looked up at Westry. As I gazed into his eyes, my resolve strengthened. I loved this man with every ounce of my being. I kissed him softly, and laid my head back on his shoulder. We listened to the French songs on the radio for a long time, forgetting people, places, even time, until my eyes grew heavy.

It may have been minutes or hours later, but I bolted out of bed when I heard the snap of a twig outside. I hurriedly dressed, fussing with the zipper on my dress as I peered out the window, where I could see a shadowy form on the beach.

"Who do you think it is?" I whispered to Westry, who quickly rose from the bed, slipping on his trousers and sliding each arm through the sleeves of his shirt. He didn't stop to button it before opening the door. I followed close behind, realizing that I had no idea what time it was. Kitty and the others must have been panicked.

"Who's there?" Westry called out to the figure in the distance.

"It's me," said a familiar voice. "Kitty." We pushed past the thicket, and the light from the moon revealed her face. I could see that she was frightened. "Anne? Is that *you?*"

"Yes," I said, suddenly aware that my hair was askew. *Did I zip my dress all the way? What would she think seeing Westry standing there half-dressed?*

"Oh," she said when she noticed Westry beside me. "I—I didn't mean to interrupt; it's just that we were getting ready to leave, and we couldn't find you."

"I'm sorry, Kitty," I said, a bit embarrassed. "I must have lost track of time."

Kitty couldn't see the bungalow from where she was standing, and I was glad of it.

"I was just leaving," I said, turning to Westry. My God, he was handsome. I didn't want to leave. I wanted to stay with him here, maybe forever. "Good night, Westry," I said.

"Good night, Anne," he replied, smiling a secret smile.

Kitty and I walked in silence up the beach, until she finally spoke. "You love him, don't you?"

"Kitty!"

She nestled her hand in mine. "It's OK," she said. "I don't care who you love. I just want to see you happy. Are you?"

I looked up at the moon overhead and then back toward the stretch of beach that led to the bungalow. "Yes," I said. "I've never been happier in my entire life than at this moment."

The bumpy road home barely disturbed any of us. Not Stella, with her head resting comfortably in Will's lap; or Mary, deep in conversation with Lou; or Kitty, lost in her own thoughts; and especially not me, with a heart that swelled with such true and perfect love. But with it came a great heaviness, for I had to make a decision. Soon, I feared.

Chapter 9

"Did you hear?" Liz said at breakfast. "The men are shipping out. Almost all of them. There's some big fight on an island south of here. It's going to be serious."

My eyes met Mary's. I could see the concern for Lou in her eyes and wondered if she could detect the fear I felt for Westry.

"Colonel Donahue is leading them out this evening," Kitty said, with little emotion, as if she was reading the *War Digest* verbatim.

"Does anyone know who's going?" I asked, hoping the panic I felt wasn't evident in my voice.

"Yes," Stella said, pulling out her handkerchief. "Go look at the list." She pointed to the bulletin board outside the mess hall. "I saw Will's name on it earlier."

"Stella, I'm so sorry," said Liz.

I turned to Mary. "Will you go look with me?"

She nodded, and we walked somberly outside to the board. There it was. His name, halfway down, in black ink. Westry Green. Lou's was there too. Mary gasped, and we clutched each other tightly.

"We have to find them," she said. "We have to say good-bye before . . ."

"Let's be confident," I said. "Let's think positively. They need that from us."

"Anne," Mary muttered, "I can't bear to lose him."

"You shouldn't talk that way, dear," I said, patting her arm. "It's bad luck."

I'd already worked the early morning shift in the infirmary, so I didn't feel guilty about sneaking out after breakfast to make a quick trip to the men's barracks, where I gazed up at Westry's window. The room, or what I could see of it from standing on a bench outside, looked empty—a tightly made bed and a coat missing from the hook near the door. *Has he already left?* Liz had mentioned earlier that a squadron had already departed. *Is Westry with them?*

I said good-bye to Mary and walked quickly to the beach, and once I'd rounded the bend, I started to run. *Maybe he's at the bungalow, waiting for me. I can see him before he leaves, if I run fast enough.* My shoes filled with sand as I sloshed along the beach—sand that had never felt so heavy, so stifling. *Can it be trying to keep me from Westry, to hold me back?* I tripped on a piece of driftwood and clutched my aching knee before standing up again and resuming my pace. *Faster. Run faster.* Each second counted.

I pushed through the brush and finally made my way to the front step of the bungalow. The morning sun shone on its palm walls, streaming

171

light all around it. I reached for the doorknob, praying that it would be open, praying that Westry would be inside. But my hand was met with a sharp click. Locked. Westry wasn't there. I was too late.

I pulled out the key and let myself in anyway, sitting down in a heap of disappointment on the chair by the desk. The little room immediately comforted me. I could sense his presence, just as he'd said I would. I searched my memories for his exact words, and found them tucked away in my heart: "Next time you worry that I am growing distant, come here. Come to the bungalow, and you will feel my love." Yes, I could feel his love. It enveloped me.

I lifted the floorboard and my heart warmed when I saw a letter inside.

My darling Cleo,

I have to leave now, my dear. I am shipping out to Guadalcanal for what the CO calls "serious combat." The men don't know what to expect, nor do I. After all, we've been sitting pretty on this rock for so long. We were almost fooled into thinking we were on vacation. It's about time we fulfill our jobs, to do what we came here for. To fight.

I stopped by the infirmary this morning to say good-bye, but you were busy, and I hated to disturb you. I watched you work from the window for a few minutes. My, you are beautiful. The way you move. The way you talk. I have never loved as I love you.

I don't know how long I will be gone. Maybe days. Maybe months. But I pray that you will hold the memory of last night in your heart, as I will. I pray that you will think of me and wait for me. For I will return, and we will be reunited. And when the war is over and done with, we will never part.

Remember me, la vie en rose, my darling.

Yours forevermore,
Grayson

I wiped away tears, then ran outside to the shore as a squadron of airplanes flew overhead in formation. I blew a kiss out into the sky.

He'd come back. He had to.

The days passed with very little news from the war front. The men who had stayed seemed preoccupied and on edge, perhaps guilty that they weren't out fighting too, or ashamed that they hadn't been chosen for such an important mission.

The Allies were closing in on the Japanese in the Pacific, and this was a critical battle to protect New Zealand, Liz had explained. Liz knew more about the war than any of us. She said the Japanese had planned to colonize New Zealand, to rape and kill. And while the allies had taken Guadalcanal, pockets of enemy forces remained scattered throughout the South Pacific. We had to win. If we didn't, well, no one talked about that, but it weighed heavily on our minds.

Every day more injured men were wheeled off airplanes. Some came in on stretchers, dazed and bloodied, mute, as if what they had seen had robbed them of their voices, their sanity. Others had such severe injuries—severed legs, missing arms, shrapnel in the eyes—that they moaned for morphine, and we gave it to them as quickly as our hands could inject needles into their pain-ravaged skin.

The steady stream of men kept us busy in the infirmary, making us wonder if the battle was going according to plan. Nurse Hildebrand, who directed us with such emotionless precision, seemed almost mechanical. "Liz!" she shouted. "Go to the storeroom and get a fresh supply of bandages. Can't you see that we're almost out? Stella! Come here and help me get this one prepped for surgery. Kitty! The man over in bed nine needs morphine. Quickly now."

She operated with the force of a drill sergeant, and rightly so. This was the most intense work any of us had ever done. And in it, emotions ran high. As each man was wheeled into the infirmary, the women crowded around to check for a familiar face.

And on one morning in early April, we heard a commotion at the entrance, where a man shouted, "I need a nurse here, fast!"

I saw a pilot standing in the entryway holding a bloodied soldier in his arms. "There wasn't time to wait for a stretcher so I brought him in myself," he said. "He bled out on the plane. I'm not sure what you can do for him, but work fast. He's a good guy."

I wheeled a stretcher to the entrance and helped the pilot lay the man on top. Though blood covered his face and neck, I recognized him in an instant. *Dear God, it's Will. Stella's Will.* "I'll take him from here," I said. "Thank you, lieutenant."

"There are more coming," he said gravely. "Just heard on the radio. It's bad out there. Lots of men down."

My heart filled with terror as I took Will over to the operating room, where Dr. Wheeler was washing his hands. "Doc!" I yelled. "This one needs you now."

I motioned for Mary across the room.

"It's Will," I whispered once she was near. I pointed to the operating room. "He's badly hurt. Where's Stella?"

She gestured toward the far corner of the infirmary, where Stella was working with Nurse Hildebrand on a leg splint. The soldier moaned as they adjusted his knee, moving it into place. "We have to tell her."

"No," I said. "We need her. We need every able-bodied nurse on this island right now. The lieutenant said more are coming. Maybe Lou. Maybe Westry. We need to keep working. We can't stop to grieve."

She nodded solemnly. "I'll do my best to keep her away."

"Thanks," I said. "I'll keep an eye on him. If anything changes, I'll bring her over."

An hour later twenty-three more men came, and then nine more, and then another eleven. Three died. More were stabilized and sent on homeward-bound planes for care we couldn't administer.

"What a bloody mess," Liz said, dabbing her eyes with her handkerchief. The intensity was getting to her, and to all of us.

"Are you OK?" I asked, patting her back. "I can speak to Nurse Hildebrand and see about you getting some leave."

"No," she said, straightening her white uniform. "No, I can do this. I have to."

I glanced over at Kitty, where she worked feverishly with another nurse on a man who had just been brought in. I could see by the bandages they were reaching for that it was a head injury. A serious one. Kitty's fingers moved fast, dabbing the man's forehead with alcohol. He winced. She wrapped a bandage around his head, but she

176

swayed a little as she did. Something was wrong. Then Kitty's legs buckled, just as they had on the tarmac that first day on the island. She fell to the floor, but this time, nothing blunted her fall.

I ran to her side, fanning her face. "Kitty, Kitty! Wake up. You fainted."

Liz handed me a vial of smelling salts. I held them to Kitty's nose, and a moment later, her eyes opened.

"I'm so sorry," she said. "Look at me. There are men here who are really in trouble, and I can't even manage to stand."

"You need to rest," I said. "I'll help you back to the room. Nurse Hildebrand will understand."

"Yes," she said. "But I won't let you walk me. You're needed here. I can go myself."

"All right," I conceded. "But be careful."

Kitty made her way outside, and I turned back to the rows of men waiting for medicine, for a bandage, for surgery, or just to die.

"We have to tell her," Mary said over my shoulder. "Doc says he may not make it."

I nodded. "Will you come with me?"

We walked over to Stella, who was searching a cabinet. "You'd think they'd restock this damn thing," she said, standing up. "Have you seen any iodine in this godforsaken place?"

"Stella," Mary said, "I need you to sit down."

"Sit down?" she shook her head suspiciously. "Now, why would I do that?"

"Will," I said, helping her into a chair. "He's been hurt. Badly hurt."

Stella gasped and covered her mouth with her hand. "No, no," she said. "No, I don't believe it." She looked at me, then at Mary. "Where is he?"

Mary pointed to the operating room. "Dr. Wheeler is with him now, but they don't know if he's going to pull through."

Stella ran across the room, and we followed close behind.

"Will!" she cried. "Will, it's me." She knelt down by the gurney, draping her arm lightly over his chest. "It's me, Stella."

Will didn't move. His breathing was shallow. "Doc, you're going to save him, right? You have to save him."

Just then Will's eyes opened. They fluttered and closed again.

"Will!" Stella cried. "Will, come back to me."

He opened his eyes again, and then his mouth, and said weakly, "I'm here, Stell. I'm here."

Dr. Wheeler took off his glasses. "By golly," he said. "He's conscious. This boy may make it after all."

Stella, oblivious to the tears streaming down her face, clutched Will's hand in hers. "You're going to pull through. Oh, Will!" She nestled her face in the crook of his neck.

Mary and I dried our eyes. Will had a chance. Thank God for that. But what about Lou and

Westry? What about the other men? Would they have the same good fortune? Would we?

We worked until the shift change at eleven p.m. But even then, many of us, including me, didn't want to leave. *What if Westry comes through the doors of the infirmary? What if I miss him?* Still, Nurse Hildebrand forbid us to stay. "You're too tired, and you're getting sloppy," she said.

She was right. Liz had forgotten to give meds to a patient, and I had reported incorrect information to Dr. Wheeler about a sergeant's injuries. It was the head wound in bed nineteen, not the leg injury in seven, that needed his attention. Nineteen. Seven. Twenty-three. Four. The beds, the numbers, the men—they all blurred together, and when I closed my eyes, all I could see was a deep red shade of blood.

As I opened the door to the barracks, I realized I hadn't thought of Kitty at all since she had left. *Is she OK?* I rushed up the stairs to the room, where I found her in bed, sleeping.

"Kitty," I whispered, "how are you feeling, honey?"

She rolled over and looked at me. "I'm all right," she said. "But how are the men? How are things down there?"

"It's crazy," I replied. "Will came in, badly hurt. But we think he's going to be all right."

"Good. And Westry? Any word?"

179

"Nothing yet," I said, feeling tears form in my eyes again.

"Mail came. I put a letter for you on your bed."

"Thanks," I said. "Night, Kitty."

I picked up the envelope and stood by the window so I could read the return address in the moonlight without disturbing Kitty. *It's from Gerard.*

My love,

I haven't heard from you, and I hate to even mention it, but yesterday, I was overcome with fear. I just felt that something was wrong. Of course, I don't want to believe it, but something in my heart flinched. Did something happen? Are you safe? Please write and tell me you are.

I am in France with the 101st Airborne Division, so far away from home, so far away from you. The conditions are tough here, as they are everywhere, I imagine. Men are dying right and left. But I have that card you made for me, the one with the little red heart on the cover, tucked into my jacket pocket. I believe it brings me luck. I will come home to you, Anne. I promise.

Yours,
Gerard

I wept as I tucked the letter back into the envelope, then reached for my stationery set, light blue, embossed with my initials, AEC. Anne Elizabeth Calloway. I had intended to write many letters home, to Mother, to Papa, to Maxine, and especially to Gerard, but the little letter set hadn't gotten much use, and I was ashamed that I hadn't taken more time to write Gerard. I sat down to compose a letter, even if I didn't know what I'd say.

Dear Gerard,
  I wanted you to know that I am well and fine. The mail has been backed up here, so I am only now receiving your letters.

I paused, considering the lie. A white lie.

  I'm so busy here, or else I'd have written more. When we're not working we're sleeping; when we're not sleeping, we're working.

Another lie.

  I think of you often, and miss you.
                                    With love,
                                        Anne

· · ·

"You know what we need to do to pass the time," Stella suggested at the mess hall one morning in early May.

"What?" Mary asked, feigning interest.

"A knitting circle," she said.

"Easy for you to say," Mary snapped. "Your Will is right here, safe and sound. And you think *yarn* is what *we* need?"

Stella looked wounded.

"I'm sorry," Mary said. "I didn't mean that."

"It's OK," Stella replied. "I was only thinking that it might busy us in the evenings when all we do is listen for news on the radio."

"It's not a bad idea," I chimed in.

"I'm sure the natives could use blankets," Mary added. "For the children. We could make them."

"I'll join," Kitty said.

"Me, too," said Liz.

"We could start tonight, after our shift's over," Mary offered.

Stella smiled. "Good. I'll gather the supplies. We can meet in the rec hall."

Stella had been right. It was yarn that sustained us those next couple of weeks. We made one blanket, and then two. By the third and fourth, we were already planning the fifth: green and yellow yarn, a palm motif in the center.

"I wonder who will sleep under these?" Liz

asked, running her hand along the edge of the first blanket we'd completed. "As insignificant as a blanket is, it's nice to be doing something for the people of this island."

We all nodded.

"Do you ever wonder what they think of all of this?" she continued. "One day, their peaceful oasis in the middle of the sea becomes the center of a raging war?"

"It must be terrifying for them," Mary replied. "I wish we could do more than give them blankets."

"But blankets are something," Liz said.

I thought of Atea, all alone and perhaps even in trouble. She might be able to use one, and if not, she'd know others who could.

I looked up at the circle of women, knitting needles clinking together. "I can take them to a woman, a native, I know who can use them," I offered. "I'll bring them to the market tomorrow."

"Nurse Hildebrand?"

"What is it?" she snapped without looking up from her desk.

"May I have permission to take an extended lunch?"

She pulled her spectacles lower on her nose. "And what is it that you intend to do?"

"Well, the nurses and I have been kitting blankets," I explained. "It's kept us busy in the evenings when we'd just be worrying—"

"Make your point, Nurse Calloway," she said sternly.

"Yes," I said, "I'm sorry. My intention is to deliver the blankets to the market today, to give them to some of the islanders who could use them."

"Blankets?" she said, a little mockingly.

"Yes, ma'am," I said. "Blankets."

She shook her head, then shrugged. "Well, I don't see the harm. Be sure that you're back by half past two. We're getting a shipment, and we'll need all hands on deck."

I smiled. "Thank you, Nurse Hildebrand, thank you. I will."

The market seemed quieter than usual, eerily so. Since most of the men had been deployed in the fight, fewer islanders turned up to sell their wares, but I hoped Atea would be there. I needed to talk to her.

It had been months since I'd seen her, since that fateful Christmas Eve scene at the chapel, and I'd worried about her. The blankets were merely an excuse to make sure she was all right.

"Excuse me," I said to a toothless woman holding an infant at a nearby table stacked with bananas and a few clumps of dusty, exotic-looking salad greens. "Have you seen Atea?"

The woman eyed me skeptically. "She no here," she said dismissively.

"Oh," I said, holding out the blankets. "It's just that I wanted to give her these."

My gesture changed the woman's demeanor. She softened, pointing to a hill a few hundred yards away. "She with Tita. Green house. You find her inside."

"Thank you," I said, turning toward the hillside. I had less than an hour before the truck returned to camp, so I walked fast along the pathway that led to the hill the woman had indicated. Dirt caked my ivory patent-leather pumps, but I didn't mind. I swatted a mosquito from my arm and started on the trail into the thicket. It was darker under the cloak of the tropical forest, and I almost didn't see the little green house ahead, for it blended into the hillside as if it were part of nature. *That must be it.*

A bicycle leaned up against the side of the small one-room home, which appeared to be constructed of scrap wood and treasures that had washed up from the sea. A chicken squawked a few feet away, startling me as I lifted my fist to knock on the door. *Am I foolish coming here like this?*

An old woman appeared in the doorway, her gray hair fashioned into a single tidy braid.

"I'm here to see Atea," I said meekly, holding up the basket of blankets.

The woman nodded and muttered something in French, or maybe Tahitian, that I could not

185

understand. I heard footsteps from behind the door.

"Anne!" Atea said, poking her head around the old woman. "You come!" She looked different then, which might have been because she was wearing a dress, one that was about five sizes too big for her small frame. It appeared to have been plucked from the Sears Roebuck catalog circa 1895. I wondered why she wore it when she'd been so comfortable with hardly a swatch of clothing before.

"Yes," I said. "I'm sorry to intrude. I—I wanted to make sure you were safe. And I wanted to give you these."

Atea took the basket from my hands and gasped. "They're beautiful. For me?"

"Yes, and for anyone else you think can use them," I said, smiling. "How have you been?"

She looked conflicted about answering the question. "Come in," she said instead. "This is Tita."

The old woman nodded.

"Pleased to meet you, Tita," I said. "I'm Anne."

Atea directed me to a grass-woven chair, and I sat. Moments later Tita produced a mug containing something warm. "Tea," she said. "For you."

I thanked her and took a sip. The beverage was sweet and spicy at the same time.

"It's good," I said. "What is it?"

186

"Kava," Atea said. "It calm you."

I nodded. Atea was right. Each sip had a soothing and somewhat dizzying effect. Everything softened around me. Minutes later, the sharp edges of the jagged window frame looked polished and the dirt floor I'd noted when I walked in began to take on the appearance of a soft oriental rug.

"Is this her?" Tita asked Atea.

Atea nodded.

Tita moved to the chair next to me. "You are the one who found the artist's home?"

Confused at first, I remembered what Atea had said on the beach so many months ago—a detail I had forgotten to share with Westry. "Yes," I said, "if you mean the bungalow."

Tita gave Atea a knowing look. "There is something you must know about this bungalow," the old woman said. Her eyes were so arresting, I could not look away. "According to legend, whoever steps foot in it will face a lifetime of"— she paused as if to consider the right word— "heartache."

"I'm not sure I understand what you mean," I said, setting the mug down on a little wooden table to my left. A fog seemed to appear in the room, and I wondered what was in the tea.

"Bad things happen there," she said.

I shook my head. No, she had it all wrong. *Good* things happened there. It was our beloved hideaway, the place where I had grown to love Westry. *How could she say this?*

"Like what?" I asked, finding my voice.

"Things too dark to speak of," she whispered, casting her eyes to a crucifix that hung on the wall.

I stood up abruptly and the room seemed to move. "Well," I said, steadying myself on the edge of the chair. "Thank you for the tea. But I really must be going." I turned to Atea. "Take care of yourself, dear. And please, remember my offer if you need assistance."

She nodded and eyed Tita cautiously as I reached for the door handle.

"Wait," I said, turning back around. "You said the bungalow once belonged to an artist. Do you happen to know who?"

Tita looked at Atea and then at me again. "Yes," she said with wistful eyes. "His name was Paul. Paul Gauguin."

The following night, Mary passed out the yarn in the rec hall just as the onslaught began. We looked up when we heard a rush of men coming through the door. "Nurses, come quick!" one shouted. "You're needed in the infirmary. It's a plane full of wounded men. Too many this time."

I dropped my knitting needles and ran with the other women along the path to the infirmary, where Nurse Hildebrand was shouting orders. "Kitty, you'll stay with me and assist Doc

188

Wheeler. Stella, you'll handle beds one through eleven. Liz, take beds twelve through nineteen. Mary, Anne, you two work receiving. Keep it orderly. There will be a lot of misery tonight. But it's why we are here. Nurses, find your strength. You will need to draw upon it hours from now."

We all scattered to our stations, and when the men began coming, it was like nothing we'd seen before. The wounds were more critical, the screaming louder, the intensity stronger than in past days.

Mary and I worked the doors, directing traffic and admitting the men, many of whom shrieked and pleaded for help, some weakly, others with such force that it was terrifying to witness. A young soldier with a head injury pulled my arm so hard he tore the sleeve of my dress. "I want my mama!" he screamed. "Mama! Where is Mama?"

It was harrowing to witness. All of it. The blood and the misery and the pain, and especially seeing men reduced to children in their suffering. But we kept on. We drew upon our reserves of strength as Nurse Hildebrand had instructed. And when that ran out, we found more.

It was two thirty in the morning when the last plane came in. Nine men were wheeled into the infirmary. I heard Mary scream at the door. The horror in her voice told me why.

I ran to her side, and there on the stretcher lay Lou—limp, lifeless, and very badly burned.

The soldier at the door shook his head. "I'm sorry, ma'am," he said. "This one died on the way over. We did all we could for him."

"No!" Mary screamed, shaking her head violently. *"No!"*

She ran to the soldier and gripped his shirt in her fists. "Did you not try to help him? Did you not do anything?"

"Ma'am," he said, "I assure you, we did everything we could. His wounds were just too great."

"No," Mary said, falling to her knees. "No, this can't be." She stood up and lay her head on Lou's chest, sobbing into his blood-soaked shirt. "Lou, Lou!" she cried. "No, no, Lou. No."

Liz ran to my side. "We have to stop her," she said. "Will you help me?"

"Mary," I said. "Mary, stop. He's gone, dear. Let him go."

"I won't!" she screamed, pushing me away. Her face was covered in Lou's blood. I gestured to Liz for assistance.

"Honey," I said, taking her left arm in my hands. Liz took her right. "We're going to take you to bed."

"No," Mary moaned.

"Liz, grab the sedatives," I said.

She nodded and handed me a syringe. Mary hardly flinched as I jabbed the needle into her arm. Moments later, her body went limp.

"There," I said, letting her down softly onto a nearby bed. The sheets had a smudge of blood on them. Someone else's blood. But there wasn't time to change them. "Lie down, dear," I said, wiping Lou's blood from her face with a damp cloth. "Try to rest."

"Lou," she muttered weakly before her eyes closed.

I watched her breathing for a few minutes, thinking about how unfair this was. After all she'd been through, she had found love again, only to lose it in such a tragic way. It wasn't right.

Kitty and I walked back to the barracks together in silence. We had now seen war, or, rather, the aftermath of war—its ugliness, its cruelty.

We fell into our beds and listened to the airplanes flying overhead for a long time. I prayed for Westry, and I wondered who Kitty was praying for, or thinking of.

"Anne," Kitty whispered to me after the skies had been quiet for some time. "Are you still awake?"

"Yes."

"I have to tell you something," she said. "Something important."

I sat up. "What is it?"

She sighed, looking at me with eyes filled with sorrow, with hurt that I could not understand. "I'm pregnant."

Chapter 10

I gasped, running to her bed. "Oh, Kitty!" I cried, shaking my head in disbelief.

"I've known for a while now," she said, her eyes welling up with tears. "I've been so afraid to tell you."

"Why would you be afraid, Kitty?"

She exhaled deeply. "Partly because I feared admitting it, even to myself, and also because I knew it would disappoint you."

"Disappoint *me?*" I ran my fingers through her curls and shook my head. "No, I'm only disappointed that you've had to carry this burden alone."

Kitty pressed her face against my shoulder and wept so intensely her body shook with grief. "I don't know what to do," she cried. "Look at me." She indicated her belly, which was obviously swollen. "I've been hiding under girdles for months. I can't go on like this anymore. Everyone will notice before too long. The baby's coming in a month, maybe sooner."

I gasped. "We'll speak to Nurse Hildebrand," I said.

"No!" Kitty pleaded. "No, we can't go to her. Please, Anne."

"It's our only option," I countered. "You can't be working such long hours in your condition, and the baby will be coming soon. We must plan for that."

Kitty looked frightened and lost. I knew by the expression on her face that she hadn't considered the reality of what lay ahead—delivering a child on an island thousands of miles away from home, unwed, in disgrace, uncertain.

"All right," she said. "If you think it's best, tell her. But I can't bear to be there when you do."

I kissed her forehead and smiled. "You don't have to, dear," I said. "I'll take care of everything."

There was little time the following day to find even a minute alone with Nurse Hildebrand, but by the final hour of my shift, I had managed to run into her in the storeroom.

"Nurse Hildebrand," I said, quietly closing the door behind us. "May I speak to you about something?"

"Yes, Anne," she said without looking up from the crate she was unpacking. "Quickly, please; I must get back."

"Thank you," I said. "It's about Kitty."

Nurse Hildebrand nodded. "I already know," she said simply.

"What do you mean, you know?"

"Her pregnancy," she replied without emotion.

"Yes, but I—"

"Anne, I've been a nurse for a very long time. I've delivered babies and had children of my own. I know."

I nodded. "She needs your help," I said cautiously. "The baby's coming soon, and she can't keep working like this."

For the first time, Nurse Hildebrand turned to me. Her face softened in a way I hadn't known it could. "Tell her not to worry about the work here. If the others ask, I'll say she has a bout of the fever going around, that she's been quarantined. You'll need to bring her meals up to her. Can you manage that?"

"Yes," I said, smiling. "Yes, of course."

"And when the time comes, come to me."

I nodded. "But what will become of the baby, after—"

"I know a missionary couple who will take the baby," she said. "They live just over the hill, on the other side of the island. They are good people. I'll speak to them in the morning."

"Thank you, Nurse Hildebrand," I said with such emotion, tears fell from my eyes. "I didn't expect you to be so—"

"Enough," she said. The softness, now gone from her face, was replaced by the stern expression I knew so well. "It's time to get back to work."

The day Mary left the island was sad for all of us, particularly for Kitty, who remained trapped in the barracks, unable to join the other nurses on the airstrip for her farewell.

The island had been hard on Mary, perhaps harder on her than on any of us. It had given her malaria and nearly taken her life, and then it broke her heart.

"Farewell, friend," Stella said to her.

"We'll never forget you, dear," Liz chimed in.

Mary looked like a shell of a woman standing there before the open door of the plane, thinner than ever, with wrists still bandaged from her self-inflicted wounds, the wounds that had almost ended her life.

She retrieved a handkerchief from her bag and dabbed her bloodshot eyes. "I'll miss you all so much," she said. "It doesn't feel right to leave. You've become my dearest friends, my sisters."

I squeezed Mary's hand. "It's your time, dear. Go home. Take care of yourself." I remembered the letter from Edward, which was now in my pocket. I hadn't anticipated keeping it from her this long. Was she ready to read it now? It didn't matter, I reasoned. The letter belonged to her.

"I guess this is it," she said, reaching for her bag.

The other women choked back tears as Mary turned toward the plane.

"Wait," I said. Mary looked back at me with a confused expression.

I pulled the letter from my pocket and tucked it in her hand. "This arrived," I said, "for you. I hope you will forgive me for keeping it from you. I wanted to protect you from any more pain."

Mary's eyes brightened when she saw the name on the return address. "My God," she gasped.

"I'm so sorry," I said, stepping back.

Mary extended her hand to take mine. "No," she said. "Don't be. I understand. I do."

"I'll miss you so much," I said, wishing that things could be different—for her, for Kitty, for all of us. "Promise you'll look me up in Seattle when the war's over?"

"I promise," she said. And with that, Mary and her letter were gone from our lives—forever, perhaps. And the island was lonelier because of it.

For a long time it felt like Westry might never return. The island was different without him, especially now that Mary had left and Kitty was bedridden. But then one morning in late May while working in the infirmary, we heard the loudspeaker at the center of camp announcing that the men had returned.

"Go," Nurse Hildebrand said to me.

I didn't stop to thank her; instead I ran out to the pathway and didn't pause until I'd reached the edge of the airstrip. Men trudged with heavy bags and even heavier hearts toward camp. Lance, Colonel Donahue, and some of the other men I knew. *But where is Westry?* I looked around for a familiar face. Elliot had gone home earlier with some of the other men whose service was up. *Would someone else know of Westry's whereabouts?*

"Have you seen Westry?" I asked an unfamiliar soldier. His head hung low.

"I'm sorry, ma'am," he said. "I don't know him."

I nodded, then noticed one of Westry's bunkmates from the barracks. "Ted," I said, approaching him. "Where's Westry? Have you seen him?"

He shook his head. "Sorry. Not since yesterday."

"What do you mean?"

"He was on the front lines, and . . ."

My heart raced. "What are you saying?"

"He wasn't on the plane with us."

"What does that mean?" I cried. "That he isn't coming home? That you just left him there?"

"There's another plane coming in tonight," he said. "Let's pray that he's on it."

I nodded as Ted tipped his cap at me and filed back in line with the men making their way back to camp, eager for a hot meal and a soft bed.

I clutched the locket that stood guard around my neck, hoping that wherever Westry was, he could feel my love. I would will him home. I had to.

• • •

A chill filled the air that night, unusual for May in the tropics. I shivered as I walked along the beach, a foolish move given Kitty's state. She'd been having mild contractions for days now, but she assured me they weren't serious. Even so, I promised her I'd only be gone an hour. I felt guilty about leaving, but I needed the comfort of the bungalow now more than ever.

I unlocked the door and draped the quilt around me, listening for airplanes overhead. *Is he coming? Please, God, bring him home.*

But instead of footsteps on the sand, I could only hear rain—just a few drops at first and then a hundred, a thousand. The sky appeared to have opened up, dumping its contents right on the roof of the bungalow.

I opened the door, extending my hand outside to feel the raindrops, like firm kisses on my skin, beckoning me outside. I took another step, and looked up to the sky, eyes closed, letting the warm drops cover my face, my hair. Moments later my dress was soaked. I unfastened the buttons on the bodice as the rain seeped down beneath my slip. And then, out of the corner of my eye, I saw a figure. It was faint at first and blurred in the distance. I walked closer, unafraid, pushing my way through the rain, like a curtain of beads extending from the sky, until I could make out his face, thin from months of fighting, and hungry for the love I desperately wanted to give him.

Our bodies collided, fitting together perfectly as his bag dropped to the sand. "Oh, Westry!" I cried. Even in the dark, I could see the scratches on his face and his ripped, mud-stained uniform.

"I came directly here," he said.

"Oh, Westry!" I cried again, pulling his lips toward mine.

He ran his hands along my dress, tugging at the fabric as if to make it disappear. I leapt into his arms, wrapping my legs around his body, kissing him again and again, before he smiled and gently set my feet down on the sand.

He reached inside his bag. "Let's do this the right way," he said. "Ever seen a proper military shower?"

Westry pulled out a bar of soap. "When we were on the ship, this is how we bathed," he said. "Right out on the deck, in the tropical rain."

I reached for his collar, running my hands down his shirt, unfastening each button as quickly as my fingers could move, until my hands caressed his bare chest and the dog tags hanging from his neck.

He slipped out of his trousers and lifted my dress over my head. We stood there for a moment, without a stitch of clothing, in the warm rain, until Westry moved toward me, running the ivory bar of soap along my neck. I gasped as he touched it to my breasts, lathering my skin with bubbles.

I moved in closer, loving the way our bodies felt against each other, and took the soap in my hands, rubbing it across his chest, his arms, and his back. The rain washed away the bubbles as quickly as I could lather them. Westry pulled me close, and I felt the intensity in his kiss, the hunger. He lifted me in his arms, and the soap, what was left of it, slipped out of my grasp and fell to the sand as he carried me to the bungalow, setting me down on the bed.

I liked the feel of the bungalow's quilt on my bare skin, and an hour later, when the storm had passed, I lay there tracing Westry's face with my finger as he gazed out the window facing the beach. The stubble on his jaw was thick. I counted the scrapes on his face. Four—well, five if you counted the gash on his ear.

"What was it like out there?" I whispered.

"It was a living hell," he said, sitting up against the pillows on the bed.

I sensed his hesitation. "You don't want to talk about it, do you?"

"I'd rather enjoy this perfect moment," he said before planting a soft kiss on my lips.

I thought of Kitty, and realized that hours could have passed. *Is she all right?* I felt guilty for being gone so long.

"Our clothes," I said, a little panicked. "They must be soaked."

Westry stood up, letting the blanket fall to the bed. I giggled shyly, studying his strong, beautiful unclothed body.

"I'll go grab them," he said.

He returned a moment later with my damp, wrinkled dress. I fit it over my head, as he slid into his trousers.

"Can you stay for a while?" he asked, combing my hair with his fingers.

"I wish I could, but I need to get back." I wanted to tell him about Kitty, but I decided against it. "I told Kitty I'd be back hours ago."

Westry nodded, kissing my hand.

We both turned to the window when we heard a rustling sound in the brush, followed by a faint knocking sound on the door.

Westry opened the door cautiously, and I peered over his shoulder to see Kitty standing outside. She clutched her belly in agony. "Anne!" she screamed. "It's *time*."

I didn't stop to think about how she found us. There wasn't time for questions. "We need to get you to the infirmary," I said, running to her side.

"No. I can't bear to have the other nurses see me like this. Besides, it's too late for that," she said. "The baby's coming *now*."

Westry's mouth flung open as I helped Kitty up the stairs into the bungalow, where she rested on the bed, moaning in such pain, it was heartbreaking to witness. *Lance should be punished for leaving her this way.* I shook my head, wiping the perspiration from Kitty's forehead with the edge of the blanket, and began to pray silently. *Please, God, let Kitty be comforted. Give me the strength I lack.*

Kitty moaned louder now. Something was wrong; I felt it. I remembered Tita's eerie warning and shuddered, forcing the thought from my mind, and tried to stay focused. I carefully positioned myself below Kitty's legs, helping her lean farther back on the bed. My hands trembled as I lifted her dress and tried to recall an ounce of what I had learned about childbirth in my nursing courses. Hot water. Forceps. Ether. Blankets. I shuddered. I had nothing but my two hands.

She was bleeding, that much was clear. "Kitty," I said as she screamed. "Kitty, you need to push *now.*"

She seemed alone with her pain, unable to hear my voice. I squeezed her hand. "Kitty," I continued, "stay with me. This baby is coming and you need to help me. Please, push. You must be strong."

"Anne, let me help you," Westry said once he finally found his voice.

He knelt down beside me. The bungalow's lantern illuminated his skin, darker from months in the sun. I could only imagine what he'd gone through, and now he returned to this.

Westry soaked his handkerchief with water from his canteen and dabbed Kitty's forehead as I talked her through her next contraction. "I can see the baby's head," I said. "It won't be long now."

Kitty looked up at Westry with eyes full of gratitude. He held her hand and stroked her hair. One more push and the baby slid into my arms.

"A girl!" I cried. "Kitty, it's a girl."

Westry helped me sever the cord with his pocketknife, then placed the baby in Kitty's arms. She clutched the newborn to her chest.

"We need blankets," I said when I noticed that Kitty was shivering.

Westry tucked Kitty's limp body under the quilt, and then unbuttoned his shirt. "Here," he said. "Let's wrap the baby in this." Carefully, he swaddled the child in his green army shirt, ragged and a little bloodied from weeks of fighting.

Once Kitty and the baby were settled, we walked outside together and sat down on the sand. I could no longer repress the emotion I felt.

"Don't cry," Westry said softly. "She's fine. You delivered that baby better than any doctor could have."

I nodded, blotting my tears with the edge of my sleeve. "It's just not what I wanted for her. Lance should be court-martialed for leaving her in a position like this."

Westry looked confused, but nodded. "And the baby? What will become of her?"

"A missionary couple here on the island is taking her," I said. "Kitty agreed to it, but"—I gestured inside the bungalow—"I know how hard this will be for her."

"When she's well enough to stand, I'll carry her back to camp," he said. "If you can take the baby."

I nodded. "We should probably get her home before sunrise to avoid spectators."

Westry paused and stroked my hair softly. "Anne," he said, "I hated being away from you."

My eyes filled with tears. "I worried about you every hour of every day."

"It was misery," he said. "And the only thing that got me through it was knowing I'd return to you."

I nestled my face into his bare chest, smooth and warm. "I don't know what I would have done if you didn't make it home," I said. "I don't know how I could have gone on."

He held my hands in his, lifting up my left hand and touching the ring on my finger. "I can't share you with him anymore," he whispered.

"I know," I said, breathing in his breath. I slid the ring off my finger and let it drop into the pocket of my dress. "You don't have to anymore. I am yours. Completely yours."

Westry kissed me with such passion, it erased

the familiar guilt I'd felt about Gerard. We might have stayed like that, locked in an embrace, until dawn if I hadn't heard the baby's cry from inside the bungalow, reminding us of the task at hand.

"We better get them home," I said to Westry, kissing his cheek and then his nose, and then the back of his hand softly. I had never felt such true and unfaltering love.

Westry carried Kitty, wrapped in the quilt from the bungalow, along the beach back to the base. It was no small feat, even for a man of his strength, and when we returned to camp, beads of perspiration dripped from his sun-kissed skin. The baby slept in my arms while we walked. She looked just like her mother, even swathed in army green. She had Kitty's nose, for sure, and those high cheekbones. I wondered if she'd one day grow a headful of curls. I hoped so.

"We'll get you settled in the infirmary now," I said to Kitty.

"But Anne, no, I—"

"Shh," I whispered. "Don't you worry. You have nothing to be ashamed of."

It was five a.m., and while there may have been a few nurses tending to patients in the far wing, it wasn't likely we'd run into any of them, except Nurse Hildebrand.

Westry carried Kitty inside. I directed him

toward a small private room to the right, where he set her down gently on the bed. I nestled the baby girl in her arms. The child fit like a puzzle piece. Kitty looked at me, and then at Westry, before running her hand along the stubble of his chin. "How can I ever thank you?"

"No thanks necessary," he said, smiling. "But you might help a fellow find a new shirt."

"Oh," Kitty said, smiling, "but doesn't my baby look lovely in this shade of green?"

Westry grinned, helping himself to a white medical coat, probably one of Dr. Livingston's, hanging on a hook beside the bed.

"It suits you," I said, winking.

We all looked toward the door when we heard the knob turn. Nurse Hildebrand walked in, startled at the sight of Westry in a white coat.

"And you are?"

"Westry Green, ma'am," he said. "I was just getting these two—I mean, these three—settled, before going on my way."

"I can take it from here, solider," she said briskly. "And you can return the coat once you've washed and pressed it."

Westry nodded, and walked toward the door. "Good night, ladies," he said, sending a final grin my way.

"Good night," I said. I couldn't help but notice something unsettled in Kitty's eyes as Westry walked out.

"Anne, Kitty, are you all right?"

"Yes," I said. "The baby is healthy. She needs to be cleaned up, though. They both do."

Nurse Hildebrand nodded and pulled a basin from the closet. "Anne, you'll give the child her first bath."

"Of course," I said, taking the baby from Kitty's arms.

"I will phone the Mayhews and ask them to come," Nurse Hildebrand continued. "You can swaddle her in this spare sheet when you're finished. They'll have clothes and blankets for her at their home."

Kitty shook her head. "The Mayhews?"

"The couple who is taking your child," she replied.

Terror appeared on Kitty's face. "But it's so soon," she said. "I—I . . ."

"It's what you wanted, Kitty. And it's what has to be done," Nurse Hildebrand said without emotion. "You can't keep a child here. This is the right choice for her, for you. The sooner you let go, the easier it will be."

Kitty watched despondently as I bathed her little girl, lathering her tiny head with soap and gently wiping the suds away with a washcloth.

"Her name is Adella," Kitty muttered.

"You can't name her, dear," Nurse Hildebrand retorted. "The Mayhews will have their own name."

"I don't care!" Kitty snapped, looking away. "To me she will always be Adella."

I rinsed the remaining soap bubbles off the child's delicate skin before lifting her out of the basin and into a towel. Once she was dry, I carefully swaddled her in a sheet, as Nurse Hildebrand had instructed, then tucked the tiny package into Kitty's arms.

"No," she said, turning away, choking back tears. "I can't hold her. If I hold her, I won't be able to let her go. Can't you see that, Anne?" Kitty began to cry, but it wasn't the same sort of cry I'd heard from her in years past. This was sorrow that emanated from someplace very deep.

I swallowed hard, trying to stay strong for Kitty's sake, and walked the baby outside the room. I waited there for some time, until a couple, maybe in their early thirties, appeared in the hallway. Kitty's muffled sobbing seeped through the closed door.

Nurse Hildebrand indicated the couple and nodded. "John and Evelyn Mayhew," she said, forcing a smile. "They'll take the baby now."

The couple looked kind, and I could see by the woman's eager smile that she would welcome the child with love. She stroked the baby's head. "She must be hungry," she said, retrieving her from my arms. "We have a bottle waiting in the car." Nurse Hildebrand watched quietly, perhaps even proudly, as the new mother bonded with "her" child.

"Adella is her name," I said quietly, on Kitty's behalf.

"It's a beautiful name," she said, "but we've chosen another. I will put it in her birth records, though, so it will always be a part of her history."

I nodded and stepped back as the couple thanked Nurse Hildebrand and left, an instant family of three.

"I'm going to go to Kitty now," I said, reaching for the doorknob.

"Anne, wait," Nurse Hildebrand said, "not yet. Please, I'd like to have a word with her first."

I wasn't sure what she had in mind, but the seriousness in her face told me to oblige. I waited outside the door for what felt like an eternity. *What is she doing in there? What's she saying to Kitty?*

I pressed my ear against the door, and heard Nurse Hildebrand say something startling. "I was in your situation once." The words shocked me, and I jumped back when the doorknob began to turn.

When the door opened, Kitty emerged with dry eyes and a blank, emotionless expression I'd never seen on her face before.

Chapter 11

Nurse Hildebrand excused me from my duties at the infirmary so I could care for Kitty in the days that followed. I stayed in the room and kept her company, though I think she would have preferred to be alone.

"How about a game of cards?" I suggested, reaching for the deck in my bedside table.

"No," Kitty said. "Thanks, but I'd rather not."

I brought her meals and tried to interest her in magazines. Liz, believing that Kitty was still recovering from an illness, stopped by to deliver the two latest issues of *Vogue*, but Kitty just set them on her bed, preferring to stare at the wall ahead rather than the latest fashions.

I knew I couldn't fix things for her. She had to wade through this on her own, which is why I excused myself two days after the birth for a beach walk and a visit to the bungalow. I craved a change of scenery, and Kitty needed to be alone.

Westry was there, just as I'd hoped he'd be, napping on the bed as the afternoon sun streamed in.

"Hi," I whispered, nestling my body on the bed beside him. He opened his eyes and smiled warmly at me, pulling me closer.

"I bet you didn't know that you were sleeping in the presence of a masterpiece," I said, grinning.

Westry ran his finger along my face and marveled. "I've known it since the day you stepped foot in this place. You are the world's greatest work of art."

I smiled and shook my head. "No, silly. Not me, the painting." I reached for the painting under the bed. "It's a *Gauguin*."

Westry sat up quickly, looking at the canvas with fresh eyes. "You're serious?"

I nodded.

He shook his head in disbelief. "I always thought it had to be done by one of the Postimpressionists, but more likely by a younger, lesser-known painter, or maybe the apprentice of one. But God, Gauguin? How can you be sure?"

"An old woman on the island told me," I said, smiling proudly.

Westry sat down on the bed next to me for a closer look. "It's not signed," he said.

"Maybe he didn't sign his work early on."

"You could be right about that," he conceded. "Monet did the same."

I nodded. "And look at those brush strokes."

"You could get lost in this painting," Westry said, still marveling at the treasure in his hands.

"What will we do with it?" I asked, smoothing Westry's rumpled shirt.

"I don't know."

"We can't leave it here," I said, "when the war's over, when we're gone. I couldn't bear to think of the painting swallowed up by a tidal wave."

Westry agreed. "Or deteriorating in the humid air. I'm surprised it's lasted this long out here in the elements."

I hung the painting back up on the little hook, and sighed. "Or maybe it's meant to stay right here." I looked at the canvas for a moment before turning back to Westry. "There's something else I need to tell you. Something about this bungalow."

"What is it?"

"The old woman, Tita, she warned me about this place. She said that all who step foot inside live with some sort of curse."

Westry grinned. "And you believed her voodoo?"

"Well, it frightened me, I will admit."

"Anne, remember what we talked about, the first day we met? You told me you believed that life is about free will." He stroked my hair lightly. "Your life will be rich and blessed and filled with love because of what you make it."

I tucked my hand in his. "You're right."

"Besides," he continued, "look at all the good that has come from these four walls. Our love has grown. A baby has been born. And we may have discovered one of the greatest artistic finds in our century. Is that what the old woman calls a *curse?*"

As we sat together listening to the waves roll onto the shore, I said a silent prayer. *God, please let him be right.*

Time was growing scarce now; we all knew that. May had blown through like a fierce storm, and Kitty and I would be leaving the island in mid-June, at the same time that Westry and the other men would ship off for another tour of duty—this time in Europe. As a result, I could almost hear the ticktock of a clock in the distance, a constant reminder that the world we'd come to know was hurtling toward an abrupt end.

I'd have to face Gerard. Kitty would have to leave her daughter's birthplace. How could we return to Seattle such changed women? How could we even pretend to resume our old roles in that foreign place we once called home?

"I think I'm going to stay," Kitty announced one morning in the mess hall in early June. "Nurse Hildebrand could use the help. Besides, no one's waiting for me in Seattle."

She hadn't meant it as a jab, but her words, and the long pause that followed, pierced. It was true. Gerard would be waiting. He was due home in June.

I wondered about Kitty's motivation to stay. So unlike the woman who had stepped off the plane the very first day on the island, she had become a shell of her former self. Vacant. Distant. Lost. She devoted herself to work, and spent every spare minute in the infirmary.

"I just don't understand," I said to her between bites of boiled egg. "Don't you miss home? Don't you want to leave this island after . . . after everything?"

She glanced out the window toward the lush, emerald hillside in the distance. Just as memories would forever anchor my heart to this place, I suspected that Kitty would always feel that a piece of her was here too.

She forced a smile. "I thought I'd want to leave when the time came," she said. "But now, well, I'm just not ready."

I nodded.

"These past months have sure turned out differently for us," she said, her voice thick with regret. "But you've met the most marvelous man. To think that you found him out here in the middle of a war."

As if on cue, Westry waved from the other side of the mess hall. Then, in a breach of protocol, he approached our table. "Well if it isn't the two most lovely women on the island," he said, a cloth napkin still dangling from his collar. "How are you, darling?" he said to me, as I pulled the napkin free and handed it to him.

"Wonderful," I replied. "I missed you in the bungalow this morning." It felt strange to speak openly about our secret, but it didn't matter now that Kitty had been there herself, and besides, there weren't any other diners at the table.

"Westry," Kitty said, perking up. I didn't like how she batted her eyelashes at him. "I found some stray floorboards in a closet in the infirmary. I thought they might work to fix that creak in the bungalow's floor."

My cheeks burned. *How could Kitty think it's her place to talk to Westry about the bungalow? And how in heaven's name does she know, or remember, that the floorboards creak?*

"Thanks, Kitty," Westry said, unfazed. "I'll stop by today and take a look at them."

"But—" I opened my mouth and then shut it again.

"What is it?" Westry asked.

"Nothing," I muttered. "I was just going to suggest that we meet at the bungalow later this evening." I made sure to look directly at Westry, making clear that he was the sole recipient of the invitation.

"I'd love nothing more," he said. "I'm off at five thirty. Just in time for the sunset."

"Good," I said, instantly feeling better.

As Westry turned to leave, Kitty stood up. "If you'd like to come by this afternoon, I'll be working until eight." She looked at me awkwardly. "I mean, if you want to see those floorboards."

Westry nodded noncommittally and walked out of the building.

We ate in silence for a few minutes, until Kitty spoke again. "So, as I was saying, I'll probably stay on for a few more months, and then who knows?" Her gaze drifted toward the window again. "There's plenty of opportunity for nurses these days. Maybe I'll sign up for a post in Europe."

I watched her mouth open and close and the words pass her lips. *Who is this woman before me?* I searched her eyes, but she looked away. "It's just that I—"

"I told Nurse Hildebrand I'd help her with the immunizations today," she said, cutting me off. "I'd better be going."

"Yes, right, you'd better be going," I said, but she'd already made her way through the door.

"There's something wrong with Kitty," I said that evening, kicking my shoes off as I walked into the bungalow and collapsed on the bed.

"Well hello to you, too," Westry said, grinning, tucking a bouquet of hibiscus in my hand.

"Sorry," I said, marveling at the blossoms, vibrant yellow—a stark contrast to the more common red hibiscus that grew like weeds all around the base. These were not typical. As far I as I knew, they were the only yellow hibiscus on the island, and they grew right here, mere feet from the bungalow. I set the flowers down on the chair and sighed, thinking of Kitty.

"It's just that I had a strange encounter with her at breakfast, and I'm worried about her. She's changed so much in these past few months. I hardly know her anymore."

Westry pulled out his pocketknife and carefully sliced a red apple on the mahogany desk. "She *has* changed," he said. "Anyone who's gone through what she's gone through would have to. Do you think you might be being too hard on her?"

I nodded. "You're probably right," I said, reaching for the slice of apple he held out to me. Its crunchy sweetness dulled my worries, for a moment.

"You're not upset about the comment she made about the floorboards, are you?"

"No," I lied. "Well, maybe a little." I sighed. "Is it wrong that I feel possessive of this place?"

He grinned, sitting down next to me on the bed. "No, but I'd rather you feel possessive of me."

I gave him a playful shove. "I do, which is why my next question is, did you go to see her at the infirmary today?"

"Yes," he said, reveling in the discovery of my jealousy.

"And?"

He shook his head. "The floorboards she had in mind were all wrong."

"Good," I said. "I like our floorboards."

He ran his finger along the nape of my neck. "Me too."

"And besides," I continued, "new floorboards would mean we'd lose our mailbox."

"It's unanimous, then," he said, striking an imaginary gavel. "The creaky floorboards stay."

He took the gold locket into his hands and carefully opened it. "Still empty?"

"I know," I said. "I've been trying to think of the perfect thing to put inside, but I haven't been struck with inspiration just yet."

Westry's eyes darted. "It needs to be something that reminds you of here, of us—something that will warm your heart with the memories of our love."

I frowned, snatching the locket from his hands. "Memories of our love? You talk as if our days are numbered, as if this is just a—"

"No," he said, putting his hand to my lips. "I intend to love you for the rest of my life, but I have another tour of duty ahead; you know that. While I'm in Europe, however long this war lasts, I want to know that you can find me, and this place, in your memories. It will help sustain you while we're apart."

Westry stood up and searched the room, running his hands along the desk, the woven walls, the curtains, before crouching down to the floor. "I've got it," he said, prying a tiny piece of wood from an edge of a warped floorboard. "A piece of the bungalow. You can carry it with you always, and with it, there I will be."

My eyes welled up with tears as he opened the locket and placed the piece of floorboard, just a mere splinter, inside. It was *perfect*. "There," he said, patting the locket against my chest. "You will always have me with you."

My kiss told him how much I appreciated the gesture.

Shortly after the sun set, Westry lit a candle on the desk, and we huddled together just listening to the breeze and the crickets chirping in the moonlight, until a startling sound caught our attention.

A man's voice, angry and determined, followed by a woman's desperate scream rang out in the distance. The voices sounded far away at first, perhaps deep in the thick jungle brush—far enough away to ignore, but when the screaming grew nearer, I instinctively clutched Westry's arm. "What do you think that is?"

"I don't know," he said, standing up and quickly slipping his arms into his shirt. "But I think she's in trouble. Stay here," he directed me.

"Be careful," I whispered. I didn't know what worried me more—Westry going out there by himself, or me staying in the bungalow alone.

He slipped through the door quietly, listening as he pushed his way toward the brush outside. We heard another scream, and then more footsteps. *Someone is running.*

I stood up and put on my shoes, wishing I had some sort of weapon in the bungalow. *Did Westry bring his gun?* It wasn't likely. The men didn't normally take their weapons out beyond the base. I swallowed hard. *Westry is out there all alone. What if I need to protect him?* I couldn't just stay in the bungalow and wait, I decided.

Quietly, I stepped outside, and when I noticed a two-by-four propped up against the bungalow, I picked it up. *Just in case.*

I crept toward the beach, but turned around suddenly when I heard a branch breaking nearby. *Was it behind me?* My heart pounded in my chest. I sensed danger lurking. Something evil was in our presence.

Then, another scream rang out, this one near the beach.

"No, no, please, please no hurt me, please!"

I gasped. I knew that voice. *Dear God. Atea. Was she trying to make her way here, to the bungalow, as I instructed her to?* Lance must have followed her. *Where is Westry?* I pushed through the brush to the clearing on the beach and saw the scene that would be burned in my memory forever.

In the shroud of darkness, it was difficult to make out faces, but as my eyes adjusted, the horror came into view. He held her by a clump of her hair; I could see that. Then a flash of steel shone in the moonlight. *God, no.* A knife. He sliced the blade along her neck, and I watched, mute, as her small, limp body fell to the sand.

"No," I muttered, unable to find the strength of my voice. *No, this can't be.*

The shadowy figure tossed the knife like a football deep into the jungle, before pitching a jog down the beach.

I ran to Atea, choking back tears. "Atea, I'm so sorry, I'm so sorry." I lifted her blood-soaked head onto my lap. She gurgled and choked for breath.

"He, he," she sputtered.

"No, honey," I whispered. "Don't try to talk. Don't say anything."

Blood pooled in her mouth. She was dying. If we could get her to the infirmary in time, Doc Livingston might be able to save her. *We have to save her.*

Atea gestured to her belly, swollen, round. *She's pregnant. Oh my God.*

"Westry!" I screamed. "Westry!"

I heard footsteps approach from the direction in which Lance had left, and I prayed he wasn't coming to finish the job. "Westry!" I called out again.

"I'm here," he said. "It's me."

"Oh, Westry!" I cried. "Look at her. Just look at what he's done to her." I gasped. "And to her baby."

Atea lifted her hand in the air, as if to reach for something or someone.

"She's not going to make it," he said.

"What are you saying?" I screamed desperately. "Of course she's going to make it. She has to. I promised I'd protect her from that monster."

Atea's breathing was reduced to a sporadic gurgle and gasp. "She will pull through," I sobbed. "We have to save her."

Westry put his hand on my arm. "Anne," he whispered. "Her neck is half-severed. The best we can do for her is ease her pain, end her misery."

I knew what he was referring to, but could I actually go through with it? It went against everything I'd learned in nursing school, and yet holding Atea's dying body in my arms, I knew it was not only the right choice, but the only choice.

"Go grab my bag under the desk," I said. "Hurry!"

He returned with my knapsack and pulled out the supply of morphine that every nurse kept on hand in wartime. There was enough inside to sedate a 280-pound man, or to send a hundred-pound woman to the gates of heaven.

I kissed Atea's forehead, and injected the first dose in her arm, rubbing the spot where the needle had pricked. "There now," I said, trying to hold back my tears and keep my voice calm and steady for her sake. "The pain will be over soon. Let yourself relax."

Her breathing slowed from choking gasps to

shallow gurgles. When I injected the second dose, her eyes turned to the stars, then fluttered and shut. I checked her pulse, and then pressed my ear to her heart.

"She's gone," I said to Westry, tears streaming down my face. *"They're* gone. How could he do this?" I screamed. "How could he?"

Westry slid Atea's limp body onto the soft sand, and helped me to my feet, holding my trembling body in his. "I should have saved her," I cried into his chest. "I promised I'd protect her. I promised I would."

Westry shook his head. "You did the best you could. She went peacefully."

"How could he?" I said, feeling overcome with anger. "How could he do this to her?" I turned to the beach where, just minutes before, the man, presumably Lance, had fled. I pried myself out of Westry's arms and started to run in the direction the man had left in.

Westry ran after me, however, and held me back with a firm grasp on my waist, which made me buckle over, planting my hands on the cold sand. I tried to break free, to stand again, but Westry's strength prevented further movement. "Anne, stop," he pleaded. "You can't."

"What do you mean I can't?" I screamed, throwing a clump of sand toward the lonely stretch of beach where the killer had escaped. "We just watched him murder a woman and her child. We have to find him, Westry. We have to take him to the colonel. He needs to pay for what he did."

Westry knelt beside me, stroking my face. I felt tears on my cheeks, and he wiped them away. "Listen to me," he said softly. "What we saw here tonight was tragic. But I need you to believe me when I tell you that we can never speak of what we saw—not to anyone."

I shook my head. "No, this makes no sense," I said. "A murder was committed; we must report it. We can bring him to justice."

"We can't," Westry muttered. His voice sounded strange, thick with defeat. "For one, an assault was committed." He paused. "We committed the murder."

"No, that's not true."

"But it's how it would be viewed," he said. "And there's something else, something far worse that could become of us, of those we love, if this secret gets out."

What does he know? What is he hiding?

I stood up, brushing the sand off my dress. "This makes no sense," I said. "How can I go back to the base knowing there's a murderer on the loose?"

He searched my eyes. "Tonight," he said, pointing to the bungalow, "you said you loved me; you said you wanted to spend forever with me."

I nodded.

"Then will you trust me?"

I held up my hands in confusion. "Westry, I just, I—"

"Just promise me you won't say anything," he said. "One day you'll understand. I promise."

We both turned to look at Atea. Even in death, she exuded beauty and gentleness. I exhaled deeply and looked at Westry's strong, steady face. No matter how uncertain his plan seemed, I trusted him. If he said this was the right course of action, I had to believe it would be.

"I won't say anything," I whispered.

"Good," he said, stroking my cheek. "We'll have her buried by sunrise."

Chapter 12

It wasn't a grave worthy of her short, beautiful life, but we laid Atea to rest forty feet behind the bungalow in a makeshift plot under a plumeria tree. Fortunately, we had a shovel; Westry had brought one over a week prior in hopes of resetting one of the bungalow's foundation beams. It took him an hour to dig the grave. I watched him for a long while, then slipped away to the beach when I could no longer stomach the gritty sound of the shovel hitting the dirt again and again.

Once my feet hit the sand, I collapsed to my knees. Never in my life had I seen such horror. And while I had agreed to trust Westry, I couldn't deny the longing in my heart for justice. I replayed the scene in my mind over and over again, hoping to find some clue, some frame I'd missed, which is when I remembered the knife.

Lance had thrown it into the brush before exiting the scene. I remembered the flash of steel in the moonlight, and my heart began beating louder in my chest. *If I could find the knife, I could at least secure proof that he did it.*

I ran back to the bungalow and retrieved the lantern, then cautiously walked to the edge of the jungle. Animals howled and snickered in the distance. The wind rustled the bushes. What used to seem like a place of beauty and serenity now felt like a safe haven for evil. I considered turning back, but I found my strength. *Atea. Remember Atea.* I nodded to myself and took one step forward, and then another. The crunch of my feet on the earth below me seemed to amplify with each step.

I shone the lantern farther down the path. *It has to be close. Just a few more steps, perhaps.* A snake slithered by, too near for my liking, and I gasped, taking an exaggerated step back, before continuing on. *Keep going, Anne.* I looked back toward the beach and tried to mentally calculate the distance the knife may have traveled. I eyed a large palm to my left, moving my search there. It had to be near.

But after several more minutes I wondered if the jungle may have swallowed up the knife, a coconspirator in the gruesome crime. I leaned against the palm and set my lantern down, and when I did, it made a little clinking sound.

I knelt down and immediately noticed a familiar shimmer of metal. My hands trembled as I pulled the bloodied knife from its hideaway in the soil. I inched the lantern closer to read the inscription on the army green handle: *Unit #432; Issue #098.*

"Anne? Anne, where are you?"

Westry's voice filtered through the thicket. *How long have I been gone? What would he think of me searching for the knife like this, especially after I promised to trust him?*

"Anne?" His voice was nearer now. I reached down to the edge of my dress and ripped off a piece of the light blue linen fabric. Quickly, I wrapped the knife inside, then dug a little crevice with my bare hands, deep enough for adequate protection, tucking the blade inside. I covered it with dirt and a pile of leaves before standing up, just as Westry approached.

"Oh, there you are," he said. "What are you doing out here? I was worried."

"Just thinking," I said, brushing off my dirt-stained hands on the back of my dress.

"Come on," he said. "I know this has been a

hard night, but we need to"—he paused to find the right words—"see this through."

I nodded and followed him back toward the makeshift grave, where I waited while Westry went to get Atea. He returned with her in his arms, and tears streamed down my face again at the sight.

He set her body inside the hole, and we both stared in silence. After a few minutes, Westry reached for the shovel, but I pulled his arm back. "Not yet," I said.

I picked three pink plumeria blossoms from the nearby tree, then knelt at Atea's grave. "She deserves flowers," I said, without looking away from her face.

I scattered the blooms across her body, then looked away as Westry began shoveling the earth over her. I couldn't watch, but I forced myself to stay until he finished. We walked back to camp in silence, for our world had changed—forever, perhaps.

It was close to three when I snuck into the room that morning. Kitty didn't stir, and with a ripped, blood-and-dirt-stained dress, I was glad of that. I slipped off my clothes, tucking them into the wastebasket, then pulled a nightgown over my head and crawled into bed. Sleep didn't come, though. I knew we hadn't committed a crime, but I was plagued with the horrible and yet very real fear that we were guilty.

• • •

The next morning, I awoke to the sound of a fist pounding on my door. I sat up in bed, disoriented, and glanced over at Kitty's bed, which was neatly made. I covered my face when the bright light from the window hit my eyes. *What time is it?*

The pounding at the door persisted. "Yes, I'll be there in a minute," I muttered, stepping one foot out of bed and then the other, stumbling to the door. Stella stood outside, with a disapproving frown.

"Anne, look at you," she said. "Asleep at half past eleven? Nurse Hildebrand is fuming. She sent me up to find you. Your shift started at eight."

I peered at the little alarm clock on my bedside table. "Oh my," I said. "I can't believe I slept this late."

Stella smirked. "Must have been some night." She gave me the once-over, and her eyes paused at my hands. "What were you doing—making mud pies?"

I looked down at my dirt-caked nails and hid them self-consciously in the folds of my nightgown. As I did, the memories of the night before came swirling back. The murder. The knife. The cover-up. Westry's words of caution. I hoped Stella couldn't see the goose bumps that had broken out on my arms.

"Please tell Nurse Hildebrand that I'll be over just as soon as I can dress," I said.

"And wash," added Stella, grinning accusatorily before walking away.

I nodded. "Stell!" I called out to the hallway after her.

"Yes?" she said, turning back to the door.

"Why didn't Kitty come wake me?"

"I wondered that too," she said, her voice free from sarcasm, rare for Stella. "Something's not quite right about her. It's like she's—"

"Like she's not my friend anymore?" I said. The words felt like grenades hitting my tired heart.

Stella put her hand on my arm. "Don't worry, hon," she said. "I'm sure whatever it is will blow over soon."

I hoped she was right.

Ever since Kitty had given birth, she and Nurse Hildebrand had struck up an unlikely friendship. Kitty would often stay late in the infirmary to help our superior with special projects, and her name was always first on the list when a special assignment or patient needed tending to.

It was good to see Kitty excelling in her work. It was what she'd wanted for her life, after all. And here, she could do something of meaning. Yet the more she poured herself into nursing, the more distant she became.

Such a division would have felt more

pronounced at home, in Seattle, but in a war zone, we could push it aside and let the fighting, the news, the misery muffle our personal problems.

"Liz heard from a corporal down at the docks that things are heating up again out in the Pacific," I said to Kitty that night at dinner. We talked about little else besides the war.

"Oh?" she replied, without looking up from the book in her hands.

"Do you think we'll have a few busy shifts ahead?" I asked, hating the formality of our exchange.

"I suppose," Kitty said, yawning. "Well, I better be off. I'm working on a project for Nurse Hildebrand. I'll be in the infirmary."

I spotted Westry on the other side of the mess hall, laughing with Ted and a few other men. *How can he be so calm, so jovial, after what we went through just hours before?*

I carried my tray to the kitchen, and waited for him outside on the path.

"Hi," he said when his eyes met mine. We walked a few paces together, toward the marina. "How are you doing?" he whispered when the other men were out of earshot.

"Not good," I said. "I keep having memories from last night and praying that it was only a nightmare. Westry, tell me it was all a nightmare."

He pulled my head close to his. "I wish I could."

"Have you seen Lance?" I whispered.

"No," he said, looking around uncomfortably. "Didn't you hear?"

"Hear what?"

"He shipped out this morning, on a special mission with a dozen others."

"Sounds to me like he's running away," I huffed.

Westry looked uncomfortable. "We can't talk about this anymore," he said. "It's too dangerous."

I nodded, remembering Liz's paranoia. Convinced that the base could be littered with hidden recording devices, she chose to share secrets only in the barracks, and usually only in the bathrooms. "Will I see you tonight at the bungalow?"

Westry rubbed his forehead. "I wish I could, but I'm working later tonight, and after last night . . . I guess I could use the solitude."

Solitude? The word pierced me like an arrow.

"Oh," I said, visibly hurt.

Westry tried to lighten the moment with a smile. "I only mean that we're both operating on such little sleep, it would make sense to turn in early."

"You're right," I said, still smarting.

"Besides," he said, "are you really ready to go back there, after—after all that's happened?"

Yes, horror had infiltrated our private world, but I couldn't shake the feeling that Westry was giving up on the bungalow, on us.

"I don't know," I muttered. "I know that what we had there was beautiful, and I don't want to lose it."

"Neither do I," he said.

It was a week before I stepped foot in the bungalow, and I did so alone. Westry had joined some of the men on a construction project on the other side of the island. He'd been vague about when he'd return. But as the days ebbed on, I felt the bungalow calling me, drawing me back, and after a particularly long shift in the infirmary, where the women spent most of it huddled over a tiny radio listening to the latest on the fight in the Pacific, I succumbed to its call.

It was dusk when I set out for the beach, and I clutched my locket as I made my way up the shore. I pushed past the brush, but took a step back when my eyes detected a figure sitting on the steps of the bungalow.

"Who's there?" I called out.

Someone stood and began to walk toward me. With each step forward, I took a step back.

"Who is it?" I cried, wishing I'd brought a lantern. But as the figure moved out into the open, the moonlight shone down. It was Tita.

"Anne," she said.

What is she doing here? Looking for Atea, no doubt. My heart pounded. *What will I tell her?*

The old woman's face looked tired and anguished.

"Would you like to come in?" I said, gesturing to the bungalow.

She looked at the hut with eyes that told me she'd been inside, perhaps a long time ago. She shook her head. "Maybe you don't remember what I told you about this place," she muttered. "It's cursed." She pointed to the beach ahead and began walking out of the thicket. I followed, unsure of what was in store.

"Sit," she said, gesturing at a spot not far from where Atea had clung to life. I was grateful that the waves had washed away the bloodstained sand.

We sat in silence for a few minutes until Tita finally spoke. "I know she is gone," she said.

Unsure of how to respond, I kept looking out at the surf, letting the soothing ebb and flow of the waves numb my heartache.

"I warned you," she said, scowling. "This place is evil. It's no good. And now it took my Atea, our Atea. She was special, you know."

I tried in vain to stop the tears from coming, but they seeped from my lids of their own accord. "Oh, Tita," I cried. "I'm so sorry."

"Hush," the old woman said, standing. "What's done is done. Now it is your duty to make justice."

What does she know? Or worse, what does she think she knows? Did she see the disturbed ground where Westry dug the grave?

I watched, bewildered, as she made her way toward the jungle.

"Tita," I said. "Please, Tita, wait. You're wrong. If you think that I, that we—"

"Justice," she said, turning toward me a final time, "is the only way you will ever break the curse."

I watched her walk into the thicket until the jungle seemed to swallow her whole. I sighed and collapsed onto the sand, wrapping my arms around my knees the way I'd done as a girl after a scolding from Mother. Lance wasn't on the island, at least for now, and there hadn't been any Japanese flyovers in months. So why did I sense evil lurking? I thought about the knife, stained with Atea's blood, buried a few hundred feet away, safely wrapped in the swatch of fabric from my dress. No one knew it was there but me. I could retrieve it as evidence. I could seek justice, just as Tita had urged me to. But how could I ignore Westry's convictions?

I rose to my feet and walked to the bungalow, unlocking its door with the familiar motions and then stowing the key back inside the book. The air inside felt thick and suffocating. I thought about the painting under the bed and knelt down to retrieve it. *Who are the subjects in it, and were they in this very bungalow? Did they meet misfortune in the way Tita spoke of? Or were they lucky enough to escape the "curse"?*

I reached for a piece of paper and pen on the desk, and sat to write Westry a letter, my heart racing at what I was about to record:

My dear Grayson,

I wish you were here now, to take me into your arms, to erase my memory of the horrors I have seen. I worry that, after what we've witnessed, I may never view these walls in the same way again, and that frightens me.

I have an idea, a plan. We've only spoken of the future in vague terms, but after the war, after this is all over, perhaps we can go to the military superiors and report the crime. Perhaps the hesitation you feel will be remedied by time. I have evidence, something that will clear our names from any wrongdoing when the time is right. My dear, please tell me when the time is right.

But, there is something else. By now you know of my love for you, and I want you to know that there is nothing else I'd rather do than share my life, share eternity, with you—right here on this island if that's what you want. What I'm saying, my love, is that I am yours, if you ask me to be.

Love, forever and always,
Cleo

I folded the page in half and tucked it under the floorboard, exhaling deeply as I reached for the doorknob.

Two days later, Kitty, seated on her bed, looked up from a magazine, startled. "Did you hear something hit the window?"

It was half past three, but instead of working in the infirmary, we'd all been ordered to the barracks after a Japanese warship was detected two miles off shore. Kitty clutched her rosary as she thumbed through the pages of *McCall's*; I pulled out a novel I'd started the first month on the island, but I found myself unable to read. The fear in the air had a paralyzing effect.

I shook my head. "I didn't hear anything."

No one knew what was going to happen next. One of the nurses said the ship was en route to another destination. Another said that a soldier had confirmed by the ship's coordinates that it was heading dead on to Bora-Bora. War here? On our island? Clinging to disbelief was a comforting defense, but we all knew an attack was a possibility. Our only option was to watch and wait.

"There's a cellar," I said, "below the barracks. Stella thinks we'll be moved down there in the event of—"

Kitty flinched. "There," she said, "that sound. I heard it again. Something keeps knocking at our window."

I forced a smile. "I know you're worried, Kitty, but the Japanese aren't outside our window—yet."

Kitty didn't return my smile. Instead, she stood up and walked to the window. "See?" she said, grinning victoriously. "It's Westry. He must have been trying to get our attention."

Our attention? I watched Kitty at the window, waving down at Westry. I didn't like how her spirits lifted instantly in his presence.

"I'll go see him," I said possessively, walking out the door and briskly down the stairs to the entrance.

"Hi," I whispered once outside.

Westry grinned. "Why the whisper?"

"Don't you know? The island may be under attack."

Westry put his hands in his pockets and tilted his head to the right, looking at me with an amused grin. "I love your spirit, you know that? Come here, let me see you."

I lingered in his embrace for longer than was proper for the base, but somehow decorum seemed insignificant now.

"You seem overly confident," I sparred back.

He shrugged. "After you've been through a fight like I've been through, a battleship on the horizon doesn't ruffle your feathers, I guess."

"But what if they're coming?" I said. "What if they're on their way to our island?"

"They may be," he said. "It's too early to tell, though."

I sighed. "And to think we've been here for so many months, and with so little time before our departure, this happens. Some luck."

Westry caressed my chin, tracing my profile with his finger until tingles ran down my back. "Let's go to the bungalow," he whispered into my neck.

"In the middle of all of this?"

"Why not?" he said, hypnotizing me with his caress.

"Because we've been given orders to stay in the barracks," I protested weakly.

Westry looked at me with his big, hazel eyes. "But it may be our last time in the bungalow together before . . . before . . ."

Neither of us knew what would happen next, and in my heart, I knew what mattered was now. I squeezed his hand. "OK."

"If we're lucky," he said, "we can slip through the jungle and not run into a soul."

I nodded. "Do you think we'll be safe out there?"

"We'll be able to see the ship from the beach, and if it gets close enough, we'll head back and I'll join the ranks."

I frowned, remembering the beating Colonel Donahue had unleashed on Westry in the barracks, then hesitated. "Will you get in trouble for this?"

"Probably," he said, his eyes sparkling in the late-afternoon sun. "But I don't care."

He reached for my hand and I glanced up to the second floor, where Kitty lingered at the window. When our eyes met, I gestured toward the beach and then waved, hoping she'd understand. But she turned quickly to the bed without so much as a smile.

Westry unlocked the door to the bungalow, and we exhaled deeply once inside. "I feel like we're fugitives," I said.

"I suppose we are," he replied, resting his hands on my waist.

"Westry?"

"What, dear?"

"I was here a few days ago, and, well, I'm frightened," I said.

"About what?"

"Tita was here."

"Tita?"

"The old woman who Atea lived with. She's some kind of shaman or spiritual leader. I'm not entirely sure, but she seems to know about Atea."

"How could she know?"

"I don't know," I said. "But she warned me again about the bungalow's curse. She said justice was the only way to break the cycle of the curse."

Westry frowned. "Don't believe it for a minute."

240

"Why shouldn't I believe her? She knows this place better than you or I."

"What she, and you, don't realize is that with justice comes something else, something far worse than the guilt we may carry with us." Westry sat down on the old mahogany chair. For the first time, I detected the weight of the secret in his eyes. He didn't want to keep it any more than I did; yet he was holding to his convictions. "How can I make you understand that we can't seek justice? Not the kind you want, anyway. It's the way it must be."

I nodded, reaching for his hand. It felt wrong to argue on what could be our final night together. I poked my head out the front window and could make out the battleship in the distance. "It's still there," I said.

He pulled me closer, and I remembered the letter I'd left for him, with my heartfelt confessions about the future. *Has he read it? Does he want to spend a lifetime with me, too?* I sighed nervously.

"Westry," I whispered.

"Yes, my love."

"Did you get my letter?"

"No," he said. "I haven't been here in days." He began walking to the floorboard to retrieve his mail, but I pulled his arm back.

"Not yet," I said a little shyly. "Tuck it in your pocket when we leave. I want you to read it alone."

"Is it bad news?"

"No, no," I said. "Just wait. You'll see."

He nodded, pulling my body tight against his. He flipped on the little radio on the desk, and the French station came through again, crystal clear.

"Let's not think about anything else but our love," he said as we swayed to the music.

"OK," I whispered. His suggestion worked like magic, blocking the war, worries of Kitty, and the lingering darkness from the murder on the beach. For a moment, the bungalow was ours again, ours alone.

Westry kissed my cheek shortly after the sun went down. "It's probably time that we started back," he said. I could sense his anxiety building, and it worried me. I didn't know whether it was the enemy in our midst that gave him pause or what we both knew and dreaded—that our time together was coming to an end.

"We probably should," I agreed, considering the prospect of just holding out in the bungalow when the Japanese appeared on the shore. *Would the bungalow's "curse" protect us?*

I smoothed my dress and refastened a pin in my hair. "Don't forget your letter," I said as Westry opened the door.

"Of course," he replied, kneeling down to the floorboard and reaching inside. "Wait, what letter?" He shook his head. "There's no letter here."

"Silly," I said, kneeling down next to him. "Of course there is. Maybe I pushed it back too far." I wedged my hand deeper behind the joists, but was horrified to find the space empty.

"My God, Westry," I said. "It's gone."

"What do you mean? No one knows about our hiding place. Unless you told someone."

"Of course I didn't," I said, confused.

A light flashed in the ocean ahead, diverting Westry's worries to a bigger concern. "We'll have to figure this out later," he said. "I need to get you back."

The door creaked to a close, and Westry locked it ceremoniously. "We'll head back through the trail in the jungle," he said. "It'll be safer."

I nodded, taking his hand. As we walked through the thicket, I thought about the letter. *Who could have taken it, and why?* Now, with so little time left, I needed Westry to know my true feelings, about him, and about what I hoped for after the war. *Will I have the chance to tell him? Does he feel the same?*

By the time we made it back to base, however, I wasn't thinking about the letter anymore. Instead, something else haunted me.

"Westry," I whispered, in a panic, as he walked me to the entrance of the women's barracks. "We have to go back!"

He looked confused. "Why?"

"The painting," I said. "We left the painting there."

He shrugged. "We can get it later."

"No, no," I said. "Whoever took the letter I wrote could take the painting."

Westry looked momentarily concerned, then shook his head. "No. Whoever may have taken the letter could have taken the painting already, but they didn't."

I shook my head. "I have a bad feeling about this," I said. "I can't bear to think that the painting could fall into thieves' hands. It belongs in a museum somewhere, a gallery, where it can be admired and treasured."

"And we'll make sure it gets there," Westry reassured me. "Just as soon as this ship passes. I promise. I'll bring it back for you."

"You promise?"

"Yes," he said, kissing my nose.

I turned to the barracks. "Be careful," I said.

"You too."

"There you are!" Nurse Hildebrand whispered in the hallway. Even her whispers sounded like shouts. "I don't have time to hear your explanation, nor do I have time to discipline you, so I will just say that you are the last of the nurses to make it to the cellar. The Japanese are coming. The colonel gave orders for the women to go under. We must hurry."

My heart raced as I followed Nurse Hildebrand down a set of stairs. I patted the place on the collar of my dress where I'd fastened the blue rose pin, the one Kitty gave to me in Seattle. I'd worn it on a whim that morning and gasped when I realized it was *gone*. I stopped suddenly.

"What are you waiting for?" Nurse Hildebrand snapped.

Distraught, I looked down at the stairs, then back toward the door. "It's just that"—I fumbled, patting my dress pockets frantically—"I lost something. Something very important to me."

"Your life is important to you, isn't it?"

I nodded meekly.

"Then let's go. We have to get to the cellar."

How could I be so careless to lose the pin? I imagined it lying on the beach, buried in a clump of sand as a wave carried it out to sea. I shuddered, thinking of Kitty. *Is it a sign of the end of our friendship?*

I followed Nurse Hildebrand farther down the stairs, through a locked door, and then watched as she pulled up a rug and pried open a hinge in the floor. "You first," she said, pointing to a dark cavern below.

I descended a ladder into a shadowy space where a few lanterns flickered. When my feet hit the floor, I could make out Liz and Stella, and some of the others in the distance.

"Kitty?" I called out. "Are you here?"

245

Only silence answered back. I turned to Nurse Hildebrand with concern.

"She's over there," she said, pointing to the light of a single lantern in the far right corner.

"Kitty," I said, walking toward her until I could make out her small, frightened face, wayward curls springing out in disarray. She sat against the wall, looking despondent.

"I was worried you weren't coming," she said, wiping away a tear.

I sat down beside her and squeezed her hand. "I'm here now."

No one knew what was happening above. After two hours, or what felt like twelve, Nurse Hildebrand enlisted Stella to help pass out rations, water, and beans in tin cans. Enough to last days, even weeks. I thought about the prospect of living in the dark, eating canned Spam, and I shuddered.

"Here," said Stella, offering me a canteen. I took a swig and swallowed hard. It tasted of rust.

We all froze when we heard footsteps on the floor above.

"Nurses," Nurse Hildebrand whispered, reaching for a rifle on the wall, "put out your lanterns."

We obeyed, and listened in the darkness, as the footsteps grew closer, louder. There was a thud, and then the creak of the trapdoor opening. I squeezed Kitty's hand harder. *Dear Lord. The Japanese are here.*

But instead of a foreign accent, a familiar voice rang out in the cellar. "Nurses, it's all clear. The ship's turned west. You can come out now."

The women let out a cheer—all but Kitty, who just stared ahead. I reached for her hand. "Come on, dear," I said. "It's over. We can go now."

She looked startled, as though I'd roused her from a dream. When she turned on her lantern, I could detect the familiar cloudiness in her eyes. The distance. "Yes, of course," she said, standing up and walking ahead of me.

"Can you believe we ship out tomorrow?" Liz marveled at breakfast the next day.

Tomorrow. I'd been dreading this day since the moment I fell in love with Westry. Leaving the island meant the end of our reality, and the beginning of a new one—one, I feared, that would be more complicated than we might know.

"The men ship out in the morning," Stella added. She didn't like that Will was joining the fight in Europe any more than I liked that Westry was.

"I was thinking," she continued. "If I went to serve in Europe, I'd at least be closer to him. In case—"

I shook my head. The war had taken its toll on

Stella, who was now shockingly thin. She needed leave more than any of us. "Going to Europe won't protect him," I said. "Go home. Wait for him there."

She nodded. "Can you believe Kitty? I hear she's heading to France, right in the middle of the action. She's joining a group headed for Normandy."

My cheeks flushed. France? *Why didn't she tell me the extent of her plans? Does she think I don't care?*

"Well, speaking of the devil," Stella said, pointing to the door.

Kitty walked into the mess hall, smiling. Her cheeks looked rosy, the way they once had. As she approached our table, I could see that she was holding a cluster of yellow hibiscus, and my cheeks burned at the sight.

"Morning, ladies," she said. "How are the rations today?"

I felt Stella's eyes boring into the side of my head.

"Fine," Liz, said, oblivious to the tension in the air, "if you like rubberized eggs."

Kitty giggled, setting the flowers, tied in a single white ribbon, on the table. "Aren't they beautiful?" she said, admiring their yellow petals against the contrasting sterile beige tabletop. I knew them instantly, of course—the hibiscus that grew near the bungalow. They had to be.

"Well, well, well," Stella said. "It looks like someone has an admirer.

"Oh, Stell," Kitty said, playing coy.

"Then where did you get them?" she said relentlessly. I wished she'd stop. I didn't want to know.

Kitty grinned and twirled around toward the buffet line, leaving us to our imaginations.

Stella cleared her throat and smirked. "What did I warn you about the first day on this island?"

I stood up abruptly and began walking to the door.

"Anne," Stella called out. "Wait. I didn't mean anything by it. Come back."

Outside on the path back to the barracks, my heart pounded as I retraced the past few weeks. I thought of the way Kitty lit up whenever Westry appeared, and the way she had pulled back from me. *Of course Kitty feels something for Westry.*

I froze for a moment. *Could he possibly share her attraction?* Every man in our past—well, except Gerard—had favored Kitty over me. She was asked first to dance. She had received a half dozen invitations to the Homecoming banquet, when I'd had one. My mind raced. *The letter. My God. Westry didn't seem at all concerned about the prospect of someone taking it. Did he pretend it had been stolen so he wouldn't have to face my declaration of love, my hope for the future—of a future together?*

I kicked a rock on the path and shook my head, dismissing the disturbing train of thought. *No, I won't think of it a moment longer, not when we are leaving tomorrow. Not when we have mere hours left together. There isn't time for nonsense.*

"That's it," Kitty said the next morning after breakfast, sighing. She bent over to zip up the side of her bag, which looked, strangely, smaller than the enormous duffel I'd lugged into this room ten months prior. Like the bag, Kitty had lost some of herself on the island.

"My flight leaves in an hour," she said in a distant voice, her gaze turned to the hillside outside the window, a scene that often captured her attention. I wondered what she was looking for up in those hills. "Nurse Hildebrand and I will meet up with a squadron flying into France tomorrow. And then . . ." Her voice trailed off.

Kitty in France. All by herself. I hated the thought of it, just like I had hated the thought of her coming here, to the South Pacific, alone. It didn't matter what I thought of her feelings for Westry. I knew that somewhere beyond the layers of emotional scars draped over her like armor, my best friend resided. But this time I wouldn't insist on going with her.

"Oh, Kitty!" I cried, leaping to my feet. *If I could only get through to her.* "Why did things turn out the way they did for us?"

Kitty shrugged, reaching for her bag. She looked at me for a long moment. "The island had its way, I guess," she finally muttered.

"No, Kitty, you have it wrong," I said, hearing the panic in my voice—panic at what seemed like the end of a friendship, the end of an era. I thought about my transgressions as a friend. *I could have spent more time with her. I might have been more supportive through her final weeks of pregnancy—but wasn't I? Most important, I should have been honest with her about the bungalow, about everything.* I had let too many secrets creep in between us. Secrets I had promised never to keep. "Kitty," I pleaded. "I haven't changed. I'm still the same old Anne. And I'd wager that you're still the same old Kitty in your heart. I want nothing more than to go on being Anne and Kitty."

She looked at me with eyes I didn't recognize. They were tired and older, hardened. "I wish that too," she said softly, turning away from me. "But I don't think we can now."

I nodded, feeling tears rise from a place deep inside. They welled up in my eyes before spilling out unbidden on my cheeks.

"Good-bye, Anne," Kitty said without turning around. Her tone was businesslike, the way I'd witnessed her speak to the servants in her home growing up, or the clerk at the drugstore. I felt the urge to scream, *"Kitty, stop this right now! Let's end this charade.*" But I could only stand there, mute, too stunned, too sad to open my mouth. "I wish you the best of luck," she said, reaching for the door handle. "With everything."

The door clicked closed and the silence in the room pulsed. I fell to the floor, sobbing into my hands for what felt like hours. *What right does she have to leave like this, to declare our friendship over? How could she behave so coldly?*

When the clock told me it was eleven, I willed myself to stand, prying my tired limbs off the floor. I'd promised Westry a farewell on the tarmac, and his flight left in a half hour, just after mine.

I set my bag by the door and glanced in the mirror at my red, swollen eyes. I hardly recognized myself.

For a moment, I feared I wouldn't find him. I squinted as I looked out at the thick and frenzied crowd of men, awash in army green. A small cohort would stay on the island, but the majority, Westry included, had been tapped for new assignments. France. Great Britain. And a lucky few, like me, would go home.

I squinted, scanning faces, and then toward the edge of the crowd, our eyes met.

Ignoring the orders over the loudspeaker for the nurses to begin boarding, I set my bag down by

Stella and Liz and ran to Westry. He lifted me into his arms and we kissed.

"Don't cry, my love," he said, wiping a tear from my cheek. "This isn't good-bye."

"But it is," I said, running my hand along his freshly shaven face. "We don't know what will happen out there." I realized the statement was as much about him as it was about me.

Westry nodded, pulling a nosegay of yellow hibiscus from his bag and tucking it into my hand. A white ribbon loosely tied the blooms in place. *Kitty.* "These flowers," I stammered. "You gave the same ones to Kitty yesterday, didn't you?"

Westry looked confused, then nodded. "Well, yes," he said. "I was—"

Another voice piped through the loudspeaker. "All men proceed to board."

"Westry," I said, feeling panicked. "Is there something you need to tell me? Something about Kitty?"

He looked to his feet momentarily and then back at me. "It's nothing," he said, "but I still should have told you. A few weeks ago, I found her weeping on the beach. I was on the way to the bungalow, and I invited her to join me."

My cheeks burned. *Westry brought her to our bungalow—alone, without me?*

I shook my head in disbelief. "Why didn't you tell me? Why didn't *she* tell me?"

"I'm sorry, Anne," he said. "I really didn't think anything of it."

I turned to glance at the plane that would take me home. Stella was standing beside it waving her arms frantically at me.

"Anne!" she screamed. "It's time to go!"

I took a final look at Westry. The wind had tousled his hair. I longed to run my hands through the sandy blond strands the way I'd done a hundred times in the bungalow, to take in the scent of his skin, to surrender myself to him. But this time, something told me no.

"Good-bye," I whispered in his ear, letting my cheek brush his a final time. I reached for his hand and placed the flowers in his palm before running toward the plane.

"Anne, wait!" Westry shouted. "Wait, the painting. Did you get it?"

I froze. "What do you mean, did I get it? I thought you were going to get it."

Westry threw his hands in the air. "I'm sorry, Anne," he said, looking panic-stricken. "I intended to go back, but there just wasn't time. I . . ." His unit had already boarded the plane, and I could see his commanding officer walking toward him. I turned toward the beach and wondered—if I ran fast—could I make it back to the bungalow to retrieve the canvas before the plane departed?

"Please," I pleaded with Stella, who was

standing at the base of the stairway that ascended to the plane's cabin. "Please tell the pilot I just need fifteen minutes. I left something on base. I promise, I'll be quick."

The pilot appeared behind her. "I'm sorry, ma'am, there simply isn't time," he said firmly. "You need to board now."

My legs felt as though they'd been strapped with lead as I climbed the steps. Before the pilot's assistant pulled the hatch shut, my eyes met Westry's. I couldn't hear him over the airplane's engine, which was roaring like a monster, but I could read his lips.

"I'm so sorry," he said. "I'll come back. Please don't you worry, Anne. I—"

The door slammed shut before I could interpret his last words. What did it matter, I reasoned, blotting my tears with a handkerchief. It was over. The magic we'd found in the bungalow was gone, and I could feel its spell lifting as the plane gained speed and altitude. I watched as the island grew smaller, until it appeared a mere dot on a map. A dot where so much had happened, and so much had been left behind.

Stella leaned over to me. "Will you miss it?"

I nodded. "Yes," I said honestly.

"Do you think you'll ever come back?" she asked cautiously. "Will and I have talked about returning for a visit. When the war's over, of course."

I looked out the window again before responding, unable to take my eyes off the speck of emerald floating in the turquoise sea. "No," I assured her. "I don't think I ever will."

I squeezed the locket resting on my chest, grateful for the scrap of wood from the bungalow nestled safe inside. With it, I could always return—in my heart, at least.

Chapter 13

We missed you, kid," Papa said as I climbed into the car, grateful not to see Maxine in the backseat. Even with months to process their affair, the revelation that had destroyed the family unit I belonged to, I still couldn't make sense of it.

I sighed, leaning back into the soft leather of the Buick as Papa started the engine and began to back away. Here there would be no jeeps, no gravel roads or potholes.

"It's good to be home," I said, taking in a deep breath of the temperate Seattle air. The return trip had been a harrowing one, with multiple flights and a four-day sea passage. It gave me time to think, to get a grip on the loose ends that plagued my mind, and yet when I stepped out of the airplane onto the airstrip in Seattle, my body trembled with uncertainty.

"Gerard's home," Papa said a little cautiously, as if to test the waters.

I looked at my hands in my lap, hands that had loved Westry, still loved Westry. Hands of betrayal.

"Does he want to see me?" I asked.

"Of course he does, sweetheart," Papa said. "Perhaps the real question is *do you want to see him?*"

He could read my heart. He always could. "I don't know, Papa," I muttered, beginning to weep. "I don't know what I want anymore."

"Come here, honey," he said. I inched closer to him in the front seat, and he draped a firm arm around me, one that told me that despite everything, I would be fine. I only wished I could believe it.

Windermere looked untouched by time, by war. As we passed the familiar estates, however, I knew that appearances were deceiving. The Larson home, for instance, still had its beautiful lawn and exquisite garden with the elaborate urns and the cherub fountain in the center of the circle drive, and yet I knew that heartache clung to every wall, every surface. The twins weren't coming home. Terry had died in a fight near Marseilles; Larry in a plane crash two days later—on the way home to comfort his mother.

The Godfrey mansion also kept up appearances, even though I knew there was a bigger story lingering behind the gates. As we drove past, I held my breath, remembering the night of the engagement party, Kitty's face, and how we'd sat on the curb outside making plans for the future. *If we'd known the way things would turn out, would we have gone anyway?*

The memories pierced, and I looked away quickly.

"He came home Friday," Papa said. "Got sent home a bit early on medical leave."

I stiffened. "*Medical* leave?"

"Yes," he said. "He took a bullet to the arm and shoulder. He may never regain functionality in his left arm, but in the scheme of war wounds, that's no tragedy."

Waves of emotion rolled through my body. Papa was right. Boys were getting maimed, dying. Gerard's injury hardly compared, but for some reason the news made me grieve in a way I hadn't expected.

"Don't cry, dear," Papa said, stroking my hair. "He's going to be fine."

"I know," I cried. "I know he is. It's just that—"

"It's hard to take," he said. "I know."

"This war," I cried, "it's changed everything, all of us."

"It's true," Papa said solemnly, pulling the car into the familiar driveway. Everything was the same, of course, just as I'd left it. But it wasn't; I knew that. And I could never get it back to the way it had been.

I heard a muffled knock on my bedroom door. *Where am I?* I sat up and tried to get my bearings. The old lace curtains. The big trundle bed. Yes, I was home. *But what time is it? What* day *is it?* The darkness outside the window told me it was late. *How late? How long have I been asleep?* The rain pelted the roof overhead, and I closed my eyes, remembering the rainstorms in the tropics, particularly the way Westry and I had showered together in that downpour on the beach. I could still feel his embrace, smell his soapy skin. I blinked hard. *Was it only a dream?*

I pulled the blanket tighter around my body and ignored the knock that sounded again at the door, this one a bit louder. I couldn't face Maxine. Not yet. *Go away. Please go away. Leave me to my memories.*

Moments later, a slip of paper slid under the door along the wood floor. I stared at it for a while, trying to ignore its presence, but it seemed to pulse, to flash like a bright light I could not block from my view. So I sat up, forced my feet to the floor, and retrieved it.

I held the square of beige stationery in my hands and took a deep breath as I took in the familiar handwriting.

My dear Antoinette,

I know you are hurting. So am I. Please let me comfort you.

Maxine

I wrapped my fingers around the cold doorknob and turned it slowly, opening the door far enough to see Maxine standing in the hallway outside, her hair pulled back in the usual fashion. An apron, pressed neatly, encircled her slim waist. She held a tray of sandwiches. A single pink rose rested inside a glass bud vase, and puffs of steam seeped from an ivory mug. I could smell the Earl Grey.

I released my grasp on the doorknob. "Oh, Maxine!" I cried.

She set the tray down on my bedside table and took me into her arms. The tears erupted with volcanic power, first in little spurts, then in great big heaves, pouring out of my heart, my soul, with such ferocity, I wondered if they'd ever stop.

"Let it all out," she whispered. "Don't hold back."

When the tears had subsided, Maxine handed me a handkerchief and the cup of tea, and I leaned against the headboard, tucking my knees to my chest under my pink cotton nightgown.

"You don't have to talk," she said softly, "if you don't want to."

I looked into her eyes for the first time and could see anguish residing there.

"I'm so sorry," she said, "about the letter I sent. I should never have sent it. I should have let your father tell you. It wasn't my place."

I reached for Maxine's hand. Her fingers felt cold. "You have always been honest with me," I said. "You were right to send it."

"Will you ever forgive me?" Her thick accent made her sound meeker, more vulnerable somehow. "Will you ever love me the way you once did?"

I took a deep breath. "I never stopped loving you, Maxine."

Her eyes sparkled as if it was the only response she needed. "Now," she said, "eat your sandwiches and tell me about the South Pacific. I sense that there is a story that needs telling."

I reached for a *croque monsieur* and nodded, eager to tell her the whole story. Well, parts of it, at least.

The rain cleared the next day, and as the clouds parted to reveal the June Seattle sun, my heart felt lighter.

"Morning, Antoinette," Maxine chirped from the kitchen. "Breakfast is on the table."

I smiled and joined Papa at the table, surveying my plate: fresh fruit, buttered toast, and an omelet—a veritable feast compared with the rations on the island.

Maxine hung up her apron and joined us at the

261

table. Papa gave her cheek a nuzzle when she did, and I realized that while I may have accepted their love, it would still take some getting used to. *How is Mother taking the news?*

"Papa," I said cautiously, "have you heard from Mother?"

Maxine set down her fork. The air felt thick and uncomfortable. "Yes," he said. "She's in New York now, dear. Of course you know that. She's written you, I gather." He produced a scrap of paper from his pocket. "She asked that I have you call her at this number. She'd like you to come out to see her." He paused. "When you're ready."

I folded the crumpled paper and set it down near my plate. She was shopping, attending fashion shows, no doubt. *But is she happy?*

"Gerard phoned this morning," Papa said, eager to change the subject.

"Oh?"

"He'd like to stop by this afternoon."

My hands instinctively reached for my locket. For a sign.

"Yes," I said, looking to Maxine for approval. "I'll see him."

Maxine's smile told me I'd made the right decision. The first step in making sense of this new reality was facing Gerard and acknowledging the life we'd planned together. I rubbed my hand along the place where my engagement ring had once resided and sighed.

"Good," Papa said from behind his newspaper. "I told him to come by around two."

I heard Gerard's car pull into the driveway, followed by the sound of his footsteps on the porch. I froze. *What will I say to him? How will I act?*

Maxine peeked into my room and gestured toward the stairs. "He's here, Antoinette," she said softly. "Are you ready?"

I smoothed my hair and walked to the top of the stairs. "Yes," I said, composing myself.

One step, and then two. I could hear Gerard's voice in the parlor talking to Papa. His nearness caused my heart to flutter in a way I hadn't expected it to. *Three steps. Four.* The voices stopped. *Five steps, six.* And there he was, standing at the base of the stairs, looking up at me with such love, such intensity, that I could not unlock my gaze from his.

"Anne!" he said.

"Gerard!" My voice cracked a little. His left arm rested in a beige sling.

"Well are you going to just stand there or are you going to kiss this wounded soldier?"

I grinned, and sailed down the final steps, welcoming his embrace before planting a light kiss on his cheek, operating on instincts, or muscle memory.

Papa cleared his throat and nodded at Maxine.

"We'll leave you two," he said, grinning. "You have some catching up to do."

Gerard took my hand and led me to the sofa in the living room before closing the double doors behind us with his good arm. "I can't tell you how much I've missed you," he said, sitting down beside me.

I'd forgotten how handsome he was, shockingly so. "I'm sorry I didn't write often," I said, frowning.

"It's all right," he replied lovingly. "I knew you were busy."

But if he really understood the reason, would he be so forgiving?

"Your arm," I said, touching his shoulder gently, then retracting my hand in haste. "Oh, Gerard. Papa says you may never use it again."

He shrugged. "I should have died out there," he said, looking at his lap. "All the men around me were shot down. All but me. I can't make any sense out of why I was spared."

I could see that, like me, Gerard carried a great burden in his heart, his a nobler one.

He reached for my hands, and then paused, holding up my left hand, bare without the engagement ring.

"Gerard, I—"

He shook his head. "You don't need to explain," he said. "Just having you here, having you back is good enough for now."

I let my head rest on his shoulder.

264

• • •

September 1944

"Can you believe I'm getting married?" I said to Maxine, admiring the white silk gown Mother had shipped from France before the war broke out.

"You look beautiful, Antoinette," she said, tucking a pin in the bodice. "We'll just have the seamstress take it in a bit here. Have you been losing weight?"

I shrugged. "It's nerves, that's all."

"Is something bothering you, my dear? You know you can tell me."

The phone rang before I could answer the question. "I'll get that," I said bolting down the stairs to the kitchen. "It's probably Gerard."

"Hello," I said cheerfully, a little out of breath. "You'll never guess what I'm wearing."

Static crackled over the line. "Anne?" a familiar female voice spoke. "Anne, is that you?"

"Yes, this is she," I said. "Who is this?"

"It's me, Mary."

I gasped. "Mary! My God, how are you?"

"I'm fine," she said. "I don't have much time, so I'll have to keep this short. I'm calling with some bad news, I'm afraid."

I could feel the blood leave my face. *Mary. Bad news.* "What is it?"

"I'm in Paris," she said. "I'm here on account of

265

Edward, but that's for another conversation. You've probably heard about the liberation of the city."

"Yes," I said, still shocked to be speaking to my old friend.

"It's a dream, Anne. The Allies are here. For a while we didn't think it would happen." She paused. "What you need to know is that today at the army hospital I saw Kitty, and . . ."

I had thought of Kitty often, especially now that my wedding date neared. And now the mention of her inflamed the familiar wound in my heart.

"Mary, is she OK?"

"Yes," she said. "She's fine. But, Anne . . . Anne, it's Westry."

I sat down as the room began to spin, feeling a stray pin from the wedding dress jab my side.

"Anne, are you still there?"

"Yes," I said weakly. "I'm still here."

"He's been hurt," she continued. "He got hit. He was part of the Fourth Infantry Division, the men who stormed the city. But his battalion was struck in the fight. Most died. He somehow held on."

"My God, Mary, how bad is it?"

"I don't know for sure," she said, "but by the look of things . . . well, Anne, it isn't good."

"Is he conscious?"

The line began to crackle again. "Mary, are you still there?"

"Yes," she said. "I'm here." Her voice sounded garbled and more distant than it had a moment ago. I knew the connection could be severed in an instant. "You need to come. You need to see him, before—"

"But how?" I cried, panicked. "Travel is restricted, especially to Europe."

"I know a way," Mary said. "Do you have a pen and paper?"

I fumbled in the kitchen drawer and pulled out a notepad. It had Mother's handwriting on it, which made me realize how much I missed her. After more than a year at home, I had yet to visit her in New York. "I'm ready," I said.

"Take down this code," she said. "A5691G9NQ."

"What does this mean?"

"It's a Foreign Service travel code," she said. "You can use it to board a ship leaving from New York to Paris in four days. And when you arrive, come to my apartment: three forty-nine Saint Germaine."

I scrawled the address on the pad and then shook my head. "You really think this will work?"

"Yes," she said. "And if you run into any trouble, mention the name Edward Naughton."

I clutched the receiver tightly, trying to hold on to the connection, to her. "Thank you, Mary." But the line had been swallowed up by static. She was gone.

• • •

"Gerard, I need to tell you something," I said that night at dinner. I pushed my plate aside. The dinner, even broiled salmon with new potatoes, hadn't interested me.

"You've hardly touched your food," he said, frowning.

He looked dapper seated across the table from me in a gray suit. The war had rendered the Cabaña Club a ghost town without the buzz of people and the familiar fog of cigarette smoke. A lone saxophonist played on the stage. In some ways, it felt like a betrayal to be there, a betrayal to those who had lost their lives, or who were in agony in hospitals. I swallowed hard.

"What is it, my love?" he continued, dabbing the corners of his mouth with a white cloth napkin.

I took a deep breath. "While I was in the South Pacific, there was a man. I—I . . ."

Gerard closed his eyes tightly. "Don't tell me," he said, shaking his head. "Please don't."

I nodded. "I understand. But there's something I need to do, before the wedding."

"What?"

"I need to go away," I said. "Just for a while."

Gerard looked pained, but he didn't protest. "And when you return, will you be yourself again?"

I looked deep into his eyes. "It's why I need to go," I said. "I need to find out."

He looked away. My words had hurt him, and I hated that. His left arm, the bad one, hung from his torso, limp, lifeless. He didn't like wearing the sling when we went out. "Anne," he said, clearing his throat. His voice faltered a little, and he paused to regain his strength. Gerard never cried. "If this is what it takes. If there's a chance I can have your whole heart again, I will wait."

Chapter 14

Papa took me to the train station the next morning. It would be a long journey to New York, but it was the only way. I'd stay with Mother for a day before boarding the ship Mary spoke of. I prayed that Westry could hold on until I arrived. There was so much I needed to say to him, and so much I needed to hear him say. *Does the grain of love that still lingers in my heart remain in his?*

"Your mother will be overjoyed to see you," Papa said, looking sheepish, the way he always did when he spoke of Mother. It didn't seem fair for him to use the words "overjoyed" and "mother" in the same sentence, given the state of their relationship, but I chose to overlook those details.

"You have the address, right?" he asked.

"Yes," I said, indicating my pocketbook, where my ticket and Mother's address were tucked inside.

"Good," he said. "Take a cab from the train station directly to her apartment. Be careful, kid."

I smiled. "Papa, you've forgotten that I lived in a war zone for almost a year. I think I'll be fine in the city."

He returned my smile. "Of course you will, dear. Ring me with your return details, and I'll be here to pick you up."

I kissed his cheek before stepping onto the train. The conductor took my ticket and showed me to the small drawing room where I'd spend the next two days traveling across the country, alone.

It was late when the train pulled into Grand Central Terminal, and as it glided along the tracks, the city lights glistened. It was hard to imagine Mother making her home in this big, bold place so unlike Seattle.

I stepped off the train, and lugged my bag through the maze of people, pushing past a woman with far too many children, a man with a monkey holding a set of miniature cymbals, and a gray-haired transient extending his cap and muttering something I couldn't understand.

Outside on the street, a sea of taxis waited. I

raised my hand and caught the attention of a dark-skinned driver, who nodded and gestured toward the back seat.

I opened the door and stuffed my bag inside before sitting down. The air smelled of cigarettes and must. "I'm going to"—I paused to glance at the slip of paper in my hand—"560 East Fifty-seventh Street."

He nodded absently.

My eyes blurred as I gazed out the window. The lights flashed—green, red, pink, yellow. Sailors on leave in stark white uniforms clung to women—blondes, brunettes, tall ones, short ones. The war hadn't ended, but the tide had turned. You could feel it—from the little suburbs of Seattle to the vibrant streets of New York.

The buildings outside flicked by like frames of a film, one after the next, composing a picture that was both foreign and lonely. The cab finally stopped abruptly on a tree-lined street.

"Here we are, miss," said the cabbie. I paid the fare, and he set my bag on the street, pointing up to a brick townhouse with a shiny red door.

"Thank you," I said, turning toward the steps. I rang the doorbell, and moments later Mother appeared. It was almost eleven, but she stood in the doorway in full makeup and a red off-the-shoulder dress. A poorly balanced martini glass sloshed in her hand.

"Anne!" Mother cried, pulling me toward her with a freshly manicured hand. An olive bobbled out of the glass and fell to floor.

She took a rocky step back, and I dropped my bag and reached out to steady her. "Let me look at you," she said in an unnaturally cheerful tone. Her eyes pored over me, then she nodded in approval. "The South Pacific was kind to you, dear. Why, you must have lost ten pounds."

I smiled. "Well, I—"

"Come in! Come in!" She turned away from the door, and her red dress swished ahead.

I followed her, lugging my bag into the foyer, where a crystal chandelier, too large and gaudy for the small space, loomed overhead. "It's not Windermere," she said, shrugging, "but it's home for me now. I've grown to love city life."

She led me into a small front room with parquet floors and a Victorian sofa. "Of course," she said, "I'm having it all redone. Leon is helping me with that." She said his name as though I was expected to know him.

"Leon?"

"My interior decorator," she said, taking another long sip from her glass. I didn't remember Mother liking martinis in Seattle, nor did I remember her collarbones protruding from her chest. "He's insisted on mauve for this room, but I'm not sure. I rather fancy a shade of teal. What do you think, dear?"

"Teal might be a little bold for this room," I said honestly.

"That's just the look I'm going for, dear," she said, running her hand along a nearby wall. "Bold. Your father was so traditional." She gulped down the last of her drink, then giggled. "I don't have to be traditional anymore."

I nodded, preferring not to discuss Papa with her in this state.

She shook her head. "Listen to me going on like this," she said, reaching for a bell on a side table. "You must be exhausted, dear. I'll ring for Minnie."

She sounded the bell, and a small woman, no older than me, materialized moments later. "Minnie, be a dear and show Anne to her room."

"Yes, ma'am," she said in a squeak, reaching for my bag.

"Good night, my dearest," Mother said, caressing my cheek. "I know you can't stay long, but I have the morning packed with fun before your departure tomorrow. Go get some rest, sweetheart."

"Good night," I said, following Minnie up the stairs as Mother made her way back to the bar and reached for a bottle of gin.

The sound of a horn outside my third-floor window woke me the next morning. I pulled a pillow over my face, hoping to fall back into slumber, but with no luck. I glanced at the clock; it was barely 6:40, but I got up and dressed anyway. Mother would be waiting, and I wanted to spend as much time with her as possible before I boarded the ship.

The light shone through the windows downstairs, revealing a lonelier space than I'd seen the night before. There were no photos on the walls, or paintings. Mother loved paintings.

"Good morning, miss," Minnie said shyly from the entrance to the kitchen. "May I make you coffee or tea?"

"Tea would be lovely, Minnie, thank you," I said, smiling.

Moments later she appeared with a cup of tea on a tray with a plate with fruit, a croissant, and a boiled egg.

I eyed the tray. "Shouldn't I wait for Mother?"

Minnie looked conflicted. "About that," she said. "Well, it's just that, well—"

"Minnie, what is it?"

"Mr. Schwartz was here last night," she said nervously, searching for my understanding, or approval.

"Do you mean Leon?"

"Yes, ma'am," she said. "He arrived after you turned in."

"Oh," I replied. "And Mother's still asleep?"

"Yes."

"Minnie, is he still here?"

She looked at her feet before gnawing at her thumbnail.

"He is, isn't he?"

Minnie looked relieved to share the secret with someone. "When he comes to stay, I often don't see her until after twelve, sometimes one."

I nodded, trying my best not to show the disappointment I felt. "Then I'll take my breakfast right here," I said, reaching for the tray. "Thank you."

"Oh, Miss—Miss Anne," Minnie stammered nervously. "You won't tell Mrs. Calloway that I—that I told you anything, will you?"

I patted her plump hand reassuringly. "Of course not," I said. "It will be our secret."

An hour later, I stepped outside the apartment and onto the street. I had five hours before I needed to make my way to the dock to board the ship. I hailed a cab, unsure of my destination.

"Where to, miss?" the driver asked.

"I don't know," I said. "I only have a few hours left in the city. Do you have any suggestions?"

The driver smiled, revealing a gold tooth. "That's funny. Everyone around here seems to know exactly where they're going."

I shrugged, looking up at Mother's apartment. The shades in her bedroom window were still drawn. "I used to think I knew where I was going. I thought I had everything figured out, but . . ."

The driver's face grew worried. "Listen, miss," he said, "I didn't mean to hurt your feelings."

I shook my head. "You didn't."

"Hey," he said, producing a folded brochure from his jacket pocket. "You like art?"

I thought of the painting I'd left in the bungalow. How I longed to have it in my possession just then. "Yes," I said. "I do."

"Then I'll take you to the Met."

"The Met?"

He looked at me in the way one looks at a child. "The Metropolitan Museum of Art."

"Yes," I said, smiling. "Perfect."

"I hope you find what you're looking for," the driver said with a wink.

"Me too," I said, handing him three crisp bills from my pocketbook.

Minutes later, I stood before the great stone building, with its enormous ivory columns flanking the entrance. I climbed the steps to the double doors, walking inside to an information booth straight ahead.

"Excuse me, ma'am," I asked. "You don't, by chance, have any paintings by French artists here, do you?"

The woman, about Mother's age, nodded without looking up from her book. "Of course we do, miss. They're all up on the east wing of the third floor."

"Thank you," I said, heading to a nearby elevator. It was foolish, I knew, to think that I'd find any of Gauguin's paintings here. Yet, I longed to know if the small canvas in the bungalow bore any similarity to his other work. *Could Tita have been right about the true owner of the bungalow? And its curse?*

I exited the elevator on the third floor. Aside from a little boy with a red balloon clutching his mother's hand, and a security guard standing near the west wall, the floor was empty.

I moved from painting to painting, reading the placards underneath: Monet, Cezanne, and others whose names I didn't recognize. When I'd scoured the entire room, I sat down, defeated, on a bench by the elevator.

"Excuse me, miss." I looked up to see the security guard walking toward me. He pulled his spectacles lower on his nose. "May I help you find something?"

I smiled. "Oh, it's nothing. I had a silly idea that I'd find the work of a certain artist here. But I was wrong."

He tilted his head to the right. "What artist?"

"Oh, a French painter, one who did the majority of his work in the South Pacific. I'd have better luck searching in France."

"What's his name?"

"Paul Gauguin," I said, standing up and pressing the Down button for the elevator.

"Well, yes," the man said, "we do have some of his work."

"You do?" The elevator's chime sounded and the door opened. I stepped back and let it close.

"Indeed," he said, pointing to a door a few paces away. A gold padlock hung from its handle. "The wing is closed for maintenance now, but, seeing how much you're interested, I might be able to open it up—for a special occasion."

I beamed. "Could you?"

"I have the key right here," he said, patting the pocket of his pants.

I followed him to the door, where he slipped a brass key into the lock and held the door open for me. "Take all the time you need," he said proudly. "I'll be right outside."

"Thank you," I said. "Thank you ever so much."

I slipped inside the door, letting it close with a click behind me. The room was small compared to the wing outside, but the walls were crowded with paintings. At first I didn't know where to begin—with the landscapes on the right or the portraits to my left—but then a canvas caught my eye, a beach scene on the far wall. It looked *familiar,* somehow. It would be too much to hope that the artist who had once lived in the bungalow could have painted this same stretch of beach, but as I walked closer, the idea didn't seem too far-fetched.

The canvas revealed a yellow hibiscus bush near a thatched-roof bungalow. *Our bungalow.* The silhouette of an island woman lingered on the shore. It looked like a companion to the scene on the canvas in the bungalow—like a photograph of a scene shot right before the other.

I took a step back, searching for a placard with identifying details—anything to hint at its origin, its date, and especially its painter. But the wall was blank.

I opened the door and leaned out into the hallway, trying to capture the attention of the guard. "Excuse me, sir," I whispered.

He nodded and walked toward me. "Yes?"

"I'm sorry to bother you, but you mentioned this room was closed for maintenance. Do you know if some of the placards near the paintings have been removed? There's one in particular I'd like to know about."

The man smiled. "Let me see if I can help."

Inside, I pointed to the canvas. "This is the one."

"I know this painting," he said. "It's very special."

"Whose is it?"

"Why, Mr. Paul Gauguin," he said, grinning. "Surely you could tell by the depiction of the island woman in the foreground, and the signature."

I shook my head in awe. "Signature?"

"Right here," he said, pointing to a spot on the lower left. The yellow paint he'd used to sign his name blended in with the hibiscus.

Of course it was Gauguin. If only Westry were here.

"And here's another," he said, pointing to a larger canvas a few feet away featuring a barebreasted woman with a plumeria in her hair. I gasped when I realized there was a resemblance. *Atea. She's the spitting image of Atea.*

I walked back to the beach scene that had captured me so. "Do you happen to know when he painted this?"

"It would have been during his time in Tahiti," he said, "in the early 1890s."

"Tahiti?"

"Yes, or thereabouts," he said. "It's rumored that he spent time all over the nearby islands. In fact, occasionally some of his work turns up from a ship captain who barters with a local. A priceless painting in exchange for a pack of cigarettes." He shook his head. "Can you even imagine?"

I nodded, feeling the same panic I'd felt the day I left the island, knowing the painting might be lost forever. "Do you know anything more about his life on the islands?"

"Just that he was reclusive," he said. "He lived in little hideaways, mingling with women half his age and often coming into misfortune. He died alone of a syphilitic heart attack. Not a very happy life, if you ask me."

I nodded. *It all adds up. The bungalow. The painting. Tita's warning. The curse.*

I looked at the security guard with new

appreciation. "How is it that you know so much about Gauguin?" I asked.

"There aren't many art thieves trolling these halls," he said with a wink. "I have a lot of time on my hands here. Besides, he's my favorite. He doesn't deserve to be sequestered away in this room. He should be out with the Monets, the Van Goghs."

I nodded, wishing I could transport myself back to the island and retrieve the painting Westry and I had left behind. I'd bring it to the museum and request that it be hung right here, right by the other, completing the story one canvas began to tell and the other could finish.

"I'm so sorry I overslept this morning, dear," Mother said from the couch when I returned to the apartment. An ice pack rested on her forehead. "I have a terrible headache."

I wanted to say, *Because you stayed up all night drinking with a certain Mr. Schwartz,* but instead I smiled sweetly. "I kept busy, Mother."

"Good," she said. "I'm afraid I'm much too ill to take you to the dock today. I've arranged for a driver to pick you up in a half hour. You'll get there in plenty of time."

I nodded. "Mother." I paused, considering my words carefully before I spoke them. "We haven't talked about what happened, about Maxine and Papa."

She looked away, unwilling to let her eyes meet mine.

"Mother," I continued, "are you all right? I know it must have been so painful."

I could sense her sadness, even when she tried to stifle it by offering me a scone from a tray Minnie had set on a side table.

"Mother?"

She sighed. "I will be, in time," she said. "I fill my days with as much as I can. And there's no shortage of men now."

I looked away, embarrassed.

"The failure of my marriage was the greatest of my life."

"Oh, Mother—"

"No," she said, silencing me. "I want you to hear this."

I nodded, though I wasn't entirely certain I wanted to listen.

"I loved your father; I always did," she went on. "But I realized, a long time ago, that he did not love me. He never had, in fact. Well, not in the way a husband *should* love a wife." She sighed, and held her empty hands out before her. "So," she continued, changing the tone of her voice from regret-filled to practical. "Let that be a lesson to you, dear. When you marry"—she paused to look deep into my eyes—"make sure he loves you, *really* loves you."

"I will."

She leaned back against a pillow. "You didn't mention the purpose of your trip to France, dear."

I looked at her with a new understanding. "What you said about love, Mother—that's exactly why I'm going. I need to be certain."

Chapter 15

The Foreign Services travel code worked just like Mary said. My hands had trembled at the dock, and a skeptical young soldier had looked me over suspiciously, but at the mention of Edward Naughton, he'd handed me a slip of paper containing my cabin assignment and waved me on.

On the final day of the grueling voyage, green from seasickness, I began to wonder whether I was making the trip in vain. Even if I did get to see Westry, would he want to see me? It had been more than a year since our strained good-bye on Bora-Bora, and he hadn't called or written. Sure, it would have been difficult, given the intensity of fighting in Europe, but he might have tried. He didn't even try.

"Coming ashore," the cabin steward called out from the hallway outside my room. "All passengers secure your belongings."

I looked out the tiny window. Through the

foggy mist, the sleepy port of Le Havre waited in the distance, with Paris just a short train ride away. Doubt seeped into my heart. *What am I doing here? It's been a year.* A very long year. *Am I merely chasing a dream that has long since died?* I reached for my bag and shook off the thought. *I've come this far; I will see this through.*

I stood on Mary's street, Saint Germaine, looking up at the stone building above—stately, with little terraces adorned with potted flowers and plants. Candlelight flickered inside. I wondered what kind of life Mary had been living here during the city's occupation, and I wondered about Edward and how their story had unfolded. *Did the letter change everything? Did he take her back? Was it a happy ending?* It was late, nearly ten, but it warmed me to see city dwellers crowding in cafes and restaurants, lovers strolling arm in arm. And yet, reminders of the horror that the city had endured were ever present. A Nazi flag lay near a Dumpster, partially burned and ripped at the center. The green awning of a bakery across the street was blackened from fire. One of its windows had been boarded up. A yellow Star of David dangled from the door.

I proceeded inside Mary's building, checking the apartment number again before knocking quietly. Moments later, I heard footsteps approaching and then the sound of a latch opening.

"Anne!" Mary cried. "You came!"

My eyes filled with tears as I embraced my old friend. "I have to pinch myself," I said. "It hardly seems possible that I *am* here."

"You must be exhausted," she said.

I took a deep breath. "Mary, I have to know. How's Westry? Have you seen him recently? Is he . . . ?"

Mary looked at her feet. "I haven't been to the hospital in a few days," she said quietly. "But, Anne, I can tell you his injuries are serious. He was shot. Multiple times."

The air suddenly felt thick, toxic. The tears stung. "I can't bear to lose him, Mary."

My old friend wrapped her arm around me. "Come, we'll get you comfortable," she said. "Save your tears for tomorrow."

I followed Mary inside, where she turned on two lamps and motioned for me to sit with her on a sofa with gold-plated trim. All around were walls decorated in toile panels.

"It's a beautiful home," I muttered, still thinking of Westry.

Mary shrugged. She looked out of place in the apartment, like a schoolgirl dressed in her mother's evening gown. "I won't be here much longer," she said, offering no further details. "Care for a sandwich? A croissant?" I looked at her left hand and noticed that her ring finger was bare. Instinctively, I covered the diamond solitaire on mine with my right hand, remembering how I'd hidden it away on the island.

"I'm fine," I said, "thank you." *What's different about Mary?* She wore her hair, the color of tawny hay, in the same fashion. Her smile still hid the crooked teeth. But her eyes . . . yes, her eyes had changed. Deep sadness had taken up residence, and I longed to know the story.

"And Edward?" The name echoed in the night air, and the second it escaped my lips, I wished I could retract the question.

"There is no Edward," she said blankly, turning her gaze out the window to the sparkling lights of Paris and the great river Seine in the distance. "Not anymore." She paused again, before turning to me. "Listen, I'd rather not talk about any of that, if it's all the same to you."

I nodded quickly. "I can't imagine what you've been through here—I mean, during the occupation."

Mary ran her hand through her thin hair. "It was simply terrible, Anne," she said. "I'm lucky to still be here, being American and all. Fortunately, my college French got me through. The papers Edward—" She paused, as if the mere mention of his name jarred her. "The papers he had drawn up protected my identity. It's a miracle I wasn't found out, given my help with the Resistance."

"Mary, how frightening. You're very brave."

Her eyes looked sad, distant. "The Nazis making their sweeps," she continued, "the fear that if you said the wrong thing, sneezed the wrong way, you'd be taken in for questioning. And the poor Jewish families, removed from their homes." She paused, pointing toward the door. "There were three in this building. A family of four just down the hall. We tried to save them"— she held up her hands—"but, we were too late. God knows if they'll ever return."

I blinked hard. "Oh, Mary."

She shook her head as if to repress another memory, one that might have been too painful to recount, then pulled a handkerchief from the pocket of her dress. "I'm sorry," she said. "I thought I could talk about this with you, but I'm afraid—I'm afraid it's all too painful."

I took her hand in mine, noticing the tiny pink scar on her wrist. Memories of Bora-Bora came rushing back. "Please," I said, "let's not speak of the past."

Mary sighed. "I'm afraid it will be with me always."

"But the city was spared," I said, searching for a positive note.

"Yes," Mary replied. "A miracle. For a while we thought it all might go up in flames, and us with it."

"Mary," I said cautiously, "how is it that you

ended up here? Did you come because of . . . the letter I gave you before you left Bora-Bora?"

She rubbed her hands together in her lap. "If only the answer was that simple," she said nostalgically. "No, I was a fool to come here."

I wished, for a moment, that I'd kept the letter in my possession, to save Mary from the heartache she felt then. And yet without that letter, Mary wouldn't have been in Paris. She wouldn't have found Westry. She couldn't have called. I marveled at how our stories intertwined, and I longed for hers to have a happy ending, just as I hoped mine would.

"Where will you go next?" I asked, searching her face for a sign that she would be all right—a glimmer in her eye, a half smile, anything.

But instead, she looked gravely out the window. "I haven't decided yet."

The lights of Paris sparkled, and my heart lightened when I thought of Westry. He was out there, somewhere.

"Will you go with me to the hospital tomorrow? I'm terribly nervous about seeing him, after . . . all this time."

For a moment, the haze in Mary's eyes vanished. "Of course I will," she said. "You know, Stella's here too."

"She is?"

"Yes," she continued. "She's been here since last month."

"And Will?"

"He's here too. They're getting married in a month or so."

"That's wonderful," I said, grinning. "I'd love to see her."

"She and Will took a train down south for a few days," she said. "She'll be disappointed to have missed you."

"What time should we leave for the hospital in the morning?"

Mary glanced out the window again. "Visiting hours begin at nine. We can catch a cab over first thing. Now, your room is down the hall—second door on the left. You must be exhausted. Go get some rest." She tried her best to smile, but the corners of her mouth seemed stiff and heavy, paralyzed with grief.

"Thank you, Mary," I said, gathering my bags.

I took a final look into the living room before turning down the mahogany-paneled hall toward the bedroom. Mary sat on the sofa, motionless, hands folded in her lap, looking out at the Seine and the shimmer of a liberated Paris.

Something had happened here, inside these walls. Yes, something unspeakable. I could feel it.

The First U.S. General Hospital loomed in the distance, and I squeezed Mary's hand tightly as we stood gazing up at its enormous facade. The sun shone in the sky, but all around the building were shadows.

I gulped. "Why does it look so . . ."

"Evil?"

"Yes," I said, squinting up at the highest story.

"Because it was a place of evil," she said, "before the Allies arrived."

Mary explained that the twelve-story gray building, formerly the Beaujon Hospital, the largest in Paris, had once been a Nazi stronghold. After the takeover, Major General Paul Hawley, a surgeon, transformed the building, clearing out rooms of medical equipment the Germans had used for gruesome medical experiments, mostly on Jews and Poles. Now it had a red cross painted on the highest story, a cross that rather looked like a bomber airplane, I thought.

Mary pointed to a window a few stories up in the distance. "See right up there? The open window on the seventh floor?"

I nodded.

"That's where I found a Polish woman and her infant," she said quietly, "starved to death. Nazi doctors used them for a research experiment. They watched through a window, documenting the whole thing. I read the paperwork. It took her nine days to die. Her baby, eleven."

I shivered.

"But the horror has ended," Mary said solemnly. "General Hawley turned this place around. There's been nearly a thousand admits in the last two weeks, and we expect many more."

I couldn't take my eyes off of the seventh floor. "Anne?"

"Yes," I muttered weakly.

"Are you ready for this?"

"I hope so," I said.

Together we walked up the stairs and into the building. Darkness lingered palpably in the stiff and heavy air. A structure could not endure such evil without absorbing some of it. Walls could be scrubbed, floors waxed, but the scent of evil remained.

Mary pressed the elevator's ninth-floor button and we began our ascent. As the lights on the panel shifted, my mind reeled. First floor, second. *Will he be conscious enough to recognize me?* Third floor. *Does he still love me?* Fourth floor. *What might be next for us?*

"Oh, Mary," I said, clutching her arm. "I'm so frightened."

She neither comforted me nor acknowledged my fear. "It's the right thing to do, coming here," she said. "No matter what, you'll have closure."

I sighed. "Have you been in touch with Kitty?"

Mary looked uncomfortable for a moment, and I knew by her expression that she'd gotten wind of our history, our troubles on the island.

"About that," she said nervously. "There's something I need to tell you. Since I called you, there's been—"

The elevator stopped suddenly on the fifth floor, and a doctor and two nurses entered the car, silencing our conversation.

We stepped off on the ninth floor, and I gasped at the sight. Perhaps three hundred, maybe more, wounded men lay on cots with dark green wool blankets pulled over their limp bodies.

"This is a tough floor," Mary said. "A lot of serious cases here."

My heart pounded loudly inside my chest. "Where is he?" I said, looking around frantically. "Mary, take me to him."

A nurse about my age approached us and nodded at Mary without a smile. "I thought you were off today."

"I am," Mary said. "I'm here on my friend's behalf. She'd like to visit Mr. Green."

The nurse looked at me and then back at Mary. "*Westry* Green?"

The sound of his name on another woman's breath sent a shiver through my body.

"Yes," Mary said, "*Westry* Green."

The nurse turned to me. Her eyes narrowed. "And you are?"

"Anne," I muttered. "Anne Calloway."

"Well," she said, giving Mary a knowing look, then glancing back toward the room of men behind her, "I'm not sure that . . ." She sighed. "I'll check."

When she was out of earshot, I turned to Mary. "I don't understand. Why did she act so strange?"

Mary looked around the room, out the window—anywhere but at my face.

"Mary," I pleaded. "What happened?"

"Let's sit down," she said, leading me by the arm to a bench a few feet behind us. A clock ticked overhead, taunting me with each movement of its hand.

"When I called you," she said, "I didn't have all the information. I didn't know that Westry—"

We both looked up when we heard footsteps approaching, clicking on the wood floors. My eyes widened when I saw a familiar face approaching. "Kitty!" I cried, leaping to my feet. Despite the past, I found myself unable to resist the urge to run into the arms of my old friend, to embrace her with the love and forgiveness we both owed one another.

But I stopped quickly when my eyes met Kitty's, the eyes of a stranger. "Hello," she said stiffly.

Mary rose and stood by my side. "Kitty," she said, "Anne has traveled a great distance to see Westry. I'm hoping we can take her to him."

Kitty frowned. "I'm afraid that won't be possible."

I shook my head, blinking hard as my eyes

began to sting. "Why, Kitty?" I cried. "Is he hurt badly? Is he unconscious?"

Kitty looked down at my engagement ring, and I wished I'd thought to take it off. The nurse who greeted us moments ago reappeared and stood in solidarity next to Kitty. *What are they hiding from me?*

"Kitty," I pleaded, "what is it?"

"I'm sorry, Anne," she said coldly. "I'm afraid the fact of the matter is that Westry doesn't want to see you."

The room began to spin, and I clutched Mary's arm for support. *My God. I traveled all the way from Seattle, and now I stand mere feet away from him and he doesn't want to see me?*

"I don't understand," I stammered, feeling waves of nausea churn in my stomach. "I only want to—"

Kitty clasped her hands together and turned back to the floor. "Again, I'm very sorry, Anne," she said as she walked away. "I wish you all the best."

I watched her proceed into the room, turning right, where she disappeared behind a curtain.

"Let's go, Anne," Mary whispered, reaching for my hand. "I'm so sorry, dear. It was wrong of me to bring you here. I should have explained—"

"Explained what?" I cried. "That I would be barred from seeing the only man I've ever loved by . . . my best friend?" I listened to my own words echoing in the air, surprised by their raw honesty. Gerard may have had my hand, but Westry would always have my heart. I broke free from Mary's grasp. "No," I said firmly.

I pushed past Mary and into the room of injured men. The sounds that had been muffled near the elevator now amplified to reveal moaning, babbling, crying, laughing. The range of human emotion on the floor was maddening.

I walked faster through the aisles of beds, scanning face after face. Some looked up at me longingly; others just stared ahead. *Where is he? Surely if I find him, if I look into his eyes, he'll have a change of heart? Surely he still loves me? I won't let Kitty stand between us. I won't let her speak for Westry.* My heart fluttered as I weaved through the rows of men, praying that just around the corner I'd see the familiar hazel eyes that had captured my heart on the island.

Minutes later, however, I had combed through every aisle without finding a trace of Westry. I looked around the floor frantically, then remembered Kitty slipping behind a curtained area in the distance. *Could he be inside?* Clutching my locket, I walked across the room, stopping in front of the gray-and-white-striped curtain. *Could this swath of fabric be all that separates Westry from me?*

My hands trembled as I lifted the edge of the curtain, just far enough to peer inside. Four hospital beds, all occupied by soldiers, lay inside. I gasped when I made out the face of the man in the bed farthest away.

Westry.

My legs weakened when I saw his face— thinner now, with a shadow of stubble around his chin, but just as handsome, just as perfect as I'd memorized in my heart. I pulled the curtain back farther, but stopped quickly when I saw Kitty approaching his bed. She pulled up a chair, and I watched as she ran a wet towel over his face, lightly, lovingly, before caressing his forehead. He gazed up at her with a smile that made my cheeks burn.

I felt a tug at my waist, and then heard Mary's voice. "Anne," she said, "don't do this to yourself. Let him go."

I shook my head. "But, Westry, my Westry!" I cried, releasing my grasp on the curtain and burying my head against Mary's shoulder. "How could she? How could she, Mary?"

Mary lifted my chin, and dabbed my cheeks with a rose-colored handkerchief. "I'm so sorry, honey," she said. "Let's go."

I followed her to the elevator, then stopped, reaching into my purse for a scrap of paper and pen.

Mary looked confused when I sat down on the bench. "What are you doing?"

Moments later, I stood and handed her a folded

slip of paper. "Tomorrow," I said, "after I'm gone, will you give this to Westry?"

Mary took the paper in her hands and looked at it skeptically.

"Kitty will intercept any letter I try to send here," I continued. "My only hope is you."

Mary eyed the paper cautiously. "Are you sure you want to say anything more to him?"

I nodded. "I need him to read this."

"Then I'll make sure he gets it," she said, but I could hear a strain in her voice that worried me. "I work the morning shift tomorrow. I can try to give it to him then."

"Promise?" I said, searching her face for the assurance I needed.

"Yes," she said softly. Exhaustion permeated her voice. "I'll do my best."

Seattle did little to take my mind off of Westry. More than a month had passed since that dark day in Paris, and even with the familiar distractions of life at home and a wedding just weeks away, I couldn't get him out of my mind, or my heart. I jumped every time the phone rang, and sat by the window each morning, eagerly awaiting the mail. Surely after he read the note Mary had delivered, he'd write, or call? *Why hasn't he written?*

Then, on a quiet Tuesday morning when Maxine and I were getting ready to go into town, the doorbell rang. I dropped my purse, and a tube of lipstick fell to the floor, rolling underneath the sofa.

"I'll get that," I called to Maxine. I opened the front door to find a postman standing outside.

"Good morning, ma'am," he said. "Miss Calloway?"

"Yes," I said. "I am she."

He handed me a small envelope. "A telegraph for you," he said, grinning. "From Paris. If I can just get you to sign right here."

My heart lightened as I scrawled my signature on his clipboard and ran up the stairs to my bedroom. Safe behind the closed door, I ripped open the envelope. A yellow slip of paper with five typewritten lines nestled inside. I held it up to the light and took a deep breath:

```
Came home early from trip
   STOP
Mary is dead STOP
Hung herself the morning of
   September 18 STOP
Edward broke her heart,
   irreparably STOP
Sending love and well wishes
   from Europe, Stella STOP
```

I stared at the paper for a long time, letting the words sink in until the haze of shock lifted. *"No!"* I screamed. *Not Mary. Not you, Mary.* I remembered the sadness in her eyes, the hesitation. She'd endured more heartache than any woman should, but to end things like *that? How could she?* Tears trickled down my cheeks as I crumpled the paper and threw it to the floor.

Moments later, my pulse raced faster. *Dear God, when did Stella say she hung herself?* I retrieved the scrap of paper. *September 18. No. No, this can't be.*

I stared at the wall in horror. Mary never made it to her shift the day after we'd visited the hospital. She died before she had a chance to deliver my note to Westry.

"Are you ready?" Gerard stood in the doorway on the morning of our wedding, two weeks later. Spurning tradition, he had insisted upon picking me up and taking me to the church before the ceremony, maybe because he was worried I wouldn't come any other way.

I looked at him in the doorway, dashing in a tux, with a perfect white rose pinned proudly to his lapel. Mother's words rang in my ears: *When you marry, make sure he loves you, really loves you.*

I thought of Westry and Kitty's tender moment in the Paris hospital. *How naive I was to assume he'd wait for me, to assume he still loved me. And what does it matter now if he got the note or not?* I looked at Gerard with new appreciation. *He loves me. He will always love me. That will be enough for a lifetime.*

"Yes," I said, gulping back the hurt, the pain, the ghosts of my past and weaving my hand in his. "I'm ready."

As I stood, my gold locket dangled from my neck, before settling itself once again over my heart.

Chapter 16

"So you married Grandpa," Jennifer said, her voice pulling me back to the present. The sun had set, leaving just a line of pink on the horizon outside the window.

I smiled, wiping away a tear with the handkerchief in my hand. "Of course I married Grandpa. And aren't you glad I did? After all, you wouldn't have been here any other way."

Jennifer looked dissatisfied with the answer. "So I owe my existence to your heartache?"

"Nonsense," I said reassuringly. "I loved your grandfather."

"But not in the same way you loved Westry."

I nodded. "There are all sorts of love. I've come to realize this in my life." I thought of Gerard—strong, sure Gerard. I missed the way he'd nuzzle my cheek or greet me with the morning paper and a poached egg on a plate with golden brown toast. He'd devoted his life to me, giving me his whole heart freely, when I let him have only a piece of mine. For in my heart, I'd kept a room locked, where a candle burned for someone else.

"Oh, Grandma," Jennifer said, leaning her head against my shoulder. "Why didn't you tell me this story sooner? How lonely to keep it to yourself all these years."

I patted my locket. "No, dear," I said. "I have never been alone. You see, when you share love with someone, even for a time, it always remains in your heart." I unclasped the locket and let the tiny bit of wood from the bungalow's floor fall into my palm. Jennifer hovered over it, marveling at the sight.

"No," I said again, "I have never been alone."

Jennifer frowned. "But what about Kitty? What about Westry? Didn't you ever try to find them?"

"No," I said. "The day I married your grandfather, I vowed to let it all go, each of them. I had to. It was only fair to him."

"But what about the bungalow, the painting? And what about your promise to Tita? Remember what she said about finding justice?"

I felt a deep exhaustion setting in. "And I haven't forgotten," I said honestly.

"I'm coming with you," Jennifer said, nodding with determination.

"Coming with me?"

"To Bora-Bora."

I smiled. "Oh, honey, you're very sweet, but I really don't think—"

"Yes," she said, ignoring my apprehension. Her eyes looked wild with excitement. "We'll go together."

I shook my head. The retelling of the story had opened up old wounds that felt raw again, as painful as the day they were inflicted. "I don't think I can."

Jennifer looked deep into my eyes. "Don't you understand, Grandma? Don't you see? You have to."

The airplane rattled and shook as it made its descent over the Tahitian islands. "We're experiencing a little more turbulence than normal, folks," a male flight attendant with an Australian accent chirped over the intercom. "Sit tight. The captain will have us safely landed in no time."

I closed my eyes, recalling the flight into Bora-Bora so many years ago, with Kitty by my side and a cabin full of eager nurses listening, with bated breath, as old Nurse Hildebrand warned us of an island full of danger. I sighed, remembering the way Kitty had softly touched my arm, thanking me for coming and promising me that I'd be glad I did. *Would I take it all back if I could?*

The plane jolted violently, and Jennifer turned to me. "Don't worry, Grandma," she said lovingly.

I squeezed her hand tighter as I looked around the cabin filled with young couples, presumably honeymooners. A young man in a seat to our right gently smoothed his bride's hair, kissing her hand as the two looked out the window to the island below. I couldn't help but feel envious. *How lucky they are to have found the island this way, without the complications of war or time.* I longed to be twenty-one again. To start over again from this point forward, with Westry seated beside me.

"Ready?" Jennifer asked, rousing me from my thoughts. The plane had landed, and I stood up quickly, following my granddaughter to the open door, where passengers were already making their way down the steps.

A flight attendant pinned a purple orchid to my shirt, so deeply colored I wondered if it had been spray-painted. "Welcome to Bora-Bora, ma'am," she said. "You will love this island."

"I have always loved this island," I said, smiling, taking in a breath of the warm, humid air. A bustling airport stood where a single runway had seventy years prior. The emerald hillside was now dotted with homes. Everything had changed, and yet the familiar floral scent lingered in the air, and the turquoise water sparkled in the distance, beckoning me to its shore. I knew it then: My heart was home.

"Take my hand, Grandma," Jennifer said, reaching out to steady me.

I shook my head, feeling stronger, steadier than I had in years. "I can do this," I said, making my way down the steps. *Yes,* I said to myself, *I can do this.*

A shuttle deposited us at our hotel, the Outrigger Suites, just a mile from the airport. Jennifer pushed the key card into the door, and we set our bags down in the air-conditioned room.

"Look at that view!" Jennifer exclaimed, pointing to the window ahead. A set of French doors framed a stunning picture of sand and surf, which is when something familiar caught my eye.

"My God," I said, walking closer to the window. "The formation of the sand . . . it's remarkable."

"What is it?" Jennifer asked, running to my side. "What do you see?"

"Well, I may be mistaken, but I think this hotel was built on the old base!" I cried. "I know that beach, the way it hooks up at the shore. The reef below the sparkling water." I shook my head, expecting to see Nurse Hildebrand or Kitty, or— I sighed—Westry walking toward me from the sea. "To be here again, it's just . . ." I opened the doors and walked outside onto the balcony. Jennifer didn't follow.

"Take all the time you need, Grandma," she said quietly. "I'll be inside."

I sat down in a wicker chair on the balcony and let my mind, my heart become mesmerized by the familiar waves.

I ventured back inside the room an hour later, and found Jennifer asleep on one of the beds. I took a spare blanket from the hall closet and spread it over her softly before reaching for a pad of paper on the desk nearby. I knew where I had to go.

> My dear,
> I've gone out walking. I didn't want to wake you. I'll be back before dinner.
> > Love,
> > Grandma

I reached for my straw hat and made my way outside the hotel, beyond the pool, where women in bikinis lay baking in the hot sun; past the bar by the beach, where couples sipped fruity cocktails; and out to the open shore, which, aside from an occasional home nestled along the edge of the sand, was just as quiet, just as pristine as it had been the day I left.

At once, I was twenty-one again, in nurse's garb, sneaking off to the beach after a long shift in the infirmary, head peeking over my shoulder to make sure I wasn't being followed, heart pounding in anticipation of seeing *him*.

I trudged along. The sand felt heavier around my soles now. I wiped a bead of sweat from my brow and pulled my hat down lower, protecting my weathered face from the sun's unrelenting rays. I searched the palm-lined shore. *Where is it? Surely just a few paces farther?*

Birds called overhead as I pressed on, scanning the thicket with every step. *It has to be here. Somewhere.*

Twenty minutes later, I stopped, out of breath, and sank into a shady spot on the sand, freeing a deep sigh from the depths of my heart. *Of course the bungalow is gone. How could I be so foolish to think it would still be here waiting for me?*

"Excuse me, ma'am?"

I looked up when I heard a male voice nearby.

"Ma'am, are you all right?"

A man, perhaps in his sixties, not much older than my eldest son, was approaching, with a woman of about the same age. She wore a blue sundress, and her dark hair was pulled back loosely in a clip.

"Why yes," I said, collecting myself.

"I'm Greg, and this is my wife Loraine," he said. "We live right here on the hillside."

"I'm Anne," I replied. "Anne Call—" I stopped myself, marveling at the slipup. I'd been Anne

Godfrey the majority of my life, and yet here on the island, the name felt wrong.

"Anne Calloway," I finished.

Loraine looked at her husband, then back at me. "Anne *Calloway?*"

"Yes," I said, confused by the recognition in her voice. "I'm sorry, have we met before?"

The woman shook her head, and then gave her husband a look of astonishment. "No," she said, kneeling down next to me. "But we have hoped to meet you for a very long time."

"I don't understand," I said, searching her face.

"Can you believe this?" Loraine marveled, shaking her head at Greg before turning back to me. "You lived on this island during the war, didn't you?"

I nodded.

"There's an old beach bungalow near here," she continued cautiously. "You've seen it, haven't you?"

"Yes," I said. "But how do you know this?"

She turned to her husband and then back to me. "He always said you'd come."

"He?"

"Mr. Green," she said.

I shook my head, feeling my heart rate quicken. I folded my hands in my lap. "I don't understand. You know of the bungalow? And"—I gulped— "Westry?"

The woman nodded, and her husband stood

307

up, pointing to the stretch of shore behind me.

"It's just back this way, near our home," he said. "The brush has grown quite a bit since you've been here. You must have missed it."

I rose quickly. The stiffness in my legs reminded me that I wasn't twenty-one anymore. "Will you take me there?"

"Yes," he said, smiling.

We walked for a few minutes in silence. Occasionally the couple glanced at me with concern, but I did not return their gaze, instead preferring to let the sound of the surf absorb my thoughts. *Do I want to know the secrets they've kept, about the bungalow, about Westry?*

Greg stopped suddenly, pointing toward the jungle, thick with palms. "Right through there," he said.

"Thank you," I replied, pushing through the brush until I came to a little clearing ahead.

"Wait, Ms. Calloway," he called out from the beach.

I turned around.

"You should know that it isn't what it once was."

I nodded and walked on, pushing past aggressive vines, some reaching out as if they intended to wrap their tendrils around my frail arms. I looked right, then left. *Where is it?* Then, an overgrown hibiscus caught my eye. Not yet in bloom, tiny yellow buds pushed up from its leaves. My heart pounded. *It has to be near.*

I pushed another vine out of my way, and there it was—still standing, but barely. The thatched roof had weakened and collapsed in places. The woven walls were thinning, completely gone on one side, and the front door was missing. I took a deep breath, remembering the way Westry and I had discovered the little hut so many years ago. Now look at it.

The front step had eroded, so I had to raise my body up three feet to the entrance, not an easy task at my age. My arms ached as I hoisted myself inside, the sound of which startled a bird that squawked and flew quickly out an open-air window.

I stood up, brushed the dust off my pants, and looked around the room with awe. The bed with its rumpled bedspread, the mahogany desk and chair, the curtains I'd made, though ragged and falling from the hooks—everything was still there, in its place. I looked up at the wall where the painting had once hung. *Will it be under the bed, wrapped in burlap the way Westry and I left it?*

I took a deep breath and knelt down, patting my hand under the bed. A lizard ran out, and I jumped back. Moments later I regained my composure and pulled up the bedspread to let more light under the bed. There, a few feet back, lay a lonely scrap of burlap. But the painting was gone.

I stood and collapsed into the chair, feeling the

weight of seventy years of emotion. Of course it was gone. *How naive I've been to think it might still be here.*

When I stood up again, the floors creaked below my feet, and I smiled as I thought of the makeshift mailbox Westry and I had once shared. It would be silly to think there might be a letter waiting inside. And yet I crouched down anyway, fighting back tears as I ceremoniously lifted the old floorboard and peered inside. I pushed my hand into the little dark space below, feeling around until my fingertips hit something soft, solid.

A book. No, a journal of some kind. I pulled out the leather-bound notebook, fanning its pages to release years of dust.

The light was growing dim, and I knew the sun would be setting soon. I squinted as I opened the cover to read the first page:

Letters to Anne, from Westry . . .

My God. He returned. Just like he promised.
I fumbled to the second page, my eyes desperate to read the words and my heart eager to soak them up, when I heard a voice outside.

"Ms. Calloway?"

Greg's voice echoed through the air outside. I closed the journal reluctantly and tucked it into my bag. "Yes," I said, rising, "I'm here."

I stood in the doorway as he and his wife approached. "Oh, good," he said. "We didn't want to leave you out here all alone too long. Let me help you down."

He reached two strong arms up and clasped them gently around my waist, lowering me to the ground.

Loraine looked at the bungalow, and then at me. "Did you find what you were looking for here?"

I glanced back at the little hut. "No," I said, "but I found something else, something better."

She smiled cautiously, as if she knew more than I did about this place, about my story. "Would you like to come back to our terrace, for some tea? Our home is just up the beach."

I nodded. "Thank you. I would like that very much."

Loraine poured black tea from a blue and white kettle. "Cream and sugar?"

"Yes, thank you," I said.

The home was quaint. Just a simple two-bedroom structure nestled near the beach with an ample deck outside. It suited them.

"We've lived here for thirty-five years," Greg said. "Loraine and I used to work in New York City, but after a trip here in the late sixties, we knew we couldn't go back to city life."

"So we stayed," Loraine chimed in. "We opened a restaurant a few miles away."

I envied them, of course. For this was the life that Westry and I might have had, the life I had longed for in my heart.

I took a sip of tea, and then set the white china cup down on its saucer. "You mentioned that you know Westry," I said quietly, afraid of where the sentence might lead.

Greg looked at Loraine and then back at me. "Yes," he said. "We knew him for many years."

My God. They're speaking in past tense. "Knew him?" I asked.

"Yes," Loraine continued. "He came here every year. His yearly pilgrimage, he called it."

"Pilgrimage?"

Greg smiled. "Pilgrimage in hopes of finding you."

I watched the cream swirl in my tea, spiraling around in confusion, just as I felt. I let Greg's words sink in for a few moments, then shook my head, remembering Kitty, remembering the way I'd left Westry that day in the hospital in Paris.

"I don't understand," I said, trying to reconcile the story I believed to be true with the story they were telling me.

Greg took a sip of his tea. "He told us your story," he said. "How you'd fallen in love on this island during the war, and how war had separated you."

I shook my head. "But why didn't he try to find me in Seattle? Why didn't he ever write?"

"He didn't feel it was his place," Loraine explained. "He knew you had a life, a family there. And yet, somewhere in his heart, he believed that you might return, that one day you might be waiting for him in the bungalow, just the way you did in his memories."

I reached down to my feet for my bag, pulling out the brown leather notebook. It pulsed with emotion as I held it in my hands. "I found this," I said. "Letters he wrote me."

"Yes," Loraine continued. "Every year he left you a new one. He left it inside the bungalow, hoping you'd find it." She clasped her hands together and shook her head wistfully. "It was the most romantic thing. Greg and I felt for him, watching him make such a strenuous journey year after year for a man in his condition." She reached for her husband's hand and patted it lovingly. "It was moving to see."

I sat up straighter in my chair. "What do you mean, 'a man in his condition'?"

Greg's eyes narrowed. "You don't know?"

"Know what?"

Loraine gave Greg a disapproving look before leaning in closer to me, as if she was about to reveal something horrifying. "Dear," she said, "Mr. Green was in a wheelchair. He was paralyzed in the war."

I held my hand to my heart to muffle the ache inside. *Paralyzed.* I closed my eyes, remembering the scene in the Paris hospital, where he lay gazing up at Kitty. Had he refused to see me not because of a budding relationship with Kitty, but because of his pride?

"I know this all must be very hard to hear," Loraine said. "I'm sorry if we've said too much; it's just that all these years we've watched this dear man's story unfold, and we hoped that one day we'd see the conclusion. To have you here, Anne, it's truly amazing. Greg and I had hoped you'd come, for Westry's sake, but after so many years, we'd given up hope."

I looked down at the notebook in my hands, trying to make sense of it all. "What about Westry? Where is he now?"

Loraine looked troubled. "We don't know, exactly," she said. "He stopped coming about five years ago. We were terribly afraid that he might have—"

Greg put his hand on Loraine's arm, as if to urge her to be silent. "The notebook you have," he said, "why don't you read it? Perhaps you'll find a clue."

I stood up. "Thank you," I said. "Thank you ever so much, for everything. I should be getting back now. My granddaughter is expecting me."

Loraine stood up beside me. "Let us walk you to your hotel, Ms. Calloway."

I shook my head. "I'll be fine. But thank you." I made my way down the steps to the trail back to the beach. I walked quickly, moving my aching legs along the sand as fast as they'd go, praying I wasn't too late.

Chapter 17

The early morning light shone on the balcony as I made myself comfortable in a wicker chair. Jennifer, out for a jog, would be back in an hour. I opened Westry's journal, turning past the water-stained first page, and let my eyes take in his familiar handwriting:

August 23, 1959

My dearest Cleo,

This is the first letter I have written you since we last saw each other on the island, that final day as the airplanes roared in the distance, taking you one place and me another. I've come back to the bungalow on this day—August 23, the very day we met so long ago—in hopes of finding you, or some memory of you, here, for nearly 20 years have passed and you have not escaped my mind or my heart. You'll be happy to know that the old place has held up well over the years. Everything is as we left it. The curtains, still swinging in the breeze. The desk and chair. The bed. Everything but you.

How I wish you were here, my love. How I wish I could take you in my arms the way I used to. I know you are out there somewhere, living your life, and I do not want to disturb that life. But my heart yearns for you. It always will. And so I will return each year on this day, in hopes that our paths may cross again. I will leave this journal here in our mailbox. I will eagerly anticipate your letter, and you.

Yours,
Grayson

I set the journal down in my lap and marveled at the letter that had taken some fifty years to reach my hands. *He still loves me. God, he still loves me. Just as I love him, as I did in 1959, and as I do today.* And the bungalow—he said it was just as we had left it. *Yet why didn't he mention the painting?* I turned to the next page and continued reading:

August 23, 1960

My dearest Cleo,

I admit, my heart leapt with anticipation as I opened the mailbox and retrieved this journal. I had hoped to see an entry from you, or better yet, to find you here waiting for me. But I've waited all these years, what's one more? I will be patient. I promise, my love.

As time has passed, I've had an opportunity to think. I often wonder why you didn't respond to the letters I sent from the hospital in Paris, or why you didn't come to see me there. Kitty said you had married, but I didn't believe it, not at first. How could you marry after the love we shared?

In any case, I've come to terms with that now, though I still hold out hope that you will return, that we will be reunited. I know that life must go on, but a part of me will never fully live until I am with you again.

Until next year, my love,
Grayson

I closed the journal tightly, too disturbed, too tormented by the unfolding story to read further. Kitty had lied to me at the hospital. She had intercepted his letters. *Why did she do it? If I'd gotten Westry's letters, might things be different?*

I turned to the hotel room when I heard Jennifer at the door. "It's a beautiful morning, Grandma," she said. "You should get out for a walk."

I stood up and nestled the journal in my suitcase, before pulling out Genevieve Thorpe's letter.

"I think we should call her now," I said, more sure of myself than I'd been in years.

Jennifer sat beside me on the bed as I punched the numbers into the phone and then listened to the ringing. One, then two, then three.

A woman's voice answered, speaking a French phrase I didn't understand. "Hello," I said, "this is Anne Call—Anne Godfrey. I'm trying to reach a Ms. Genevieve Thorpe."

The woman's voice switched from perfect French to perfect English. "Why yes, hello, Anne, this is Genevieve speaking."

"I'm here," I said, a little more hesitantly than I'd expected. "I'm here in Bora-Bora."

"My goodness," she said. "What a wonderful surprise! I'd mailed the letter unsure if I'd ever hear from you, much less see you in person. Would it be possible to schedule a meeting before you go?"

"Yes," I said. "It's why I came."

"Is today too soon?"

"No," I said, "it's perfect. We're staying at the Outrigger Suites. Would you like to meet us for a drink?"

"I'd love to," she said. "I've been waiting many years for this visit."

"I suppose I have too," I said. "See you this evening."

I hung up the phone, hoping I hadn't made a mistake.

"Just two tonight?" the hostess asked as Jennifer and I walked into the restaurant.

"No," I said. "We're expecting another guest." Just then, a woman at the bar stood up and waved from across the room. She was striking, petite, with rosy cheeks and light brown curly hair fastened in a gold clip.

"Hello," she said, walking toward Jennifer and me. She couldn't have been much older than my sons, maybe in her sixties. "You must be Anne."

"Yes," I said, trying to place the familiar feeling I sensed when I shook her hand. "And this is my granddaughter, Jennifer."

"Hello to you both," she greeted us warmly. "I'm Genevieve."

"It's so nice to meet you," I said. "Shall we sit down?" She carried a large canvas bag with navy stripes. I wondered what was inside.

"That would be lovely," she replied.

The hostess directed us to a table by the window. When the waiter appeared, I ordered a bottle of white wine.

Genevieve smiled. "I can hardly believe you're here," she said, shaking her head. "You seemed like such a mythical figure. I mean, your name was in the registry of nurses during the war, but you still seemed like such a figment."

A hush fell on the table as the waitress filled our glasses with wine. I took a sip and it warmed me as it traveled down my throat. "So I take it you know of the bungalow about a half mile from here," she said, turning to Jennifer. "Just a little hut. You'd miss it if you blinked."

I nodded. "I know the place."

"It's funny," she said, taking a sip of wine and leaning back in her chair thoughtfully. "The locals won't go near the place. They say it's cursed. I avoided it all my life, especially as a girl. On a picnic with our parents down on that very beach, my brother and I stumbled upon it, but neither of us would dare step inside." She shrugged. "But at some point I suppose my curiosity got the better of me. About twenty-five years ago, I climbed through one of the windows, took a look around. Wouldn't you know it, a week later I found out my husband was having an affair and my mother was dying of breast cancer."

"I'm so sorry," Jennifer said, topping off each of our glasses with more wine.

"So you believe in its curse, then?" I asked.

Genevieve swirled the wine in her glass for a moment. "I don't know," she said. "Part of me does, and yet part of me feels there is so much good that resides there too. I felt it when I was there." She scrunched her nose. "Does that even make sense?

"It does," I said. "It's how I've come to feel about the bungalow myself. I spent a great deal of time there alone."

She reached into her bag and pulled out a small white envelope.

"Here," she said, smiling. "I found this on the floor in a corner of the bungalow. I believe it belongs to you."

I took a deep breath before lifting the flap of the envelope. My fingers felt around inside and met something hard and cold. The sparkle of the blue jewels refracted the setting sun. My pin. The one Kitty had given me. I gasped, reading the inscription on the back, an inscription lost in time. Thick tears welled up in my eyes and the room blurred.

"Surely there were a dozen Annes on the island at one time or another," I said, puzzled. "How did you know this belonged to me?"

"I did my research," she replied, smiling.

"And in your research," I said, pausing, "did you happen to come across a Westry?" I looked at Jennifer. "Westry Green?"

Genevieve nodded. "Yes, I found a book of his, in fact—in the drawer of the desk in the bungalow."

"A book?"

"Yeah," she continued. "Just an old novel from

the nineteen thirties. His name was written on the inside cover."

I grinned, remembering Westry's hope to keep our ties to the bungalow hidden.

"It took me a great deal of time," Genevieve continued, "but I found him. We spoke many years ago, before I'd taken on the project I wrote about. I've tried reaching out to him since, with no luck." She sighed. "The phone number's been changed, and no one seems to know what became of him."

I looked at my lap, folding the ivory napkin there in half, and then in half again.

"I'm sorry," she said. "I don't mean to imply that he—"

"What did he say?" Jennifer asked, swooping in to lighten the moment. "When you spoke?"

Genevieve smiled and gazed up at the ceiling as if to recall the exact details. "It was out of the pages of a novel," she replied. "He said that he once loved you a great deal, and that he still did."

"Why didn't he just call or write?" I said, shaking my head.

Genevieve shrugged. "I suppose he had his reasons. He was eccentric, Mr. Green. I suppose all artists are, though."

I frowned in confusion. *"Artists?"*

"Why yes," Genevieve replied. "Of course, I haven't seen any of his work, but I know that he has, or rather had, quite an impressive collection to his name. Paintings, sculpture. He studied art in Europe after the war, and settled down somewhere in the Midwest, where he taught art at the university level."

"Genevieve," I said, "you said he *had* an impressive collection. What do you mean?"

"He donated it all to various galleries," she said. "I recall him saying that art was meant to be shared, to be seen, not cloistered."

I smiled. "That sounds like the Westry I knew."

Jennifer cleared her throat. "Genevieve, you mentioned that Westry did sculpture," she said, looking at me for approval. "Do you know the medium? Clay? *Bronze?*"

I knew where her mind was going. The island had a way of drawing connections that weren't real.

"I'm not sure," Genevieve said, shrugging. "He was very brief about his work. And I could be wrong entirely. It was so long ago. My memory has faded some."

Jennifer and I watched as she pulled a yellow notebook out of her bag and set it on the table.

"Do you mind if I ask you some questions?" she asked cautiously.

"Of course not," I said, using my right hand to steady the clinking water glass in my left.

"As I said in my letter, a young woman was murdered on this island long ago," she began. "I'm trying to put the story to rest, to find justice."

Jennifer and I exchanged a knowing look.

"I understand that you were a nurse here and

that you were off duty the night of the tragedy." She leaned in closer. "Anne, did you see or hear anything of significance? There's been such a shroud of secrecy around the circumstances of the murder. It's like the island swallowed her up without a single clue. You may be my last hope for justice."

"Yes," I said, "I do know something."

Genevieve opened her notebook. "You do?"

I clasped my hands in my lap, thinking of Westry's convictions about keeping the secret. Even after years of analysis, turning the story over and over again in my brain, I'd never understood his intentions, or whom he'd been protecting. Perhaps bringing the secret to light would give me the answers I'd longed for.

"Atea," I said. "Atea was her name."

Genevieve's eyes widened. "Yes," she said.

Jennifer squeezed my hand under the table.

"She was a beautiful woman," I continued. "I knew her only briefly, but she exuded the goodness of the island."

Genevieve nodded and set her pen down. "Many of the islanders never came to terms with her death," she said. "Even today. The ones who are old enough to remember still speak of it as a great evil that occurred on their shores. It's why I've made it my mission to find justice, for her, for all of them."

"I can help you," I said. "But I'll need to take

you somewhere. I know of a clue that may bring you the justice you're seeking."

The sunset, orange with violet hues, caught my eye outside the window. "It's too late tonight," I said. "But can you meet us near the shore in front of the hotel tomorrow morning?"

"Yes," Genevieve said, smiling gratefully. "I can be there as early as you like."

"How about nine thirty?"

"Perfect," she said. "I can hardly wait."

That evening, Jennifer's cell phone rang inside her purse on the balcony, where I sat watching the waves roll softly onto the shore. The sea sparkled in the light of the crescent moon overhead. "Honey," I called out to her through the French doors, "your phone's ringing."

She bounded out to the terrace in a pair of green pajama pants and fumbled through her bag. "That's funny," she said. "I didn't think I'd get any reception out here."

"Hello?" she said into the phone. I listened halfheartedly to the one-sided conversation. "You're kidding." She listened for what seemed like an eternity. "Oh." She paused, disturbed by something, then smiled. "Well, I'm very grateful. Thank you. Thank you so much. I'll ring you when I'm back in Seattle."

Jennifer ended the call and sat down in the wicker chair next to mine. "It was the woman from the archives," she said, stunned. "They found him. They found the artist."

I blinked hard, remembering her exchange with Genevieve earlier. *Can it be possible?* "He's not . . . is he?" I hated to admit it, but Jennifer's imagination had me hopeful.

"I'm sorry, Grandma," she said. "No. It's not Westry."

I nodded. "Of course," I said, feeling childish for linking the stories the way I had.

She watched a seabird fly overhead, following it with her eyes until it was out of sight. "The artist died four years ago," she continued.

"Sorry, honey," I said, patting her hand.

"It's OK," she replied, forcing a smile. "At least the mystery's solved now—well, sort of. Now that I know who he is, I might be able to talk to his family."

"That's right," I said. "Wish we had a bottle of champagne around."

"Why?"

"To toast the occasion."

Jennifer gave me a confused look.

"Honey," I said, "you finally found your guy."

Jennifer leaned her head against my shoulder. "You'll find yours, too," she said. "I have a feeling that it will all work out."

"Maybe," I said, hoping she couldn't hear the doubt in my voice, because my heart told me I was too late.

• • •

Just as we had planned, Genevieve met us on the beach the next day after breakfast. "Morning," she said, approaching with a cheerful smile. She carried a backpack, and her curly hair pushed out of her white floppy sun hat.

"Thank you so much for meeting me today," she said once we were a good distance away from the hotel. "I can't tell you how exciting it is to be closer to the answers."

"I hope I have the right ones," I said quietly, preparing myself for what lay ahead. "Tell me what you know about the crime already."

"Well," she said, adjusting her backpack, "I know only what the islanders know, or believe they know—that the man who committed the murder was responsible for a series of pregnancies on the island, several native women and an American nurse."

Kitty.

I nodded. "I didn't see him," I said quietly, looking out at the stretch of white sand before us. "It was too dark. But the only man it could have been was Lance."

"Lance?"

"Yes," I said. "He was the man my best friend, at the time, was seeing. He left her in a terrible predicament—pregnant and alone, while he continued his philandering with the native women."

Genevieve stopped suddenly and turned to me. "Anne," she said, "I don't understand. If you knew all of this, why didn't you tell? Why didn't you report it?"

I sighed, clasping my hands tightly together. "I know how it must sound, but it's more complicated than that." The bungalow was close, so I gestured to a bit of driftwood near the shore. "Let's sit for a moment. I'll tell you what I know."

We sat down on a beam that had washed up on the shore, gray and smooth from years of battling with the surf. I pointed behind us. "That," I said, "is where I watched him put a knife to her throat."

Genevieve covered her mouth.

"I hovered in the shadows until he was gone, then ran to her. I held her in my arms as she fought for life, for air." I shook my head. "There was nothing I could do for her. She was dying. Westry appeared moments later. He and I remembered the stash of morphine in my bag. The nurses always kept supplies of it in their medical cases. It could end her pain; we both knew that. I was reluctant at first, but as I watched her labored breathing and heard the way her lungs gurgled, I knew it was the only way. The morphine was more than enough to end her suffering, and end her life. She died in my arms."

Genevieve patted my arm. "You did the right

thing," she said. "It's what any of us would have done in the same situation."

I wiped away a tear. "It's what I've told myself all these years, but in my heart, I knew I could have done more."

"Like report the crime?" Genevieve asked.

"Yes."

"Tell me why you didn't."

I nodded. "It was Westry's idea to keep quiet. He told me it was for our own good, that we would be charged for the murder. But I don't think that was the real reason. Westry would never run from justice unless there was an important reason." I looked out to the shore, remembering him on that night, so sure, so strong. He had known something I hadn't. "He spoke of protecting someone," I continued. "If we went to the authorities on base, he feared that something terrible might happen. I trusted him."

"Do you have any inkling of what he may have meant by that?"

"I don't," I said, throwing my hands in the air. "Believe me, I've thought about that night for seventy years now, and I'm no closer to understanding his concerns than I was seventy years ago."

Genevieve sighed.

"But," I continued, "as I mentioned last night, I do have something to show you. A clue. I tucked it away the night of the murder, hoping it may be of use one day years from then, when the truth was ready to be told. That time may be now."

I stood up, and Genevieve and Jennifer followed my lead.

"Would you like me to take you to it?"

"Yes," Genevieve said eagerly.

Jennifer steadied me as we pushed through the brush and made our way farther into the jungle. *Look at me, schlepping through the jungle at my age.* But age didn't matter now. Nothing mattered but truth, and I was intent on finding it.

I stared ahead, attempting to get my bearings. "Yes," I nodded to myself. "It should be right over here."

The landscape looked different, of course, but I knew when I saw the large palm in the distance that we were close. I pushed ahead of Jennifer and Genevieve and hastened my pace until I reached the base of the old palm. I knelt down and sank my hands into the moist soil, excavating as much dirt as I could. *It has to be here.*

"Can I help?" Genevieve asked, hovering over the pile of dirt I'd amassed with my bare hands.

I shook my head. "Just a few minutes longer, and I should have it." Soil caked my hands and arms. It got under my nails in a way that may have bothered me years ago, but I didn't care now. I'd never been so close to justice. I could smell it. And a moment later I could feel it.

My hand hit something hard about a foot below the surface, and I worked harder to secure an opening to retrieve it. I gasped.

"Grandma, are you OK?" Jennifer whispered, kneeling beside me.

"Yes," I said, producing the package I'd hidden so long ago. I unwrapped the ragged fabric, formerly the hem of my dress, which was now in shreds from moisture and insects, and produced the knife.

"The murder weapon," I said to Genevieve. "I searched for it after he threw it into the jungle, then I buried it hoping to find it again when the time was right."

Like a forensic expert, Genevieve pulled a ziplock bag from her backpack and carefully placed the knife inside. Then she handed me a wet wipe for my hands. "The time is right," she said quietly. "Thank you."

"Don't thank me," I said solemnly. "Just bring Atea the justice she deserves."

"I will," Genevieve replied, examining the knife through the bag. "These inscriptions—the unit and issue numbers—they have to mean something."

"They do," I said. "They'll lead you to Lance."

"Good," she replied, tucking it into her bag. "I can look this up with help from the army's historical society. They keep records of everything from the war. It's how I found you, after all."

I smiled to myself as we walked in silence back to the beach. It felt good to set the truth free, and I felt lighter for it.

Genevieve's cell phone rang inside her backpack, and Jennifer and I excused ourselves to the shore, where I submerged my hands in the salty water, cleansing them of any residual dirt—and evil—that had clung to the knife.

"I'm proud of you, Grandma," Jennifer said, kneeling down next to me. "That took a lot of courage, what you did."

"Thank you, dear," I said, patting my hands dry on my pants. "I should have done it years ago."

We walked back up the beach to where Genevieve stood, still talking on her cell phone. "Yes, honey," she said. "I promise, I'll be home later and we can have that dinner together we talked about." She paused. "Love you too, Adella."

The hair on my arms stood on end. *That name. I haven't heard it uttered since, since . . .* I looked at Jennifer and the expression on her face told me she'd made the connection too.

"Excuse me," I said to Genevieve moments later. The hotel was in sight now, and I could hear the splashing and laughter of swimmers echoing up the shore. "I couldn't help but overhear you say the name Adella."

"Oh," she said, "yes, my daughter."

"It's such a beautiful name," I said. "You don't hear it often."

"You don't," she said. "I've never met another Adella in my life, actually. It's my middle name. I was adopted, you know, and it was supposedly the name my birth mother had chosen for me."

I looked away, unable to hide the emotion rising in my heart.

"My parents felt compelled to keep it," she said, looking thoughtful for a moment. "When my own daughter was born, it was the only name that felt right."

"Anne," she said, concerned, "is something wrong?"

"No," I said, collecting myself. "I'm fine. I was just wondering if you ever met your birth mother or tried to find her."

"Believe me," she said, "I've tried. My parents would tell me nothing of her." She looked lost in thought for a moment, then her mouth formed a smile. "A schoolteacher once told me my mother had to be French because I had a perfect French nose. But, I'll never know. The records were destroyed long ago."

Kitty's daughter. Right here before my eyes. The very baby I helped deliver in the bungalow.

"Well," Genevieve said, clasping her hands together. Now that I'd put the pieces together, I could see that her eyes were the eyes of Kitty in her youth. "Here I am, going on about myself and keeping you out in the hot sun. It's been an emotional morning. I should let you rest. Why don't I come by tomorrow when I have some news about the serial numbers on this knife? I should know something by the afternoon."

I nodded. "That would be lovely," I said, my head spinning.

"We'll have a lot to talk about, then."

"We will," I replied, tucking a stray curl behind her ear, the way I might have done if Kitty had been standing in front of me just then.

Chapter 18

"I'm going to run down to the beach for a while," Jennifer said the next morning. I could smell coconut shampoo in her freshly washed hair as she leaned in close. "Want anything? A croissant? A latte?"

I smiled. "I'm fine, dear."

As the door clicked shut behind her, I pulled out Westry's journal and continued reading his letters. I pored over the yellowed pages, learning about the life he'd led without me, and the love he'd harbored, a love that seemed to grow stronger and clearer by the year. When I reached the final page, dated five years ago, my heart seized:

August 23, 2006

My dearest Cleo,

Here I am again—another year, another August—too old now, to be here, to be here without you. This year hasn't been kind to me. I only hope it was kinder to you, wherever you are.

Do you remember the song we heard transmitted over the radio that night in the bungalow, "La Vie en Rose"? The verse went, "Give your heart and soul to me and life will always be la vie en rose." I suppose this is true of my life. For even without your presence, without your touch, I have still had you with me, always. You gave your heart and soul to me once, and I have never let it go.

Whether we meet again or not, that's all that matters.

La Vie en Rose, my dearest.

Yours, always,
Grayson

Genevieve arrived at our hotel room at three o'clock. Jennifer let her in, and she set her bag down on the desk. "You're never going to believe what I found."

"What?" I said eagerly.

Genevieve sat down on the bed beside me. "The inscription on the knife," she said. "I looked it

335

up." She shook her head in amazement. "It doesn't belong to Lance, Anne."

"My God," I said, shaking my head. "Then who?"

She retrieved her notebook from her bag and opened it to the first page. "It may come as a frightening surprise," she said. "The knife was issued to Colonel Matthew Donahue, the commanding officer of the entire base." She looked at me for an explanation. "There must be some mistake."

I got it all wrong. "No mistake," I said, sitting up straighter. Images from the past ran through my mind—of Kitty, crying on her bed; of Atea, confused and distraught the night of the Christmas service; of Westry's bloodied face in the men's barracks. *Of course it wasn't Lance.* I could see that now. The colonel had been behind it all, every bit of it.

Genevieve looked confused. "No one will ever believe that a commanding officer, a respected one, at that, could have committed such a brutal crime." She paused to retrieve her notebook from her bag. "The only way we can know for sure, the only way we can get our proof, is if we find the American nurse he was involved with and talk to her. Maybe she's the missing piece in all of this. The knife is much too corroded for fingerprints, and the islanders who are old enough to remember won't talk. Believe me, I've tried." She

336

shrugged in defeat. "What are the chances that we could get that nurse on the phone? Not likely, huh?"

"Maybe," I said quietly, pausing to consider what I was about to say. "I happen to know the woman."

Genevieve's eyes widened. "You do?"

"Yes," I said. "Well, I did, anyway. She was a very old friend of mine. My *best* friend, actually. We traveled to the island together, in fact." I paused to survey her face, so like Kitty's. Would it be too late for them?

"What's her name?"

"Kitty. Kitty Morgan." I sighed. "Of course, I don't know what became of her. We haven't spoken since, well, it's been a very long time."

Genevieve's eyes lit up. "I know that name, Kitty. Yes. I believe I took down her information from the staff roster records for the infirmary. At one point I looked up her phone number, though I never called—didn't see any reason to at the time." She thumbed through her notebook, then paused on a page. "Yes, here it is," she continued. "Kitty Morgan Hampton. She lives in California now—well, at least she did two years ago. Anne, would you call her?"

I felt weak all over. "Me?"

"Yes," she said, looking at me expectantly.

"But this is your project," I said. "You should be the one."

337

Genevieve shook her head. "She's more likely to talk to you than . . . a stranger."

If you only knew.

I thought of Kitty's coldness to me in our final month on the island, the way she'd acted toward Westry—the way she'd put herself between us, severing our love forever. No, I couldn't speak to her.

I felt Jennifer's chin on my shoulder. "Time changes people," she whispered. "You loved her once—don't you want to hear her side of the story?"

I did love her, yes. And maybe still. Her memory still affected me, still moved me, after all these years. "All right," I conceded. "I'll make the call."

Jennifer handed me the phone and I hesitantly punched in the numbers written in Genevieve's notebook.

"Hello?" Kitty's voice was raspier now, but the tone was still the same. I froze, unable to find my voice.

"Hello?" she said again. "If this is a telemarketer—"

"Kitty?" I finally said in a squeak.

"Yes?"

"Kitty," my voice cracked, and tears began streaming down my cheeks. "Kitty, it's Anne."

"Anne?"

"Yes!" I cried. "Anne Calloway, Godfrey."

"My God, Anne," she said. "Is it really you?"

"Yes, it's really me."

Jennifer handed me a tissue, and I blew my nose quietly, just as I heard Kitty do on the other end of the line.

"Anne, I—I—" Her voice faltered. "I don't know where to begin. How are you?"

"It's funny," I said. "I'm not sure how to answer that question after all these years. Where do I start?"

"Well," Kitty said softly. The edge in her voice, the one that had shaken me so in Paris, was gone now. The years had softened her tone, and perhaps her heart. "I can start by saying I'm sorry."

"Kitty, I—"

"No, let me finish," she said. "I am not well, Anne. I may not be able to say this to you again, so I must say it now." She paused, as if to collect her thoughts. "I should have reached out to you years ago. I don't know why I didn't. I'm ashamed."

"Oh, Kitty," I said, wiping another tissue under my eyes to sop up the tears seeping out.

"I regret everything about the way I behaved on the island, and in Paris," she continued. "I froze after the birth. I sank into a dark place I didn't understand. I know now it was depression—what they call postpartum depression, my daughter tells me. But I—"

I looked at Genevieve watching quietly from the chair near the desk, so like Kitty in more ways than I could count: beautiful, vibrant, impulsive. "Kitty, you have a daughter?"

"Well, yes, I have three—well, four. . . ." Her voice trailed off. "I married a good man, you'll be happy to know. I met him in Paris after the war, a Marine. We moved to California. It's been a nice life." The line went quiet for a moment. "Has your life been nice, Anne? I've often thought of you."

"It has," I said quietly. "In almost every way."

Kitty sighed. "Anne, there's something I need to tell you, about Westry."

How can his name still stir up such emotion in me? Such pain? I closed my eyes tightly.

"He talked about you incessantly in Paris," she said. "He was always asking about you and hoping you'd come."

"I did come," I said. "You remember, of course."

"Yes." I could hear Kitty's shame, feel it ricocheting across the Pacific. "I was jealous of what you had," she said.

"So you intercepted his letters to me?"

Kitty gasped. "You know?"

"I only recently found out," I said.

"Anne, I'm ashamed of myself," she said tearfully. "To think I may have changed the course of your life by my actions. I can hardly bear it."

In an instant, the anger that had churned in my heart lost its steam. "You have my forgiveness," I said. "What you said earlier about time running out—I feel that too."

"I still have my pin," she said after a pause. "The one I gave you at the Cabaña Club. It's in my jewelry box. Anne, I look at it often and think of you."

I remembered the exact moment she'd given me the piece, her gesture of enduring friendship. I closed my eyes and could immediately picture the little box wrapped in crisp blue paper and tied with a gold ribbon. The smoke of the Cabaña Club swirled around us. If only that pin could have held our bond. Or maybe it had. I retrieved it from my pocket and turned it over in my hand, eyeing the engraving.

"I still have mine, too, Kitty," I said. "I have it right here."

"How I'd love to see you again," Kitty said. "Where are you? Seattle?"

"No," I said. "I'm in Bora-Bora."

"Bora-Bora?"

"Yes, I'm here with a woman who's researching a crime that was committed on the island, a murder."

Kitty was quiet for a moment. "You're referring to Atea, aren't you?"

"Yes," I said. "You remember."

"Of course I remember."

I decided not to ask her how she knew of the story. That didn't matter now. "I wanted to ask you some questions," I said cautiously, "if you don't mind."

"Go ahead."

"We never spoke of who the father of your baby was," I continued. "I'd always assumed it was Lance, but now we have evidence linking the murder of Atea to—"

"To the colonel?"

"Yes," I said. "You know?"

"I do," she explained. "And so did Westry."

"I don't understand."

"He was protecting me, Anne," she said, "by not telling. Before the murder, he'd gotten wind of my situation, even before you. He saw us together and overheard a conversation on the beach. Westry also knew the colonel had had similar encounters with island women. I was headstrong and naive. Westry warned me about him, but I wouldn't listen."

I recalled the brutal beating in the barracks. "He threatened Westry, didn't he?"

"Yes," Kitty continued. "The colonel warned him that if he tried to intervene or report any of it to his superiors on the mainland, he'd do something terrible to me."

"My God, Kitty!" I exclaimed. "So by keeping quiet about Atea's murder, Westry was protecting *you?*"

"Yes," she said. "Looking back, I think I was in more danger than I ever knew. Westry spared me from all of that."

I sighed. "It's why you began to develop feelings for him, isn't it?"

"I suppose," Kitty said honestly. "After being treated so terribly by men all my life, here was a man, an honest man, who cared, who wanted to protect me. And yet, he was already in love with my best friend."

I gazed out the window to the shore, remembering the way Kitty had looked at Westry. I couldn't blame her for loving him.

"Anyway," she continued, "Atea was murdered because he got her pregnant, and she refused to keep quiet, just like the other women."

"The other women?"

"Yes," she said. "There were at least two others, one barely fourteen." She paused in the wake of such a disturbing revelation. "I should have come forward about this long ago, but I've had to move on. And after I heard of his death, I decided that he would burn in hell anyway."

"When did he die?"

"Nineteen sixty-three," she said. "A heart attack, alone in a San Francisco hotel room."

I sat up straighter, looking at Jennifer, then at Genevieve. "It doesn't mean justice can't still be served," I said. "He's a decorated war veteran. We'll have the military revoke his status posthumously. I'll see to that."

Genevieve nodded in agreement. *How will she feel when she realizes the man at the center of this evil was her own father?* I took a deep breath, for what I was about to say would

343

change everything, for both of them.

"Kitty," I said, gesturing for Genevieve to come over to the phone. "There's someone I'd like you to speak to. Her name is Genevieve. I think you two have more in common than you know. Her daughter, for instance . . . well, I think you two should talk."

Genevieve gave me a confused look, but reached for the phone and smiled. "Ms. Hampton?"

I walked away from the bed, and gestured for Jennifer to follow. She nodded knowingly, and we closed the door quietly behind us.

"That may have been the best thing that could have come from all of this," Jennifer said, smiling at me in the hallway.

We walked arm in arm down the stairs to the open-air lobby, where we sat together watching the waves crash fiercely on the shore, catching sunbathers off guard and scattering them with sea-soaked towels up to the higher bank. I marveled at the sight. It was as if the island knew that justice had come and was cleansing its shores of the evil.

I ran my finger along the chain of my locket, wondering if what Tita had said could be true. *The curse she spoke of, will it now be broken?* Only time would tell.

Chapter 19

The phone rang in the living room, and I groaned. Answering it meant standing up, leaving my bed, and feeling my bones ache with every step. But the persistent ringing enticed me to make the journey. One step, and then another. My legs ached, but they moved, and I reached the phone in time to pick it up and utter an out-of-breath hello into the receiver.

"Grandma, it's me," chirped Jennifer. "Today's the day."

More than three months had passed since we'd returned from the island. The trip had been satisfying in more ways than I'd expected, and yet I wasn't prepared for the emotional exhaustion that persisted upon our return. While I'd made peace for Genevieve, Atea, Kitty, and perhaps even for the island, I had left with a tsunami in my own heart, with only whispers of Westry and a book of old letters to cling to.

"Grandma?"

"I'm here, dear," I said into the phone. "I'm just not feeling like myself today."

"But you're still coming, right?"

"Oh, honey," I said, sinking into the sofa before pulling a blanket over my icy feet. "I don't think I can."

Jennifer's silence pierced my heart. *She accompanied me on my journey and stood by me with such compassion—how can I abandon her on this day?*

"You can do without me, can't you, dear?" I asked, rubbing my aching back. Jennifer had turned in her final article a week prior, and the newspaper had gotten wind of the project, as did the university's public relations team.

"Oh, Grandma," she said. "I know it's a lot to ask, especially since you haven't been feeling well, but I would love it if you came. So many people will be there, and I can hardly stand to face them alone. I'm so nervous. It would be comforting to have you there. I can pick you up in an hour. We'll park close so you won't have to walk far."

I forced my legs out in front of me and stood up. *I can do this. For Jennifer.* "Well," I said, taking a deep breath, "then I will come. For you, dear."

"Oh Grandma, thank you!" she exclaimed. "I'll be over soon."

I set the phone down and reached for the letter from Genevieve on the coffee table. It had arrived yesterday, and I'd already read it a dozen times.

Dear Anne,

I wanted to thank you for coming to Bora-Bora. Your visit was transformative—for the island, for me, for Atea. I hope it was for you, too.

I write with good news: I have been in touch with the army and they have all the details. They've agreed to put a case together against Colonel Donahue. It all feels very strange, knowing my relation to this man, but it doesn't stop me from seeking justice for Atea, for my unborn sister or brother.

While the army can't prosecute him in death, my contact tells me they are working with officials here on the island to assemble the facts of the case. He will likely be stripped of his honors and distinctions, at least in all military records.

The island officials are talking about erecting a monument, a memorial for Atea somewhere in town. Isn't that just wonderful, Anne? Of course, we'd love to have you here, when the time comes, for the ceremony. None of this would have happened without your courage.

Oh, and I almost forgot—I am meeting Kitty for the first time in California next month. She's invited me to stay with her.

I'm bringing Adella. I have to pinch myself, as I can hardly believe any of this is real. But it is, wonderfully real.

I will always think of you with warmth, fondness, and appreciation.

With love,
Genevieve

Quiet lingered on campus, and my heels clicked loudly on the brick path, shiny from a recent rain shower. A clock chimed in the distance: noon.

"Just a little farther," Jennifer said, gauging my face for signs of strain.

"I'm all right, dear," I reassured her. The crisp fall air felt good on my skin. It energized me in a way I hadn't anticipated. "You lead the way."

We walked past a row of maples, their leaves tinged orange and red. A stately brick building stood at attention nearby. I recognized it instantly, of course. Gerard had taught finance here after he retired from the bank. How I'd loved taking walks with him through campus, especially in the fall.

"Right through here," Jennifer said, taking my arm in hers as we approached a narrow path that curved around the ivy-covered building. She held up a tree branch so I could duck underneath. Of all the times I'd been on campus with Gerard, I'd never thought to walk behind the building. Not even once.

"There it is," she said, pointing ahead proudly.

I squinted, letting the sculpture come into focus. I could see why it captivated Jennifer so. It told a story. I walked closer, intrigued, and eyed the bronze couple huddled in a crude doorway. *Why is my heart racing?* The man looked at the woman with longing, while her gaze drifted out to the left somewhere in the distance.

"It's beautiful," I said, looking closer. The man held in his hands a large box with a lock, and at his feet a few possessions lay scattered: a painter's canvas, a shattered bottle, and a book. My hands trembled as I knelt down. In that moment, my heart *knew*.

Jennifer stood quietly a few steps behind me. *Where are all the people, the fanfare she spoke of?* I ran my hand along the bronze book at the base of the sculpture, cold, wet from the rain, until I secured the corner of its cover. *Could it be?* I lifted the heavy edge and stared at the tarnished steel key inside, my heart beating faster by the second.

I gestured for Jennifer to come closer. "I can't do this alone," I said, wiping a tear from my cheek.

She steadied me as I slid the key into the lock on the box, its edges sealed tightly to protect its contents. *A perfect match.* I turned it to the right but it jammed.

"The weather must have corroded it," I said. "I'll try it again."

I pulled the key out and inserted it in the lock a second time, giving it a light shake. A faint click sounded as the lock released its stubborn grip.

Jennifer hovered as I lifted the lid and peered inside to find a blue velvet case. I removed it from its bronze crypt and walked to a nearby bench, where Jennifer and I sat down.

"Are you going to open it?" she whispered.

I turned to her with heavy, moist eyes. "You knew, didn't you?"

Jennifer smiled quietly, nodding. "When the woman from the archives called in Bora-Bora, she told me the artist's name, Grayson Hodge, but I didn't recognize it. I should have remembered, but the name didn't click until a few weeks after we were home." She paused, searching my face for approval. "He used the pseudonym in his work. I didn't want to keep it from you, but I wanted you to see this for yourself."

I carefully opened the case and peeled back the brown paper wrapping inside.

Jennifer gasped. "The painting? The one from the bungalow?"

I nodded in awe. The old Gauguin warmed my hands as I held it, as if the Bora-Bora sun had lingered in the canvas all these years. The colors, just as vibrant; the composition, just as moving as the day I first laid eyes on it. And for a moment, I was there again, on the island, feeling the warm air on my cheeks, the sand on my feet, the love of Westry all around me.

"He found it!" I cried. "Just as he promised." *Of course he kept his promise.* "And to think it was here, waiting for me, all these years—right under my nose—and I didn't even look." I turned to Jennifer with eyes of gratitude. "Thank you, dear," I said, looking at the statue and then back at the painting. "This is a gift."

She eyed the nearby building anxiously before turning back to me. "Grandma," she whispered, "are you ready?"

"Ready for what?"

"To see *him.*"

My heart swelled. "But you said, you said he was . . ."

"Dead?" She shook her head. "Yes, Grayson Hodge, a ninety-year-old man from Barkley, Utah, died. But not Westry Green."

Westry. Here? Can it be true?

"I don't know," I said, choking back tears. "But your project?"

Jennifer smiled. "It's concluded beautifully."

I felt weak, unsure. "I've been dreaming about this day for as long as I can remember, and now that it's here I'm . . ."

"Scared?"

"Yes," I muttered, smoothing my wispy hair—what was left of it, anyway. *Why didn't I put on a dress? And some lipstick?*

351

Jennifer shook her head, sensing my insecurity. "Westry will only see what I see: your true *beauty*."

She handed me a handkerchief to dry my eyes. "Now, you wait here. I'll go around front and tell them we're ready."

"You mean," I said, fumbling, "he's here already?"

"Yes," she said, smiling proudly. "His son brought him over this morning. They traveled all the way from New York."

Jennifer gave me a passing smile as she turned toward the path, disappearing around the front of the old building. Alone, I looked up at the sculpture, gazing at the man's eyes. Even cast in bronze, they did look like Westry's, very much so. All those times I'd walked this stretch of campus—I exhaled deeply—if I had only stopped once to notice, to see the clue he'd placed in my path, I might have found him.

I heard the crunch of gravel in the distance and I turned my eyes back to the pathway. When a man appeared, a flock of sparrows startled, fluttering away to a nearby tree. Even in a wheelchair, he had a familiar presence—the way he held himself, the outline of his chin. When our eyes met, he waved away the middle-aged man behind him and took the wheels in his hands, pushing the chair with a strength that didn't match the white of his hair, the wrinkles on his face. His eyes remained fixed on my face, holding me in his gaze.

He stopped in front of the bench where I sat, reaching his hands out to me, cradling my icy fingers in his strong, warm palms. "Hello, Cleo," he said, extending a hand to my face. He stroked my cheek lightly, before his fingers found my locket.

"Hello, Grayson," I said, wiping the tears from my cheek.

"You're a little late, my dear," he said with the same mischievous grin I'd been so charmed by on the day we met.

I searched his face. "How can you ever forgive me? For not knowing, for not looking. . . . I was—"

Westry brushed his finger against my lips and smiled in a way that calmed me. *He could always calm me.* "Just a little late," he said softly, "but not too late." In an instant, he was twenty-five again, and I, twenty-one. Age disappeared. Time faded into the distance.

He buttoned his brown corduroy jacket and set the brakes of the wheelchair, then inched closer to the edge of the seat before pushing his body to a standing position.

I gasped. "But I thought . . ."

He grinned. "That you'd like to take an autumn stroll?" He retrieved a gray cane from the side of the chair, securing it in his left hand and holding his right out to me. "Ready?"

"Yes," I said, beaming, marveling at him standing next to me, so tall, so sure. I tucked the painting under my arm before taking his hand in mine, blinking hard to make sure I wasn't dreaming.

We started down the path through campus, unsure of our destination. But none of that mattered, not now. For our story had an ending that suited me. I loved him, and he loved me, up until the very end. This is the story that would whistle in the winds of Bora-Bora, haunt the weathered remains of the bungalow, and live on in my heart forever.

Westry came. The curse ended. Together, we walked slowly, but surely. I nestled closer to him, wrapping my arm around his just as two wine-colored leaves fell from a nearby tree branch, dancing in the autumn breeze on separate paths before falling softly to the ground, where they settled on the damp earth, side by side.

Acknowledgments

A big, heartfelt thanks goes to my extraordinary literary agent, Elisabeth Weed, for teaming up with me on another book and offering encouragement and guidance (and sometimes free therapy sessions) along the way. It's a joy and a privilege to work with you. Also, much gratitude to Stephanie Sun, who, along with Elisabeth, was the very first reader of this book. Your kind comments cheered me on and your suggestions made the book better. (I also love that you found Westry to be as dreamy as I still do!)

It is not advisable to write a book when one is deep into the second trimester of her pregnancy and also on the heels of the debut of another book. But I wrote one anyway. And I thank my lovely editor, Denise Roy, for sticking by me as I juggled the baby and the book revisions while prepping for the launch of my first novel. Denise, your sharp editorial eye and creative ideas continually amaze me. In you, I've found a great editorial partner. (Thank you, too, for being so understanding when the baby screamed sometimes during our phone conversations—because he did scream, quite loudly.)

I have much appreciation to Jenny Meyer of

Meyer Literary Agency for sharing my story with foreign editors and for being so enthusiastic about my stories. To Nadia Kashper, Liz Keenan, Milena Brown, Kym Surridge, and everyone at Plume, you're the best. Dear friends, Sally Farhat Kassab, Wendi Parriera, Camille Noe Pagan, Lisa Bach, Natalie Quick, and many more all cheered me on along the way—thank you, lovelies. And to my editors at *Glamour*, *Health*, *Redbook*, and other magazines, who gave me a deadline extension or two so I could get book stuff done— I'm ever grateful.

I am thankful in more ways than I can count to my parents, Terry and Karen Mitchell—for loving me, for putting up with me, for encouraging me, and especially for sharing Great Uncle Michael Handgraaf's journal from wartime in the South Pacific. To my brothers, Josh Mitchell and Josiah Mitchell, and my sister and closest friend, Jessica Campbell—I love you so much, but you're still no match for me at Tile Rummy. I also remember my late grandfather James Robert Mitchell, whose stories of wartime in the South Pacific remain etched in my memory.

I have three sons, Carson, Russell, and Colby, all who were under the age of four when I wrote this book. There's only one thing I love more than writing, and it's being their mother.

Last but not least, Jason—my best friend, partner in child wrangling, and loving husband, this story wouldn't have been born had it not been for our 2001 journey to Moorea and Tahiti. For in that rustic little beach bungalow we shared (complete with geckos and lots of tropical ants!) was the first glimmer of this story. You are my inspiration and my rock. I write for you, and because of you.

SARAH JIO is a journalist who has written for *Glamour*; *O, The Oprah Magazine*; *Real Simple*; *SELF*; *Cooking Light*; *Redbook*; *Parents*; *Woman's Day*; and many other publications. She is the health and fitness blogger for Glamour.com and lives in Seattle with her husband, their three young children, and a golden retriever named Paisley, who steals socks. Learn more about Sarah at www.sarahjio.com.

Center Point Large Print
600 Brooks Road / PO Box 1
Thorndike ME 04986-0001 USA

(207) 568-3717

US & Canada:
1 800 929-9108
www.centerpointlargeprint.com

E